The Book of Phoebe
MARY-ANN TIRONE SMITH

"You can't help liking Phoebe. . . . Like the best narrators, from Huck to Holden, she talks to us, tells us a story, lets us get inside to find out what's really happening."
—*Los Angeles Times*

"Very nice . . . a quirky first novel full of likable, brave characters."
—*Detroit Free Press*

"Hilarious. . . . Reading *The Book of Phoebe* is like peeling a very funny onion."
—Evelyn Wilde Mayerson,
author of *Princess in Amber*

"A love story for the eighties; a tale of a gutsy and irreverent heroine who knows precisely what she wants."
—Jessica Auerbach, author of
A Winter Wife

"A tremendous talent. The theme, the writing, the plotting . . . are all a joy. A wonderful first novel, immediate, imaginative, and important."
—William Wharton, author of *Birdy*

The Book of Phoebe

MARY-ANN TIRONE SMITH

LAUREL

Readers Service Dept ??? ??? ???, NY ?????

A LAUREL TRADE PAPERBACK
Published by
Dell Publishing Co., Inc.
1 Dag Hammarskjold Plaza
New York, New York 10017

Laurel ® TM 674623, Dell Publishing Co., Inc.

ISBN: 0-440-50742-1

Reprinted by arrangement with Doubleday & Company, Inc.
Printed in the United States of America

November 1986

10 9 8 7 6 5 4 3 2 1

W

This book is for Tyler, with love

PART ONE

Chapter One

I didn't have an abortion for two reasons—both people. First, my mother. My mother aborted what would have been my brother or sister. She didn't want to know which, naturally, so that she could continue to think of the child as an inconsequential, microscopic fishie. I wished I knew what it was even though I understood my mother's frame of mind exactly. My own state of mind at the time was feverish, teenage curiosity.

Second, an emotionally disturbed, not quite middle-aged man named Tyrus. By emotionally disturbed, I mean crazy. Nuts. Cuckoo. Not so crazy that you couldn't carry on a conversation with him. You could, and if you were lucky, fifty percent of it would make sense. Tyrus was an even bigger reason for my not having an abortion than my mother. I loved Tyrus, and he more than loved me; he depended on me, but I betrayed him.

When I didn't have an abortion, I was nineteen and a senior at Yale. Consequently, it wasn't such an easy or *de rigeur* decision, but because of that non-brother or -sister, and that insane Tyrus, I wanted my personal little fishie to become a human being. At the same time, I also wanted to graduate not more than six months late from Yale. I can be a selfish person. I wanted to have a baby whom I had no plans for, and still graduate just one semester later than my class. In addition, I didn't want a single person to know I was pregnant or to know about my giving birth, particularly little fishie's father, who had turned out to be a real shit-heel. My grandmother calls people "shit-heel" a lot. She is one of those rare personalities able to eclectically and successfully mix the old with the new, the genteel with the gauche. Instead of honking her horn, she sticks her head out the window and shouts "Fore!" Someday Grandmother will come up against a jaywalker who knows nothing about golf, and splatter him.

Anyway, since my embryo was not quite a baby, the father, as far as I'm concerned, was not quite a father, and the shit-heel, believe me, didn't deserve to be the father of even an embryo. Even a little fishie.

I pulled it off. I have pulled off great things since I was a kid—a gifted kid.

God, was I a gifted kid; and it was so nice to go to Yale and be a gifted college student among a thousand others equally and sometimes more gifted. At Yale, when you compute the slugging average of each player on both teams after a ball game in your head, nobody bats an eyelash. I enjoyed, for the first time, not being a freak. No one believes this, but in public school it is just as tough on a kid to be gifted as it is to have some other handicap, like cerebral palsy. You're different; hence, weird; hence, made fun of; hence, miserable. When I was a kid, I felt like I had the plague. Anyway, that one contented period of my life with all my fellow freaks at Yale ended abruptly when I finally and foolishly fell in love enough to . . . well . . . to fuck.

Don't be offended. That's the way we Yalies talk. Nobody at Yale has sexual intercourse. They'd laugh you right out of New Haven if you dared to refer to fucking as sexual intercourse. That's like calling tailgating picnicking.

I fell out of love just as fast, but not so fast that I was able to undo what had been done. About three weeks after I'd had an IUD inserted, I got tremendous pelvic pains, and went to the gynecologist who had put it in.

He said, "Oh my! The little devil is hanging half out of your cervix. You ejected it." This from a doctor at Yale.

I said, "Doc, don't tell me I ejected it. It ejected itself. Now give me the essentials. Has the goddamn thing been working?"

"Of course it hasn't been working. You ejected it. I gave you specific instructions to feel inside your vagina for anything unusual."

"When you told me that, Doctor, I didn't have the

heart to disappoint you and tell you I usually don't go around feeling inside my vagina. I've never felt inside my vagina before, so I didn't know what unusual type thing I should be feeling for. The essentials, Doc. Could I be pregnant?"

"How often have you had sexual intercourse since I saw you last?" (The Yale doc, as you can see, has not been laughed out of New Haven yet, but someone'll do it. Soon, I hope.)

"I've been averaging three times a day."

He finally looked up from between my legs. Men will never know the extreme wonder of holding a conversation with a disembodied head floating above a sheet between their knees, level with their belly. "Miss Desmond, when did you say your last period was?"

"Three and a half weeks ago."

He got up off his little stool, threw the IUD at the wastebasket, and missed by a foot. It lay on the waxed linoleum, bloody and disgusting. "Make another appointment for a pregnancy test. The lab isn't open today. I'll talk to you in my office."

He walked out shaking his head. I sat up and continued to stare at the repulsive IUD. It looked like a part from a Milton Bradley board game. The nurse came in, spotting it right away. She winked at me and said, "Doctor is so careless." Then she scooped it up with all his other crap.

"Doctor," I said, "is an inconsiderate slob, Nurse, and if I were you, I'd put that sickening thing into the next cup of coffee you will no doubt be serving him."

She told me to get dressed. I wonder why nurses are the last females on earth to liberate themselves.

"Doctor" was writing on his prescription pad and began speaking to me without looking up. I become rather annoyed when being addressed by a bald scalp, but even men get to hold conversations with the tops of doctors' heads. However, that's American medicine. Or, as Agatha Christie would put it, there it is.

"You've got a little infection in there, Miss Desmond, caused by the IUD piercing your cervix. Take this antibiotic, and don't have intercourse for a month. You'll have to go on the pill. Some of us girls just aren't made for IUDs now, are we?"

Obviously not, Doc. "Perhaps," I suggested, "my boyfriend could use condoms."

He didn't look up. "Many men don't receive the full pleasure of intercourse using condoms, Miss Desmond."

I said, "Many women don't feel the full pleasure of intercourse with infectious IUDs hanging out of their cervixes."

He ripped off the prescription. "Good luck, Miss Desmond," he smiled.

I never went back to him. I took a home pregnancy test and the penicillin. When I told old Shit-heel the story, before I could even get to the pregnancy part, he interrupted me and said, "I think, Phoebe, our relationship is becoming too intense, perhaps."

What's wrong with intense, I wondered, when it comes to fucking all day and all night? He also told me that we needed to expand our perspectives, get in touch with our innermost emotions, develop new frames of reference. In short, we should date others. The phone rang, too. I recognized Wendy Gurnée's silky voice asking for him. Apparently, Shit-heel had been able to expand his perspectives, get in touch with his innermost emotions, and develop new frames in the six hours since I'd last seen him.

Falling immediately out of love with him, I looked into his sly hazel eyes for the last time, and I will go to the grave knowing that he'll never know he had a baby.

Chapter Two

Since my mother is half the reason I didn't have an abortion, a further look into my background is essential. My grandmother can shed more light on my genes than I. When I was ten, prior to my meeting Tyrus, I overheard my grandmother say to my Great-aunt Virginia, "Phoebe's just like Ma, isn't she, Ginnie?"

And Great-aunt Virginia said, "How the hell would I know?"

Grandmother forgets that Great-aunt Virginia was a year old when their mother died. My great-grandmother had a baby every other spring for twenty-four years, Virginia the last. Then she died. She died of having babies. I cornered my grandmother and asked her why she'd said that. Here is the story in Grandmother's words taken from my journal, dated Easter Day 1973. I have the conversation written down verbatim because, as I explained, I am gifted and can recall a conversation of up to forty-nine minutes. At ten I was only up to half an hour. I will precede the entry with a bit about Grandmother herself.

She has ash-blond hair, golfs eighteen holes a day, drives a Silver Cloud, and used to say to my sister when she was a baby, "Don't come near Grandmother, darling. Grandmother has on a pair of twenty-dollar stockings. Baby might run Grandmother's stockings."

Then she would hand Maribeth, my sister, an entire bag of Oreo cookies to keep her the hell away. But don't let me give you the wrong impression, either. She's not rich. The way she got the Silver Cloud was like this; when her youngest kid left home, she sold her big old Victorian house with the wraparound porch—an "in" kind of house these days—and consequently, got her price. Then she bought a small condo near the club. With the leftover money, she got the car. My grandfather never even knew anything about it until she told him it was moving day, and he didn't mind at all. He watches a lot of TV, and she just kept giving him papers to sign during "General Hospital." Wisely, she had the movers leave his La-Z-Boy and his Sony till the last minute, so he only missed one show. Here is that journal excerpt.

§   §   §

"You see, Phoebe," Grandmother explained, "Great-grandmother was what you'd have to call, I guess, bitter. In those days Catholics weren't allowed to practice birth control, so—"

"Excuse me, Grandmother, they still aren't."

"Oh. I thought they changed that when they told us there was no such thing as St. Christopher. Well, never mind. I've passed that stage in my life, thank God. Where was I? Oh yes. Your great-grandmother went to confession one day, and told the priest that the doctor told her that it would kill her to have another baby, and that her husband was going to have to start practicing birth control. Now, in those days, there was only one method of birth control, and it was rather . . . uh . . . primitive."

"You mean baggies?"

"Phoebe, really. I swear this sex education business in our schools today is going to ruin our youth. Of course, they're all ruined anyway, so what's the difference? I have told your mother repeatedly that if she would only send you to St. Timothy's Academy, you wouldn't be hearing all this . . ."

"So what happened then, Grandmother?"

"To whom? Oh. Well, as I was saying, the priest told her that she was disgusting, and that to even consider such a filthy thing was a mortal sin. He told her to live like brother and sister with her husband, and if you had known my father, Phoebe, you would realize that there was about as much chance of getting him to agree to that as there is getting Uncle Edmond to quit hiding under the head table at all our weddings and barking."

"Don't get into Uncle Edmond, Grandmother. What did she do about it?"

"She had more babies. Three more. And the last one was Aunt Virginia. Ginny ripped her to pieces, so she suffered from infection for a year until she died. And when she lay there dying . . ."

"You don't seem too terribly broken up about all this, Grandmother."

"Phoebe, dear, when you have eleven brothers and sisters, your mother is a stranger. Your Great-aunt Gert was my mother, God rest her soul."

"Did she die of having babies?"

"No. She ran off with a Cuban musician and we haven't seen her since. Or him. Cubans were very big when I was a girl. Now, Phoebe, do you want to hear what happened or not?"

"Yeah, I do."

"Well, she was dying, and everyone wanted to send for a priest. But, of course, she wouldn't hear of it. She said, *'Le prêtre est mon assassin.'* (The great-grandparents were Canadians.) But just the same, the priest came because he always knew when a member of his flock was on the way out. That's what they pay priests for, Phoebe. He pushed us all aside and paraded right into her bedroom. God, when I think back. She was forty-one and looked a hundred. Get my bag, Phoebe, so I can freshen up my lips. Then the priest said (I'll give you this in English), 'Margaret, I've come to hear your confession.' And Ma said, 'All right, Father, but first I must tell you something.' Lord, how our ears perked up.

" 'What is it, my daughter?' the priest asked. So your great-grandmother said, 'Father, at dawn on this day I saw a vision. A holy vision.' He asked her what kind of a holy vision, and she said, 'I saw, sitting at the foot of my bed, right where you are now, the Blessed Virgin, all in blue, and holding a white rose.'

"Well, Phoebe, you can imagine what we all thought —that she'd gone completely mad. Then the priest asked,

'Did the Virgin say anything?' and Ma said, 'No.' And he asked, 'Did she do anything?' and Ma said, 'No.' And he asked, 'What exactly happened, my daughter?' Well! Ma smiled sweetly, looked him right in the eye, and shouted at the top of her lungs:

" 'I farted, and blew her right off the bed!' "

§   §   §

If my great-grandmother could still hold her own on her deathbed, I feel I have inherited enough of her feistiness to get through having this one baby. Not that I'm a martyr, and certainly I'm no hero. To be honest, I may be pregnant, but I don't feel pregnant. I don't feel any different at all. Always make your decision before the event actually registers, because when it does register, it's too late to change your mind.

Chapter Three

More than my great-grandmother's genes, Marlys Hightower helped me get through the consequences of my decision not to have an abortion. Marlys has been my closest friend all my life, and is gifted, too. She is also black. We met on the first day of nursery school. When you are in nursery school, and it's your first day there, and you are only three years old, you don't notice that the kid sitting next to you is black. You only notice that she's crying her eyes out. She stopped crying when I threw up. Tears and vomit will bind Marlys Hightower and me together for life.

Conveniently for me, as it turned out, Marlys decided against going to Yale with me. She also declined Harvard. Her mother told her, "Marlys, I'm real proud you got into all those nice Ivy League schools, but why don't you go to Howard and meet some spades?"

At the time, Mrs. Hightower didn't know her daughter had decided not to go to any college at all. Marlys' mother has a hell of a sense of humor. Her dad is a prude. Black or white, a prude is a prude. When it came to Marlys' future, Mr. Hightower's only concern was that she remain as pure as the driven snow until she married an upwardly mobile black with an MBA from Penn State. No matter that she scored a perfect eight hundred on her college boards, or that she was covaledictorian of a large class (yours truly being the other co). He spent all their time together pointing out to Marlys that she was just a girl. Poor Mr. Hightower.

Marlys and I, throughout our lives, were deeply fascinated with Paris. Marlys did something about this fascination. She chucked it all, flew to Paris, and became the most famous American expatriate in France in less than six months' time. Marlys is presently the star of the Folies Bergère. She is the toast of the town; the Josephine Baker of the eighties. Rich, too. Very rich. So when I found I was pregnant, I called her and filled her in on my pregnancy. I explained that I needed to hide out, have my baby, give it to someone, and then I wouldn't bother her again till my next crisis.

Marlys started saying stuff like *"Sacrebleu!"* and *"Ooh la la"* and all her French crapola. I almost killed her. She should have known I wasn't as blasé as I sounded, though it was a transatlantic call. The Paris operator kept calling me "Monsieur Desmond." Marlys just laughed.

"Get your bad ass over to Frog City, Phoeb, and I'll take complete care of you. Jesus, Phoeb, you'll love it. In Paris there is an actual law that if a pregnant woman hops on the Métro, you have to give her your seat or go directly to jail, do not pass Go, do not collect two hundred dollars. It's a law. In New York you could give birth in the aisle, and no one would budge to make room. Then they'd step on the poor newborn thing."

"Marlys," I said, "you're making me sick. I sicken easily these days. I'll come in September. No one will know I'm pregnant till then, and I have some loose ends to take care of besides. You're sure it's okay?"

"It's great! I don't know what the hell I'll be doing then, but I know I'll be back from Cap d'Antibes."

"Yeah. And I'll be back from Great Pond." That's our local lake where you get ear infections that no antibiotic can cure.

Marlys hooted. "Bring me a jar of Great Pond, and we'll pour it into the Seine. After all, they gave us syphilis. We'll give them chronic ear. Far, far worse."

"I think, Marlys, it was the Italians who gave us syphilis."

"Then we'll take a side trip to Florence and pour it into the Arno."

Marlys would be the silver lining behind my inconvenient cloud. As soon as I spoke to her, I calmed right down. Six months in Paris with Marlys. We'd have a great time. In my excitement, I was a bit unrealistic, but I hadn't seen her in over two years. Oh, I'd seen her in all the newspapers and *People Magazine* just like everyone else—with glitter on her eyelids, half naked, and her hair pulled back by a crane.

Once, in *National Geographic,* they had a story about a tribe called the Fulani who are cattle herders in West Africa, and I thought immediately of Marlys. This particular group considers home base the highlands of Cameroon, which look exactly like Scotland, only warmer, I would presume. Their houses are round, wide, and low, and in one of the pictures, standing in front of their compound was a Fulani woman in cornrows and about a thousand strings of thin gold necklaces covering her chest. The Fulani have a monopoly on cattle herding in West Africa, and have more money than they know what to do with. Once a year, during Ramadan, they all head for the nearest international airport, and fly to Mecca, first class. They used to walk to Mecca right across the desert back in the days when the British were living in caves. Subsequently, all Fulani men are hadjis, because if you are a Moslem and you make it to Mecca, you automatically become a hadji. All Fulani women are slaves, naturally, like the rest of us.

This particular woman, like Marlys, fit the old adage "You can't be too rich or too thin." Add "too tall" in this case. She was the exact color of Root Beer Barrels after they're half sucked; a golden, translucent, honeybrown. I swear to God that growing up, sometimes I had a tough time keeping myself from licking Marlys' cheek. Anyway, the Fulani woman had a little girl standing next to her smiling. Instead of cornrows, the girl had great, fat sausage curls hanging down to her shoulders. In the Fulani woman's arms was a chubby, drooling baby with stars in his eyes. His name was La-Lee-Loo.

La-Lee-Loo. What wonderful people the Fulani are to name their babies songs.

I know that a few hundred years ago, Marlys' great-great-great-grandmother with sausage curls like La-Lee-Loo's sister went wandering out of the lovely Cameroonian hills only to be grabbed by those same slavers that got good old Kunte Kinte. You'd agree if you could see Marlys and that picture of the Fulani woman.

As I've said already, Marlys also has a great deal of physical charm in common with the late Josephine Baker. And if you could see a picture of Josephine and Marlys, side by side, you'd know one of the reasons for their fame. They both have legs that climb and climb on up to their perfect, spherical little butts.

Chapter Four

In September when I was around four months pregnant, I left for Paris after a summer spent working, saving every penny, conning my parents, and conning
Yale. Thank God we have a bathroom in the basement
family room. That's where I'd throw up every morning
at five-thirty. My father began to complain about how
the downstairs john smelled, but my mother told him it
was just mildew, what with the high humidity and all.

   Aside from eating two breakfasts each morning,
once before throwing up, and once after, my life as a
pregnant person remained fairly ordinary. I didn't date,
of course. That was all right, though. The college boys

around my neighborhood who were also home for the summer I considered undatable. I went to Yale, they went to Western Connecticut State. They held me in awe.

So I took my little sister to the beach whenever I wasn't working. The highest-paid summer job where I live pays the minimum wage, but at least I found something interesting. Two gay craftsmen rented the Pilitz house on the pond. The Pilitzes had to rent out the house because they couldn't sell it, but then again, who'd buy a house that once contained the Pilitz twins? The twins used to have contests to see who could flush the most things down the toilet before the water started to back up. That game ended when Stacy tried to flush away Tracy.

The gay craftsmen used me as a professional gofer. I'd pick up their packages at the post office, make them their lunch, clean up their brushes and saws and glue buckets. They crafted all summer and never made a damn thing. They'd whittle and paste, and cut, and leave a big mess. Then they'd throw everything away and start a new project. My biggest responsibility was driving all their refuse to the dump in their Mercedes pickup. They weren't friendly, but they were pleasant, same as me. At that age you're much too confused about your own sexuality to be friends with gays, and being pregnant made things doubly confusing.

I went to Yale to talk to my dean. I told him I was going to take a semester off and would be back in February. I told him I might miss the first couple of weeks of classes, but that I'd make it up.

He took his marijuana-filled meerschaum out of his

mouth and said, "Would you like to discuss the possible ramifications of this decision?"

I said, "No."

He said, "See you in February. Sign up for your spring courses by mail. Don't forget to leave your address with my secretary. Have fun in Paris."

Good old Yale. They always ask you if you want or don't want the option of them bugging you. I guess I couldn't really consider that a con job, but the grief my family gave me made up for it.

One evening after dinner I brought home a six-pack of Michelob for my Dad and one of those little bottles of Harvey's Bristol Cream for my mother. They looked at me warily as we don't say in Creative Writing 202.

"I've got something I'd like to discuss with you guys. The booze is to soften us all up."

My parents consider talking to each other an unnatural act. My mother chats nonsense all day with her friends, and my dad yaps business all day with the jerks at E. F. Hutton. My twelve-year-old sister, however, was right there in the middle of the family-room floor sucking on a bottle of Diet Coke, raring to go. My mother took her shot glass of Harvey's, and my father twisted the top off the Michelob, and they sat down at opposite ends of the room.

Did you ever try to talk to two people when one is sitting ten feet off to your left and the other is ten feet off to your right? "Mom, Dad," I said, swiveling my head, "I've decided to leave Yale for six months. I'll just be missing the fall semester."

"Leave Yale?" My mother.

"You can't leave Yale." My father.

"Ooooh, Phoebe, how come?" The kid sister.

"I've called Marlys and invited myself to Paris for six months. I need a break."

"A break from Yale?" Mom.

"Of course you don't need a break. The point of Yale is to get in, not out." Dad.

"Ooooh, Phoebe . . . Paris . . ." My sister swooned.

The conversation basically went on like that for a few minutes, my mother disbelieving, my dad trying to establish a power base, my sister acting like your typical twelve-year-old Judy Blume idiot. Then my mother started one of those precry whines. My dad, who can't handle whining, got up and went to the john, which smelled worse than ever. My sister watched, on her third Diet Coke.

With my dad gone, my mother didn't cry. "You haven't grown up yet, have you, Phoebe? After all these years you're going to pull one of your silly stunts that could ruin your entire life."

"Ma, Paris isn't a silly stunt. I'll get some course credit. I'll be back at Yale in February."

"Your Great-aunt Virginia's son left college and never went back."

"Virginia's son enlisted in the Navy. Rest assured I will not choose the Navy over Yale."

"You'll miss your graduation ceremonies."

"I'll get you tickets, anyway. You'll never miss me. Oh, Ma, this is important. I will broaden my perspective in Paris. It's time I left this country and looked at things from an international viewpoint."

My dad stuck his head in the doorway, "What's wrong with this country?"

"Who cares, Dad? Listen, I don't have to tell you all this. I'm doing it to be civil. I have a full scholarship to Yale, and I work for my expense money."

"You've been living under my roof all summer."

"You sound like Ann Landers. Throw me out. I'll find a place to stay till I go."

"Where? Or have those queers asked you to live with them?"

"What's wrong with that? I should think that would make you happy. I could walk around naked in front of them, and all they would say is 'Oh, yuck!' "

"Please, Phoebe, not in front of Maribeth."

Maribeth smiled her best Judy Blume smile with the Coke bottle halfway down her throat. She dribbled Diet Coke on the carpet.

"Maribeth! Don't drink your pop in here. Go up to the kitchen."

"Oh, Ma," Maribeth moaned, spilling another mouthful.

"You heard your mother, Maribeth. You don't leave the kitchen with food or drink until you learn to get it all into your mouth."

Maribeth started whining, and my father went back to the bathroom to relieve himself of his fourth Michelob.

"Quit whining, Blob," I said. "Look, Ma, there's so much garbage on this carpet that nobody'll notice a few drops of Coke. You're just looking for an excuse to get off the subject. I'm leaving the day after Labor Day in case you're wondering where I am."

"Phoebe, it's just that I can't keep up with you. All I ever wanted was a nice, normal little family. And don't call your sister 'Blob.' "

"C'mon, Ma, what the hell is normal? Look at the Hightowers. Look at Virginia. Unusual problems are much more exciting than normal, boring problems. Besides, if you want normal, remember you've got . . . uh . . . Maribeth. Every kid her age in the country is now being yelled at for spilling Diet Coke on the family-room carpet. Count your blessings. Blob could be snorting cocaine."

My mother sighed. "Phoebe, I've never worried about your being unable to take care of yourself, but Paris . . . and that Marlys! She leads a wild life now."

"We don't know that, Ma. She's a dancer. An especially illustrious one. If the jet set or whatever chose to adopt her, she's still my old pal Marlys. This is very generous of her. I can't pass up such an opportunity. Yale thinks it's wonderful."

"Yale does? Oh. Well, maybe it will help you decide what you want to do with your life once your education is through."

My dad was back. "If it's ever through."

I ignored him. "Maybe, Ma. Maybe I'll find my destiny in Paris. In fact, I hope so. I really do."

"Phoebe?"

"Yeah, Ma?"

"I hope you won't be a dancer."

"You have to be beautiful to dance, Ma, otherwise you look like an idiot."

"You are beautiful, Phoebe."

"Thanks, Ma, but I'm not." Some day, though, I will be. Right now I couldn't handle beautiful. Gifted is plenty. Pregnant, more so.

Chapter Five

In Paris, in September, you get to see something most Americans never get a chance at because they can only go in the summer. You get to see Parisians. This is what Marlys told me in the limo from Orly. You get to see those dowdy housewives with the three-foot loaves of bread sticking out from under their arms. You get to see the Parisian kids in their little designer uniforms marching off to school in two straight lines, in rain or shine, the smallest one is Madeline. And you get to see Paris' equivalent of New York's bag ladies. They stake out a section of boulevard and claim all the pigeons who land in that particular territory. All day long they feed the pigeons crumbs and other junk, and God forbid you should enter the area. The pigeons peck at your ankles, and the weird old ladies hurl obscene French invectives at you. I look forward to learning the best French curse words in such a manner, eavesdropping on the pigeon ladies. I will stamp my foot, shake up the pigeons, and memorize the ensuing string of curses.

Marlys and I hugged and hugged. She didn't have her famous makeup on, but her hair was still pulled back by a crane. It was also slicked with mineral oil, and as shiny as anthracite. Marlys was dressed, however, like a slob, as I was. I could tell Marlys couldn't wait to take a vacation from *haute* and punk *couture*, and be a good old American slob again.

She had arranged, as she put it, to disappear for a week, and during that week we would have a lot of fun, and plan what to do with me and, eventually, the baby. I told her there was no way I could ever hope to repay her, and she said,

"Well, Phoeb, according to Jimmy Breslin, a friend in need is a pest. This is your turn to be a pest, which will never make up for all the times I came up to your room and cried about the torment that goes with being black and you took all my misery so seriously. And all those times you protected me, and then taught me to protect myself, which of course is how I really got to where I am now. Good old ruthless Phoebe. Remember when we were roller-skating and those kids at the playground kept calling me Nigger Baby?"

"No. How old were we? Four?"

"Seven. And the leader's name was Chuckie Magnaferrio."

"Oh God, that kid who quit school in sixth grade because he turned sixteen? The one who carved his entire name into his arm with a razor blade? Who had all those infected scabs from his wrists to his undershirt?"

"The very one. You took off your skate, went up behind him, and swung the skate around by the laces, and let it go at his head."

"Oh yeah. I remember feeling like David and Goliath except that I snuck up behind him. Then we ran like hell, right?"

Marlys looked at me solemnly. "Phoebe, you never once complained about losing that skate. It was a new skate, too, and you never mentioned it."

"That skate was nothing. Besides, you would never go skating again without me, so you lost out, too."

Marlys reached under her seat and came up with a large box. She pulled out a pair of beautiful, genuine leather, bright white roller skates with my name stamped in gold on the side. The wheels were red. "Want to go roller skating, Phoebe?"

"Yeah, Marlys, I'd really love to."

Marlys picked up a microphone from where most cars have ashtrays. *"Jean-Pierre, le Bois, s'il vous plaît."*

"Marlys," I said, "what if someone calls you Nigger Baby at the Bois? These skates are too nice to throw at someone."

She roared. "In Paris Chuckie Magnaferrio wouldn't dare call me anything. I'd have him kneecapped."

I looked at Marlys when she wasn't looking at me. Marlys has come very far. My first day in Paris I went roller-skating in the Bois de Boulogne, and I got stung by a weak bee. It was so much fun to be seven years old again. And most important, I was reassured knowing that Marlys realized I was scared stiff. She and I were the only people in the world who knew that I was not only pregnant, but that I was going to give birth to a real living child in four and a half months.

Chapter Six

"Phoebe," Marlys said, "every job you ever hold lends you experience that might turn out to be invaluable. Wouldn't you agree?" We were sitting on her white eyelet bed eating French pastries.

"Of course not. What are you getting at, Marlys?"

"For instance, that job you had with those gays this summer?"

"Yeah?"

"Would you mind a similar job until you have the baby? To keep busy, I mean. It seems I'm going to be busy myself. Very busy."

"Sounds good to me," I lied.

"Well, there's this painter named Ben who lives here in Paris . . ."

"Gay?"

"Oh no. He's always falling madly in love. You'll have a ton of empathy. He's kind of a hermit while he's creating, although he comes out every few months and turns the town upside down."

"Does he live far from here?"

"Actually, Phoebe, he lives in a garret over the Pension Rapp on the Avenue Rapp. It's near the Eiffel Tower—possibly the dullest section of Paris, but close to everything. And the thing is, he wants someone to live with him. He's lonely."

I looked at her. Marlys looked guilty even with apricot jam on her chin. "You want me out—right, Mar? How much is this guy going to cost you?"

"Phoebe, I don't want you out. And this guy is for real. If he was going to charge me, he wouldn't be an acquaintance, and you are my best friend, so don't say things like that."

"Marlys, you never meant to let me stay with you. I can tell."

"Don't make it sound so awful. I have to go on a tour of the Continent. You don't understand what it will be like around here. Starting tomorrow this house will be full of people who are mostly jerks. My manager, and choreographer, and costume designer, and all that. Then . . . oh, Phoebe! Try to understand . . ."

"It's okay, Mar. I understand." I didn't, though I was trying.

"No, you don't. It's just that if I told you this before you came, you wouldn't have come, and then what

would happen to you? I'm going on several tours, the
last one to Japan when the baby is due. Ben promised
me he'd take care of you if you take care of him. He
loves to get up in the middle of the night and have a cup
of cocoa. That's what pregnant women like to do, too,
right? But Ben doesn't like to make it himself. He's used
to being rich."

"I thought you said he lived in a garret."

Marlys smirked. "Phoebe, believe me, you'll love it.
The Pension Rapp is a total dump run by this hilarious
redhead who only hires young, gorgeous Greeks for
help. She always has six simultaneous Greek lovers who
all look alike, and take turns at the desk. The people
who are guests there are people who come to Paris with
no reservations. Imagine. Madame Besette, the redhead,
doesn't accept reservations, so she has such an unusual
and mellow clientele. Ben has the entire fifth floor under the eaves. Twenty-five hundred square feet. He
spent fifty thousand renovating it, and it's all bleached
oak floors, and incredible lighting, and all that. A spectacular place to live."

"Where'd the guy get the fifty grand? I hate cocaine."

"His mother's maiden name was Hoover. Not related to the President. Related to the vacuum cleaners."

"Oh."

"His parents told him he costs them less than his
brothers who are studying to be specialists. They're already plain doctors. His father's a doctor, too. A Jewish
doctor. Ben almost was a doctor, but quit. His parents
were thrilled. They always told him he had artistic talent."

"So I get to clean his paintbrushes?"

"Nah. He has all these cleaning people do that sort of stuff. Or, more likely, he throws his dirty brushes away. I think he just wants some plain old American company. Safe company."

"He figures pregnant is safe."

"Exactly."

"He's right."

"I know."

"Marlys, I know shit about art. In my house, after you finish a thousand-piece puzzle, you glue it together and hang it on the wall. From twenty feet away you might mistake it for a cheap print. I don't think he's going to be too happy living under the same roof with someone who can't talk to him."

"Listen, Ben knows beans about life. You're an expert. Even Steven."

"Okay."

"Okay, you'll do it?"

"Sure, Marlys."

God, her forehead had been so wrinkled. I tried to act blasé about the whole thing, but of course I had no idea what I'd be getting into. Also, I'd reached a point in that period of pregnancy where my lower tummy had now begun to appear hard and a little bit rounded. Sitting in Marlys' sunken bath, I'd cover it with a washcloth, but when I took the washcloth off, it was still there. Whatever was inside was still there, too. So while I sprawled panic-stricken across the eyelet spread listening to Marlys prepare me for the big move out, my real stomach up above the pregnant one turned hard too, with that helpless pit feeling. But I had to be tough, like my great-grandmother.

In these seconds of Marlys' wrinkled forehead, I told myself—Phoebe, this will be a terrific opportunity for you. You really will learn something about art. Besides, you trust Marlys. If you can't trust Marlys, you can't trust anyone. After all, I'd spent a solid month screwing around with her all over Paris. Whenever she wasn't working at the Folies Bergère, she'd take me on little two-day trips to Bruges, and Madrid, and of course, Florence. When she had to rehearse, her secretary saw that I was entertained. Barbara, the secretary, told me about the best walks, and where to find the tour office that gives guided tours of the Paris sewers, and took care of my appointments with my French gynecologist, who was efficient, abrupt, and businesslike. None of this "we girls" stuff.

Barbara, a blonde with horn-rimmed glasses, was the most competent secretary in the world, and seemed more like a friend than a secretary. I could see she was great for Marlys, because Marlys' schedule was so hectic she didn't know which end was up. Barbara was always shooing me off to some exciting place so Marlys could meet her responsibilities to her public, as Marlys would put it when she was drunk. So I was fit neatly in between Marlys' parties, dinners, facials, photographic sessions, interviews, etc. We were hardly ever in Marlys' house except to sleep. The house was seven steps from the Arc de Triomphe on an avenue where you had to be a billionaire to live, and it looked like the inside of Prince Saud's palace. Barbara's room adjoined Marlys' in case Marlys needed her even in the middle of the night. I don't think Barbara was too fond of me, though she was certainly a devoted secretary.

Marlys touched my arm and looked up at me. "Ben will take you to the doctor and all that, Phoeb. And I have all these detective types working on finding a real nice couple who want a baby . . . that's if you still want to give it away when it gets here."

"Great."

"C'mon. I had all your stuff packed during breakfast. Ben's expecting us."

"Now?"

"Phoebe, my new rehearsals start tomorrow. They'll be daylong rehearsals. And I'll be at the Folies Bergère every night until I leave."

"I still haven't even seen your show."

"We can never wake you up for my show. Ben will take you."

"Good."

"It's really the best I can do, Phoeb."

"I know. Thanks, Mar."

Then I started to cry. Marlys stood right up. "Don't do that, Phoebe, okay? It will make me barf, and even though I love you, I have no time to barf."

So I stopped crying, she didn't barf, I packed my tack, and we went to Ben's garret. As I left, Barbara gave me a little goodbye present—perfume, naturally. I wondered if Marlys knew that her secretary really didn't like me.

Chapter Seven

Waiting for us at the desk was Ben's spare key. Apollo gave it to me. Apollo had lips like Sophia Loren. He had blue-black curls, skin like marble, and eyes the color of the Aegean. Either that or aquamarine contacts. A minute later I felt for the first time that I was really and truly in Paris, because Marlys and I had to get into one of those skinny black cages to which Marlys was, of course, completely acclimated. We went straight up through the air supported by a squawking, rusty cable a quarter of an inch thick. When we got to the fifth floor, we were surrounded by a purple wall, and there was a little catwalk to get out. We stepped out onto the catwalk in front of a huge cherry door, from some cathedral, no doubt. Marlys unlocked it with the key, and we entered a mauve room about the size of a bowling alley with track lighting reflected on the bleached floors that Marlys had mentioned. All scattered around were pale gray seats and sofas. Dark, navy blue low tables had Imari vases on them with those skinny Japanese flower arrangements sticking up, but not silk. Real larkspurs. Alive.

"This is Ben's garret?" I asked.

"Not entirely. This is the living room."

"Only the living room? What the hell was it before he glued mauve flannel onto the walls? A dance studio?"

"Not quite just the living room, Phoebe. It serves as a dining room and kitchen when the boy eats."

"A kitchen with no stove and fridge, Marlys? What about a sink. Does the boy wash?"

Marlys pointed to the far wall.

"You're telling me those strange sculptures are appliances?"

"Yeah. Here, let me hit the lights on this side."

She did. The lights were recessed, naturally, and you could see the faucets right under a tiny window covered by an opaque mauve shade. "Actually, Ben is rather embarrassed about all this, but the guy who did the room was a gift from his mother. An offer he couldn't refuse. It's nice, though, isn't it?"

"Sure, but I wouldn't want to live in it."

Marlys cast me an apprehensive glance. I bit my tongue too late. "Don't worry, Phoeb, the bedroom is much more cozy. C'mon."

The wall at the other end of the room, opposite the

kitchen statuary, concealed a door. It was concealed by
the artwork surrounding it. Some sort of wall sculptures. We went through and entered into a new decor
commonly known as early dorm. Two beds, desks,
stereo, a surfboard, junk, books and clothes all over the
place.

"Where does our friend do his surfing, or does his
mother ship him the Pacific Ocean now and then?" I
said in a shit-heel voice intended to hide my growing
nervousness.

"On the Seine."

"Naturally. Not much chance of getting wiped out
as you pass the rose window, I imagine."

"*Au contraire.* Ben surfs all the way from the Quai
d'Orsay to the Quai d'Austerlitz on the wake of the *ba-
teaux-mouches*, those little sight-seeing boats you went
on. He gives the pilots a little something to speed up the
tour. It's illegal, but the gendarmes don't have time to
arrest surfers; they're too busy posing for Japanese tourists. Here's a note."

Marlys bent over one of the beds and picked up a
piece of paper. "Dear Star over the Paris Night, your
buddy can park her stuff anywhere. This bed is hers.
Your admirer, Ben." She laughed. "Phoebe, Ben is really so sweet."

"And where does sweet Ben paint?" I asked, dump-
ing my stuff on the bed.

"Follow *moi.*"

We went back through the living room toward the
closet that held the elevator, and Marlys drew aside a
heavy mauve drape. In flooded the famous north light
that artists can't do without. Parallel with the living

room and bedroom was a room equal to their size combined with a skylight covering the roof above our heads which sloped down to where it met the far wall. The slope was evenly spaced by three Parisian windows with wrought-iron balconies. You could see the Eiffel Tower right near by, the Arc de Triomphe off to the right, and the entire Bois in the distance.

"Oh, Marlys, how breathtaking."

"Told ya."

"Can I go out on one of those balconies?"

"No, dear, but you can open the windows and sit on the window seats. You can sit there eating croissants to your heart's content."

I looked around. There were easels everywhere, and paints, and rags, and some finished and unfinished canvases all the same size; about four feet by four feet. It wasn't too untidy—not like the living room, of course, but a far cry from the boudoir.

"Where's Ben now? Mountain climbing up the towers of Notre Dame?"

"Don't be fresh till he gets to know you. He's over there, concentrating." She pointed.

I looked past a row of easels, and there was the back of this guy holding up a twenty-foot-long piece of ticker tape between his thumb and forefinger. He let it fall onto a smooth white bed sheet. Then he studied it. There were a few rocks around the sheet, cut in half.

"What does he paint besides rocks, and sheets with ticker tape on them?"

Ben laughed. "I paint things the way they fall, pregnant friend of black star."

He and Marlys gave each other a bear hug. "Ben Reuben, this is Phoebe Desmond."

"Welcome."

"Thanks. Excuse me. I have to go to the bathroom."

I zipped out, and heard Marlys say, "She's at some sort of pregnancy stage where something presses on her bladder. She hits the john about every twenty minutes."

"At night, too?"

"Every hour at night."

"Good. That's how often I wake up with all these great ideas that never make sense during the day. Maybe she'll make some sense out of them on the way to the john."

I stuck my head back in. "Where's the bathroom?"

"Sorry," he said. "Behind the coromandel screen in the bedroom."

A coromandel screen is four black panels twelve feet high with Chinese scenes made out of coral and ivory and other pretty stuff. I hadn't noticed it before because all his underwear was draped over it.

Ben was an average-looking guy. He was about five nine, nice build, brown beard, but not too hairy for an artist, although I could see that he gave himself his own haircuts. His beard was reddish though his hair wasn't. He wore jeans and a T-shirt, and sneaks all covered with paint. For the first time since I got to Paris, I wanted to go home, but all I could do was pee, and try not to cry. I couldn't go home, I knew, but I was entitled to momentary lapses. I hoped my great-grandmother would understand.

Chapter Eight

Every minute that Marlys isn't doing something, she is late for doing something. She left Ben and me right away and I became alarmed, seriously wondering if I'd have been better off at the Saint Agnes Home for Unwed Mothers in Hartford. But Ben enjoyed a certain saintlike quality, and it steadied me some. I yawned, and yawned again. Yawning works against panic when it's coming on you like a freight train with a drunk brakeman, I find.

"Phoebe," Ben said, "I'm one of those people who loves being in love, mostly for the company, but I'm really into something with my work, and I can't fall in

love with anyone for a couple of months. I'm so afraid
I'll lose this creative binge I'm on, so I hope you don't
mind me using you like this." He paused to scrutinize
this person in front of him whom he presumed to be
either very bored or very tired. "You don't look pregnant."

Forced to respond, I prattled between yawns. "I'm
small because I threw up every meal for four months,
and my sweatshirt is two sizes too big. But you've got it
all wrong. I'm using you. And I'll make lousy company.
I don't know art at all."

"Art who?" he asked, innocently. His eyes har-
bored a waggish gleam. I stared at them. Never before
had a man been able to put a stop to my panic-induced
yawning with just two little words.

His eyes were a very pale brown. Golden. Not only
that, but Ben is one of those people who have wondrous, thick eyelashes. Long is commonplace, thick is
divine. I knew deep in my heart, right then, that Ben
was special in that Gandhi-like way. Marlys had chosen
carefully. A person like me who tends to fall victim so
effortlessly to love at first sight also tends not to learn
from experience. At Yale it had taken two meetings. In
Paris it was taking two seconds. I was in love with this
Ben. Imagine Marlys finding someone it was okay to fall
immediately in love with. All the same, I had to put my
hand up to my mouth to hold back those rising yawns.

"Phoebe," he said through one of my ears and out
the other, "all there is to it is this—you look at a piece of
art, and say to yourself, 'That pleases me,' or, 'That
doesn't please me.' Art demands nothing more."

My voice was artificially calm. "What I saw in your

studio, Ben . . . all those stripes you painted? The colors were pleasing."

"Thank you. We can talk about other things, though. What have you been doing in Paris that you'd like to talk about?"

"Well, every morning since I've been here, I run out to get the *Tribune*, and come back to Marlys' where everyone is asleep. I check the standings while I drink my *café*. I'd love to talk about the pennant race. Do you like baseball at all?" I'd come to love baseball since Tyrus' mother died.

"Where's your team?"

"Four and a half out."

Our eyes locked as only losers' eyes can, his golden, mine mud. "Phoebe, you're a Boston fan?"

"I saw them beat Detroit just before I left for Paris."

"Did Wade Boggs look as good as he sounds?"

"Better."

"Think Yaz will be back?"

"Sure. He'll only quit if they have a real bad year. If they end up in the cellar."

"I thought they had a good shot this year."

"Best shot they've had since '78."

"But they're not going to make it, are they?"

"Nah, but they'll come in ahead of the Yankees. Winning the World Series would be anticlimactic after that."

"True."

"I have to go to the bathroom." (Before I throw my arms around you.)

"I have to paint."

I ran out faster than I normally run to the bathroom, but I do recall Marlys half warning me about Ben
being the love-at-first-sight type, too. Fortunately, nobody falls in love spontaneously with a pregnant
woman, I didn't think.

§   §   §

I was still organizing my stuff when he knocked.
"Come in," I called. "It's your bedroom."

He put his head in. "I didn't want to interrupt any
pregnancy stuff." He came in. "I thought of something
I should do." He picked up the gargantuan black screen
and dragged it over between my bed and his. He figured
I needed pregnancy privacy. I wondered what he
thought pregnant women did when they were alone.

"That screen looks like a million bucks, Ben."

"About half that."

"Oh."

"I'm going out, Phoebe," he said while he changed
behind the screen. "There's food, and you can putter
around or sleep—you really seem tired—or whatever
you want to do. I don't know when I'll be back."

" 'Bye."

" 'Bye."

"Thanks again."

"You're welcome, but don't thank me again."

"Okay."

I think I was the force behind his sudden depar-
ture, but I hoped not. I didn't want to bring him any
trouble—I just needed a place to stay. Besides that, I
was in love with him, so I felt bad about making him
leave even though it was not on purpose. But I was

starving. My stomach was quite unfeeling in its quest to make up for months of lost meals. As soon as he was out the door, I headed for the "kitchen." The mauve refrigerator had three shelves and a drawer. The top shelf had seven hundred kinds of cheese; the second shelf had a case of Budweiser; the third shelf had milk, half-and-half, butter, and hot dogs (Fenway Franks); the drawer was full of giant peaches and plums and bags of fresh raspberries. The inside of the fridge door had a handle. I pulled on it to reveal a lining of a dozen bottles of wine and a thermostat set at fifty-two.

I gorged myself before I noticed the freezer. Initially, I assumed it was a dishwasher. Lifting the heavy mauve lid, I found it loaded with Popsicles, Good Humor Bars, frozen homemade pies, and other American necessities.

While I nibbled my toasted almond bar, I decided I would have to avoid Ben as much as possible so he wouldn't know I was in love with him. Besides, I didn't want to disappoint Marlys. What she'd done for me was above and beyond the call of duty. Avoiding someone who slept in the same room seemed hard at first, but then I thought of my parents.

I looked out the studio window. Anyone who had been in Paris as long as I had and still hadn't been to the Eiffel Tower was a disgrace to the Stars and Stripes. I stuffed one of my last two ten-dollar bills in my pocket and left the apartment.

It took me a good hour to figure out how to operate the goddamn elevator. We pregnant ladies have short fuses due to hormones raging beyond our control. I pulled levers and knobs, and the thing would scrape down one flight and stop. Then I'd press the same levers and knobs, and it would go right back where it came from. Finally, I pushed everything at once, and the cage jerked, and bobbed, and twitched its way down five flights. I threw up, I'd estimate, between the third and second floors. Raging hormones cannot compare with a scorned, vengeance-seeking stomach rudely squeezed out of its accustomed position. I stepped out into the lobby and said to Adonis, "Do you speak English?"

He smiled and said, "Not too many."

I had to pantomime vomiting. He grew concerned, came around from his counter, and looked at the mess all over the grilled floor. Fortunately, most of it had gone through the grating. He went back, disappeared behind a curtain, and came back with a big bucket of water. He dumped it into the elevator. He dumped three buckets all together, and the elevator was as good as new. He then came out with an atomizer of L'Air du Temps, everybody's favorite aphrodisiac, and sprayed it at the cage, at me, and all over himself.

It's lovely how Parisians never concern themselves with things like flooded basements. Especially Parisians who are gorgeous Greek gigolos. They say strong smells also make pregnant women nauseous. Not L'Air du Temps, even when fired at point-blank range.

I walked down the Avenue Rapp in order to approach the tower from the rear. From Ben's view I noticed that an empty park hid behind the tower. The Avenue Rapp has no personality whatsoever aside from a building decorated in metal. New York City has some metal buildings, but this one has metal fruits and vegetables, and sassy cherubs, and ugly gargoyles all over the front of it. Someday this one pear hanging by its stem alone is going to fall off and kill someone.

I took a right into the middle of the park and joined a group of tourists with a guide speaking English. They were a real ragtag group. It was probably the cheapest tour in the city. We walked toward the tower, and I couldn't help but notice that this park was the longest, narrowest park I'd ever come across. I wondered why. I paid attention to the guide.

"The park is called the Champs de Mars; at one end, the Eiffel Tower, at the other, the École Militaire, where army officers are trained, as was Napoleon Bonaparte, who is entombed at Les Invalides just over there."

I didn't bother to look where he pointed. I never go into tombs anymore because of what I did to Tyrus.

"The Champs de Mars was used as a parade ground during the Revolution by the peasants, who often would display severed heads secretly sequestered from the site of the guillotine."

I left the group. "Secretly sequestered" is redundant. As in all Paris parks, you couldn't meander across the grass. The French rope off the grassy areas of their parks so that the kids can't have any fun. Every French park has rows of little kids sitting on benches staring miserably at the Keep off the Grass signs.

Just as I reached the tower, I felt the baby move. I was half sure it had been moving all along, because I'd feel these little butterflies fluttering around in there. But this was a whomp, and my belly lurched to the right. I got so excited I forgot all about the Eiffel Tower, crossed the Pont d'Iéna, and ran right through the rush-hour traffic all the way to the boulevard where Marlys lives. I couldn't help it. Here was an event in my life I felt compelled to share. Marlys' house was chock full of people, but not Marlys. I almost told my news to Barbara, the secretary, who didn't seem especially sympathetic to my need to see Marlys. In fact, the way she took a quick glance surreptitiously over her shoulder made me wonder if maybe Marlys was there after all. But what could I do? Scream "Hey, Mar! Come out, come out, wherever you are!" I think Barbara was a little sick of me busting up her organized routine. I got very depressed because she looked at me as if I was pitiful. I was.

Instead of telling anyone my news, I walked along every street that fell in front of my feet until long after dark. In the Tuileries Gardens, I wrote with a stick in the dirt under the bare rose bushes, "I felt my baby move."

I went over to a vendor and bought a pastry with some loose francs I found in my sweatshirt pocket. I never needed the ten-dollar bill. I headed home.

Home, right? What home? I didn't know how I could feel so alone when I had this baby doing cartwheels inside me, but I did. My poor little baby. At a time in life like this, there is only one person that you want to talk to—one person you want to share the miracle with. Your husband. I cried because I had no husband and no home to return to with my baby.

It was very dark. Trying to keep from getting lost took my mind off my sorrow, and it was late when I reached the Pension Rapp. No one was at the counter. I walked five flights up the stairs because of the elevator I couldn't control. I knocked on the cherry door, but there wasn't any answer. Then I remembered the key Ben had given me. He'd laid it on the bureau. That's where it was now.

I struggled all the way back down the stairs, hanging on to the railing for dear life. They were just like the stairs that twirl all the way up to the Statue of Liberty's head. Tyrus and I went in there once. I tapped the little bell on the counter, and the redheaded woman appeared. She looked like Tyrus' Aunt Lettie.

I wiped my nose on my sleeve before saying, "*Excusez-moi, madame. Je m'appelle Phoebe Desmond, et* I forgot my key. *Je reste avec Ben Reuben.*" I pantomimed turning a key in a lock.

"Ah, I understand this, *chérie*," she said. She should; the French invented pantomime. She shook her head sadly. "But this was the last key, I think, that Ben gives you. Wait, I check this.

"Stavros! Demetrios! Constantine!" she shouted.

Greek triplets appeared. Madame spoke some French, and they all started searching about. It was a half-baked search—they knew they were looking for a nonexistent key. I sniffled.

"*Chérie*, I do not have the skeleton key. And my maid does not come until morning."

"Do you have a vacancy? I can take a room for tonight."

"Ah, I have filled up, *chérie*, but is all right." She must have seen the new tears filling up my eyes. "You will stay with me and my boys. I have the guest room for you. Because of my Ben, I do this. My Ben will leave my pension one day, and leave me with the most beautiful apartment in all Paree. Come."

What could I say except *"Merci beaucoup, Madame . . . Madame,* uh . . ."

"Besette. I am Yvonne Besette. Come."

I followed her behind the curtain into what I'd call a parlor. The Greek boys were all smiling at me. God, they were beautiful.

"Stavros, boys, listen. Tonight we try to speak *anglais.* We have this friend of Ben's. She is . . . hmmm . . . *enceinte."*

"Pregnant," I translated.

She said, "Ah yes, pray-nyant."

"Ben told you, huh?" I had to make conversation, but God, I felt depressed.

"Mais non, mais non! He does not need to tell. I see the color of your cheeks, and how high the breasts."

The Greek boys stared at my cheeks and breasts, all four of which were beginning to appear bigger than normal—normal being practically nonexistent. The Greeks nodded in agreement.

"So," Madame smiled heartily, "we have a little party to welcome you to my pension, and for the happy occasion, also. I have the babies, too. They are all with their grandmother in Évian. You know, near the lake. Better for children than this, no?"

She gestured toward the swarthy Greeks, who had materialized to a group of four. The new one was the guy who had cleared the decks for me in the elevator. He was stretching and wore no shirt. He smiled sleepily at me. I suppressed my desire to hug his golden chest, the hair in perfect symmetric waves, like a sandbar. Instead, I cleared my throat.

"I understand, madame. I am going to give my baby to a couple who want a child but can't have one. Yale is a worse place to raise a baby than this, madame. Much worse."

"Yale?" the boys chorused.

"Yes, where I go to school."

"You are a scholar," Stavros said, impressed.

"My boys are all students, too, mademoiselle."

"Please call me Phoebe." I realized I was relaxing. My baby, too. "What do you guys study?"

One said, "City planning"; one said, "Economics"; the golden sandbar said, "Medicine,"—God, imagine that bedside manner—and the fourth one, his arm hugged by Madame, said, "Hotel management."

"I give all my nice boys . . ." Madame said a French word.

"Scholarships!" translated the Greek chorus.

I grinned. I couldn't help it, and not two seconds ago I was convinced I'd never grin again.

"Ah, she laughs, my boys. Good! I was sure the large tears were soon to come. Now we party."

God, did we party. They kept giving me this concoction of egg yolks, cream, and a French version of Marsala, all of which is the French version of zabaglione, a dessert to be found in overpriced Italian-American restaurants. It was to "build up the blood, and the milk." I guess it didn't occur to her that I wouldn't be needing the milk. To be honest, it hadn't occurred to me either until that moment, but I tried not to think about it.

We danced, and how I love to dance. I probably danced as wildly as I did because I wouldn't be needing the milk. I taught them the old James Brown, one of my all-time favorites, and they taught me cheek to cheek, rounded pregnant belly to flat Greek belly. Each Greek maintained a chronic state of erection, and I thought Madame better get ready to man the dikes once the party was over.

After the dancing, we ate tremendous platters of "Greek nouvelle" food; stuffed grape leaves, moussaka, and all that, but the portions were tiny and arranged sparingly on white plates with sculptured raw vegetables on the side. That half-naked Greek was going to have the best hotel restaurant in all of Paris, or Athens.

I woke up the next day just after dawn in a bed with a red church candle glowing beside it. Madame on the other side of the wall was having violent multiple orgasms, which came as no surprise. I found I was wearing some sort of cozy long flannel nightshirt so I quickly sat up and felt all over the bed for spare Greeks, but none of them were in there with me.

I went back to sleep hugging my fat little belly. I was okay. I didn't mind so much being alone anymore because I really wasn't. A pregnant woman can never be alone once she's felt the baby move.

Chapter Nine

Ben was pissed. Very pissed. Pissed is another favorite locution at Yale, second only to fuck.

"Phoebe, I've got a great arrangement here, and I can't have you taking advantage of Madame Besette."

"Okay. Next time I'll sleep on the sidewalk."

"No. Next time, you'll remember to take the key."

"Okay."

"Here. This is for you. For the next time you forget the key."

"What is it?"

"It's a French checkbook."

"What do I do with a French checkbook?"

"Same thing you do with an American one—write checks."

"Hey, this account is in my name."

"I know. Marlys told me you had no money. Now when you forget the key, you can sleep at the Ritz. Don't protest. I found the last three checks my father sent me in an empty paint thinner can. I won't need them, so I opened an account for you. I don't want to have to worry about you."

"Listen, Ben. All I need besides a place to sleep is food, and God knows you've got plenty of that. And I intend to earn my keep. I'll do your chores, run your errands, and make you hot cocoa. I don't want any money."

"I have a feeling your shirt size is going to change a few times. I don't know if I'm mature enough to handle a naked, pregnant lady walking around my studio. And you'll have to pay your doctor. Before you know it Christmas'll be here, and you'll probably want to send some presents home to your family. Spend it. My mother will get anxious if my balance builds up and start sending me matzo-ball soup."

"I forgot about all that stuff."

"Don't worry about it. I'm loaded. Write all the checks you want. Really. Buy clothes. Buy French sneakers; they're hilarious."

"Ben, can I tell you something important? Would you mind?"

"Shoot."

"I felt the baby move for the first time."

"You did? When?"

"Yesterday. I had no one to tell."

"Don't cry."

Of course, I truly couldn't help it, though I tried. Ben got me some Kleenex, sat down next to me on one of his pale gray Ultrasuede seats, and nestled me under his arm until I stopped.

"Shall I make you some hot cocoa, Phoebe?"

"That's nice of you Ben, but cocoa was supposed to be my job."

"I'd burn the pan, to tell you the truth. I admire good cooks for their ability to keep their minds on what's happening in four different pots and in two different ovens."

"It's true. It's not easy. Before she had to go to the nursing home, my nana used to make Thanksgiving dinner for her enormous family, and she managed to bring fourteen different vegetables to the table all steaming hot."

"My grandmother does that, too."

Instead of saying "Gee, we have something in common," I said, "I'm afraid this conversation is making me hungry."

Fetuses must have a fairly powerful will to survive, since a pregnant woman can so easily supersede a crisis with the will to eat. I hated to feel Ben's snug arm leaving my shoulder, though.

"Let's go get some food then, okay?"

"Okay."

"And here's something to keep in mind the next time you feel glum."

"What's that?"

"The Red Sox came in ahead of the Yankees."

I laughed. "You know, Ben, as serious baseball fans, we really should check on who took the Series."

"But it doesn't matter."

"Yeah."

We went out for brunch. I ate for two. Ben ate for five. We spent the afternoon together, with me finally seeing the Eiffel Tower up close. I loved Ben, but I could tell Ben was the type who loved everyone. I could tell he especially loved Marlys. That night Ben took me to see Marlys at the Folies Bergère. He warned me of the bizarre nudity. It was worse than bizarre. It started out quite innocently as the all-bosom review. A row of fifty pairs of breasts is about as sexy as a row of teeth.

Things got nuder, and kinkier, but nothing I couldn't handle. The big moment came when six huge blond men in Viking skirts and boots with horns on their heads escorted a twenty-five-foot-high banana onto the stage. Gilt stairways rose out of the stage all around the banana, and the blonds climbed the steps to the top of the banana. Slowly, they peeled it while the audience started going crazy, shouting "Marlee! Marlee!" Marlys has no last name in Paris.

Inside the banana skin was Marlys, naked and oiled. Her Root Beer Barrel skin was aglow, and the men began to lick her. I didn't stay for the rest of the act.

Ben told me he didn't mind leaving because he'd seen the act about a thousand times. We could still hear the throng shouting "Marlee! Marlee!" out on the side-walk.

We ended up where we should have gone in the first place rather than the Folies Bergère—Saul's. Saul's is a cozy Jewish bistro behind Les Invalides. It's Jewish because Saul is Jewish and a lot of people who go there are Jewish, including Ben. The rye bread is definitely Jewish, i.e., delicious.

§   §   §

At Ben's, one week followed the next easily and quickly. While Ben painted, I read and wrote all this that was happening in my journal. I grew fatter all over, not just my stomach, and my face became softly attractive. I'd always had a scrawny, sallow look about me, and for the first time I had round, healthy-looking cheeks. The baby swam around all the time. I had forgotten Halloween, but I remembered Thanksgiving. In fact, the day of Thanksgiving proved memorable for me. I actually communicated with the baby. Ben called it Mr. Fetus.

Mr. Fetus pushed its foot out just under my right rib cage. I looked down, and there was this lump. It didn't hurt, but it didn't feel good either. So, I pushed on the bump. Mr. Fetus pushed right back.

"Ben," I whispered.

"Yeah?"

"*Sh-h-h* . . ."

"What? What?"

"Look at the baby's foot."

His face fell a mile. He was afraid the foot was sticking out of my pants. "No, Ben. Right here. Quick. Push on this bump."

Ben sat down beside me and pushed on the bump. The bump pushed back. "Holy shit, Mr. Fetus pushed back."

"That's what I'm trying to tell you."

"Do you mind if I try something?"

"Like what?"

"*Sh-h-h* . . ." Ben reached under my shirt and very gently rubbed the bump. Mr. Fetus' little foot withdrew.

"Oh, Ben," was all I could think of to say. Ben kept rubbing my side under my shirt, and then his other hand seemed to slide under my shirt. His hands felt so good, and smooth, and warm that I wanted to do the same thing to him. I put my entire arms under his old, ripped Brooks Brothers pinstripes, and we started kissing each other so continuously I nearly choked from no air. Then Ben's head was under my shirt, and his beard tingled across my breast, and I was out of my shirt, hugging his head hard against my chest. I looked down and had a hard time believing those swollen breasts were actually mine.

When we were both naked, and rolling over and over between the sofas and chairs on the mauve carpeting, I couldn't get over how my round stomach fit perfectly into his concave one, and neither of us wanted to release the other because so much of us was touching.

He said, "I didn't mean for this to happen."

I said, "I love you, Ben."

He said, "Shit."

I said, "I have to go to the bathroom bad."

He said, "Me, too."

I beat him there out of instinct.

We took a shower, and we started to make love in the shower, but Ben got afraid that I'd fall, so we went to bed and made love all day long; me, Ben and the

baby, who remained completely blasé. She would soon
be the kind of kid who would sleep through house-shak-
ing thunderstorms, just the way old Blob used to do.
And she'll be the kind of adult who casually takes over
the controls of a 747 after the crew becomes incapaci-
tated by ptomaine, and saves three hundred and sixty
lives, although I doubt highly that Blob will ever progress to that level of capability. Blob will sleep through
the crash itself.

That night we went to a restaurant that served an
"American Turkey Dinner." The man who owned the
place must have cleverly copied the dinner from a picture rather than a cookbook because the canned, jellied
cranberry sauce turned out to be sliced pickled beets.

When we came home, I asked Ben to tell me what
he was trying to do with his art. He told me for about
three hours. He wanted to tell me—or tell someone—as
badly as I had wanted to tell someone about the baby
moving.

His studio was dark because Ben only paints in the
daylight, although maybe all artists paint in the daylight—I wouldn't know. We brought in some candles
and sat on either side of a canvas laid out on the floor.
On the other two sides of the canvas were lying several
chunks of rocks that I've mentioned. The rocks looked
as though they had been broken open by a diamond
cutter; each had one flat, smooth surface revealing wavy
colored lines. The canvas was painted with those same
curving stripes bending softly together.

"See, Phoebe, these rocks are agate."

I picked one up and looked at it, trying to act fascinated. "Oooh, agate."

"Be quiet. I'm trying to paint lines inspired by natural substances, like agate."

"But your stripes don't look like these. Yours have symmetry, agate lines don't."

"I know. My lines aren't meant to copy nature, just represent it. And I further interpret nature with color."

He lost me, but so what.

"Then, Phoebe, I take something man-made, like this." He took off his watch, and dropped it. "I paint the watch just the way it lands on my stripes. So far, it's only worked once."

He pulled me up and took me over to see a canvas turned against the wall. He carried it into the living room, turned up the tracks, and showed me his one completed work. The stripes were lovely, and sitting just slightly off-center was a pile of ticker tape so real, so three-dimensional, that it made you want to pick it up.

"How do you do that, Ben? You must have a gift." Remember, I know all about gifts.

"It pleases you?"

"It amazes me."

"But it doesn't please you."

"Ben, it would, but I have such an uncontrollable urge to brush off the ticker tape to see your pretty colored stripes."

He let the painting fall, took me by the shoulders, and said, "I love you, too, Phoebe. You've just given me the support I've craved so that I can try it again."

"I thought I insulted you."

"*Au contraire.* I'm trying to show through my art man's desire to brush away what's artificial and find what's natural."

I kind of looked at my feet. Ben lifted up my chin and made me look into his thick, golden eyes. "Corny, huh, Phoebe?"

"I'll say."

"Now that's an insult."

"So look at Kahlil Gibran. Nobody's cornier than him, and he's a zillionaire."

"Kahlil was dead before he became a zillionaire. I'm one already."

"I keep forgetting, though I don't know why, considering." I swept my arm across the living room.

§   §   §

Later, when we were stuffed into Ben's bed, me against the wall, Ben said,

"Phoebe, may I ask you a personal question?"

"Sure."

"How come you didn't have an abortion?"

"Funny."

"What's funny?"

"Funny you should ask. Marlys didn't."

"That's what happens to friends when they grow up. They stop prying."

"But she's the only one who would have understood."

"Unless she's had an abortion."

"Oh, Ben, has she?" I sat straight up, ready to run to Marlys.

"Not that I know of. I was just giving her an excuse for not prying."

"Would you mind prying, Ben? I'd like to tell you."

He pulled me down on top of him. "Go."

"Two people are the reasons, one my mother."

"That's not surprising."

"My mother never knew I got pregnant."

"How about the father. Is he the other reason?"

"No, just my mother. My father doesn't effect my life at all."

"I didn't mean your father. *The* father."

"Oh. *The* father is a jerk. He effects me less than my father. Don't ever mention *the* father again."

"Okay, but if it wasn't for him, you wouldn't be here with me."

"Shut up, Ben, and try to not be nice."

"You were nice when I made you look at the rocks."

"Do you want me to tell you, or not?"

"Go."

"Once, when I was sixteen, I came down to the kitchen for breakfast, and my mother was sitting at the table with my little sister's red plastic record player going. She had on the record 'Strawberry Fields Forever.' She was really crying, and not hiding it, so I knew things were serious. I asked her if someone had died, because my first instinct was that my old nana died at the nursing home, but she said, 'John Lennon. Someone shot him. Someone had to shoot John Lennon.'

"Then she banged her fist on the table, and the needle jumped, and the record kept skipping. John Lennon singing and static and clicking and skipping—over and over. Round and round and round. It was awful. The worst was when she finally looked up at me, so bedraggled, and said, 'The killer was holding *Catcher in the Rye.*' The book, Ben."

"Why was that the worst?"

"My mother named me after Holden's sister. She loved that book."

"Oh."

"So I made her a cup of tea, and I told her that even if that killer wasn't holding *Catcher in the Rye*, he'd still have murdered John Lennon. I didn't feel too bad myself because I was too young for the Beatles. Then she was okay, but it spoiled her Christmas. She got pregnant right after that.

"We all knew she was pregnant—she didn't hide it or anything—and everybody gave her all kinds of advice before she went to have amniocentesis. There were two arguments. First, those self-righteous bastards who kept telling her that Down's syndrome children are an absolute delight, and full of love, and don't abort it even if it was mongoloid. Then, there were those flip bastards who kept saying, 'Oh, Brenda, get rid of it if it's not normal. So what.' As if my mother's fetus were a mosquito.

"So I took it upon myself to do a survey. I went to the mothers of twenty Down's syndrome children in our area. While other people were around, they were all cheerful and patient. Alone with me—and I can really ingratiate myself with people when I want . . ."

"You're telling me."

"Alone, Ben, they said, if you have a Downs baby, you manage fairly well because she'll goo and coo, smile and crawl just like other babies. But when the child reaches puberty, you have an adult retarded person in your house who looks like a cockeyed blimp and who is a million times more demanding than any ten babies.

She'll menstruate all over the furniture, then her siblings will end up hating you because of all the attention they were deprived of, and because they have no choice when it comes to inheriting the kid when you die. One poor lady told me her son spent all his time trying to have sex with their Irish setter, the vacuum cleaner, with cold cuts . . . oh, a whole bunch of disgusting stuff. Once, even her, she told me.

"And every one of them loved their kids too much to send them to some state hellhole, but they weren't rich enough to send them somewhere good. What I found out, Ben, was that there is a lot more to this sort of thing than meets the eye.

"At the sixteenth week, my mother went to the hospital for a couple of hours, and after that no one mentioned the baby again because she was no longer pregnant. A year later, on the anniversary of the abortion, she was crying at the table again, and I made her tea and went into all that stuff I had learned about Down's syndrome kids, trying to convince her that she made the right decision. She finished her tea and said, 'Phoebe, the fetus didn't have Down's syndrome. It was perfectly normal. I had an abortion anyway because I couldn't survive a baby right then.'

"I guess, Ben, I had to choose between her kind of suffering and this kind. I picked this kind. She'll go through life wondering what it would have been like, and I'll go through life wondering how he's doing."

"Didn't your father take some of your mother's burden . . . some of the guilt?"

"My father is a very lucky man. He is able to amputate whole sections of his brain that contain things he chooses not to involve himself in. I forced him to tell me why he wouldn't take part in the decision to have the abortion, because I heard my mother tell my aunt that.

"He told me he had a job. The job required making decisions which would effect his entire family's well-being, and that my mother was in charge of family decisions. He said that when me and my sister were born it was at a time when fathers were left out. In so many more words, he said he liked being left out. He was grateful to be left out, and would continue to be left out. Women and children, he said, are part of a world he wasn't at all interested in. Nice, huh?"

"Well, at least he talked to you. My dad said his father never even noticed him. My dad used to brag about how Grandpa was so important, so involved in his business, and had so many friends. Everyone loved him, and wanted his company, and he was such a great and busy man that he just didn't have time for his children. Then my grandfather died, and my parents got the biggest funeral home in Chicago to accommodate all his friends and business associates. Guess how many people came to his funeral besides family?"

"How many?"

"None. He was just a selfish bum. I caught my dad crying once. It was when he could no longer deny that his father was a selfish bum."

"What is your father like, Ben?"

"He's great. He loves me. He'd love you."

"I'm real tired now, Ben."

"But who's the other person?"

"What other person?"

"The other person who was the reason you didn't
have an abortion."

Suddenly, I was wide awake. "Oh, him."

"Shall I get out the hot cocoa, Phoebe?"

"Yeah."

Chapter Ten

Him. Tyrus.

When I learned to write at age four in Miss
Wright's nursery school, I started a journal. This is still
the journal that I'm writing in now. At my home in
Connecticut I have this huge trunk in the attic, my journal trunk. Every time I finish a notebook, I pitch it into
the trunk. All except July and August of 1977. I take
that notebook with me wherever I go now. It's all about
Tyrus. I can't talk about Tyrus without getting that tremendous buildup of saliva in my mouth that says, "You
are about to vomit." So I always figured that if I could

just bring myself to read the entry about Tyrus, I'd soon be able to talk about him, too.

I pulled the notebook out of my duffel bag, and brought it out to the kitchen table where Ben and I drink our cocoa and eat the tollhouse cookies his mother sends him monthly.

"What's this?"

"Part of my lifelong journal. It's the section about Tyrus. Ben, I really decided not to have an abortion because of Tyrus. Even more so than my mother."

"Don't get nervous. You're talking so fast."

"For the last year," I explained, still talking fast to get it over with, "I've been carrying this around with me. It's from 1977. I want to read it, but I get nervous."

"Let's see, when Marlys was thirteen, you wrote it?"

"Yeah, and I was thirteen, too."

"Is she in it?"

"Sure." I'm beginning to think Ben loves Marlys as much as me, but so do I as much as him.

"I'll read it if you want me to, and then we'll talk about Tyrus."

"Well, I might not want to talk about him, but it will be nice to have someone understand."

"Okay. You saw my important painting. I even explained it to you. Being understood is great, even if only one person is involved."

"Now listen, Ben, you don't have to read it all at once. I mean, it's a hundred pages and who cares what a thirteen-year-old has to say in one sentence, let alone a hundred pages. And my father, when I was thirteen, would not allow swearing in the house, so my language in the journal is quite foul. The section about Tyrus begins, unfortunately, with a short story. I don't recall the reason I did that."

"Phoebe, you never told me you write short stories."

"I don't. Not now. I did when I wanted to be a writer."

"Why don't—"

"Just read, okay?"

PART TWO

reason, I need all upward mobile and outward for
that. I'm a low I rather have a sweet potato and
. . .

Chapter One

KIDNAPPED

by

Phoebe Montague Desmond

July 18th was one of those God damned, boring, hot summer days when all the other kids were on vacation, and where the hell was I? Europe? Disney World? Lake George? God damned Jones Beach? No. I wasn't anywhere because my money-grubbing old man is such a capitalist that he wouldn't even take a lousy two-week vacation. I need an upward-mobile accountant for a father, right? He'd rather have a heart attack at fifty than a vacation at thirty-five so he can retire to a golf cart at

Heritage Village Condominiums while the rest of us go screw. However, when he wheeled home on the night of July 18th in his used, beloved, little Porsche, he sure as hell was sorry because July 18th was the day of The Big Kidnapping. Mine.

That morning, I was over at the Monsoons'—actually known as the Munsens and actually known also as the two biggest farts on the cul-de-sac, whose house sports a front porch slightly larger than the stage at Radio City Music Hall. I was tapping out an old soft shoe routine choreographed by myself, and looking quite a lot like old Ginger Rogers on "The Late Night Movie" who, by the way, is still the world's greatest dancer and my idol, when out of the Monsoons' front door came the two most clumsy-assed morons I've ever seen, carrying the Monsoons' silver chest, jewelry boxes, color portable, and rushing their balls off. Naturally, they collided head-on into me, and there I was tripping like a God damned maniac over eight million spoons, knives, and God damned dessert forks.

"For Crissake, where the hell did this fuckin' kid come from?"

"Never mind the kid. Let's just get outa here."

"The hell with you. I'm grabbin' this fuckin' kid."

I, of course, stood there like a dolt, and the next thing I knew, one of the guys grabbed me around the waist, ran across the Monsoons' front yard trampling every God damn prize begonia in sight, and threw me into the back seat of some shit-smelling old '64 Ford Galaxie 500 while I stupidly checked out the duals instead of the license plate.

So, off we went at eight million miles an hour through eight million development streets without a God damn cop in sight with two of the biggest jerks I've ever met in my life, one of whom had his fat, clammy hand slapped over my mouth. After about five minutes, the guy in the front seat, who by the way had more zits on his face than all my baby-sitters put together, started slowing down. The clammy hand relaxed.

I, being incredibly pissed off, naturally, pulled my head away and yelled, "Hey! What the hell do you assholes think you're doing?"

"Shut up, brat. We oughta kill ya for stompin' around that porch, scarin' the shit out of us."

Stomping? He was talking about one of my best routines which I had spent at least ten woman-hours on. Well, I was pretty nervous about this whole thing, but I wasn't going to waste my time letting that no-class slob injure my ego, so I gathered up all my strength, and yelled my God damn head off.

Unfortunately, all I could get out was one good, "Help, police," when that disgusting hand clamped back into position so tight that I could taste it. And, boy, did it ever taste like pure dog turd.

"Listen, brat, if you open that God damn trap of yours once more you can kiss your Barbie Dolls chowsito." This incredibly lousy line drew a real horse-laugh from old Zit-face in the front seat who had slowed down to about forty now that we were out of the proverbial woods and into the real thing. I mean, there was nothing but trees, dirt roads, and crummy old Milky Way wrappers all over. Being a rather vindictive person I couldn't resist a little comeback, so I jerked my head away again.

"Only assholes have Barbie Dolls, so what's so funny, you giant Zit?"

Old Zit-face immediately started to choke, and the guy choking me said, "Shut your trap, or I'll break your skinny little neck."

"Yeah," says old Zit-face, "so you do what Turk tells ya."

I immediately burst into eight million gales of laughter. "TURK! Turk? Your name is really Turk? Ha! You must be a regular asshole gangster or something."

But I stopped laughing fast when old Turk grabbed a fistful of my hair and nearly yanked my head off. The pain, of course, brought me immediately to my senses, so I decided to just relax and try and figure out where the hell these guys were taking me. All I could think was, boy, did it ever serve me right for not paying attention to the roads when I was out with the family, because for the next ten minutes we drove on unfamiliar cowpaths through nothing but scraggly pines and empty Bud cans the latter of which made me think of my old man who sure was going to wonder what the hell happened to me.

I didn't have time to worry for long, though, as we soon pulled into a stony imitation of a road at the end of which was a tiny little house with roof shingles falling off, and not a blade of grass on the front lawn. My two friends piled themselves out, and pulled me with them, and wouldn't you know I was too busy eye-balling the place to resist. Out the front door comes a big, fat old lady who, except for the bright orange beehive hairdo, looked exactly like old Sister Mary Bonaventure who had taught my second-grade religion class.

"Hey," she yelled, "did you two guys pull off a house job or rob the local orphanage?"

"Very funny," said old Zit-face. They proceded to tell old Lettie (that was her name) about how I was jumping around the Monsoons' front porch when they were coming out with the goods.

"So ya had to take her with ya?"

"Well, whatcha expect us to do? Leave her to squeal?"

"You two jerks oughta have your heads examined," Lettie said. "This kid woulda been too excited to remember what you looked like." She was right, too, except for the zits. I could see who was the brains of this outfit.

"So bring the stuff in, and I'll try to figure out what to do with the kid." Old Lettie put her arm around my shoulder.

"So what's your name, kid?"

"Phoebe."

"Ya hungry?"

"Starved."

She made us some liverwurst sandwiches on that delicious Wonder Bread which my mother hasn't bought in a dog's age because she thinks it'll make her a better mother if she forces me to eat that foul-tasting whole wheat shit. So, we chowed down while Turk and Zit-face brought in the load of junk that used to belong to the Monsoons. They talked mostly business, about how they were going to meet up with their fence in The Big Apple, and how it would bring them a few hundred bucks until they met up with Hairy Gene and the boys. (Although it might have been Harry, Gene, and the boys.)

The whole afternoon was a lot like watching a three-hour comeback of "Hawaii Five-O," and I was really enjoying myself until they all started looking at me kind of funny. I never did find out old Zit-face's name since they basically called each other "Hey!" but he, in particular, began to look awfully sinister. In fact, he really gave me the creeps what with his zits being bigger than his squinty little eyes.

"Hey, kid. You rich?"

"Nah."

"How much does your old man make?"

"What's the difference? The selfish old workaholic spends it all on himself, anyway." Lettie got all concerned.

"Now, honey, that ain't no way to talk about your old man, is it?" (Old Turk and old Zit-face didn't bat an eyelash. They probably talked that way about their grandmother.)

"Well, it's true. My mother hasn't even got a dishwasher, and he keeps taking his crummy Porsche to the garage every other day at fifty bucks a throw." Old Lettie had hit on a sore point, and idiot Zit-face hit on it further.

"Your old man makes the dough. The heada the house should have a set of classy wheels."

"Yeah, but seeing as he's never around when my jerk of a sister shits her pants instead of the potty, my mother deserves a little break now and again."

"Hey, I think we got a little bra-burner here," said Turk, as he whapped me on the back. I figured I'd better humor them while they weren't looking sinister.

"Actually, I'm an undershirt-burner."

Well, that sent them into eight million gales of laughter, and old, smart Lettie said, "So let's forget her old man's dough. We'll dump her when it gets dark so we don't get ourselves into some real trouble, and then we'll take off."

They all agreed, and while Turk and Zit-face went out for some Kentucky Fried, Lettie and I had a little chat, which consisted mostly of Lettie asking me the usual asshole questions grownups ask kids: what grade are you in, what's your favorite subject, what are you going to be when you grow up, etc. She was very interested in my future as a dancer, and she said she used to be one herself. In fact, when Turk and Zit-face got back, there she was, teaching me a few of her snazzy old steps.

We had a real nice dinner as they had even brought bean salad, rolls, and mashed potatoes (unlike my old man who would have gotten plain chicken, three pieces of which he'd have eaten on the way home, and then made like he got gypped).

While we finished up, Turk flipped on the Monsoons' TV to catch the news, and right after those assholes got through singing about how they'd like to buy the world a Coke, there was old Meredith Viera of "News at Six" interviewing none other than the old tightwad himself, my old man. I couldn't help but think that if they'd found me in a gutter somewhere, good old anchorman Jim Jensen would be doing the story instead.

When Turk finally got a decent picture, I could see that dear old Dad was as white as a God damned sheet, which actually reflected the fact that he was more nervous about being on the tube than he was about me.

". . . so please, whoever you are, there will be no arrests. Just bring our little Fifi back to us." Holy shit! He stopped calling me that when I was five. If any of my friends start calling me Fifi, I thought, I'll kill him. Old Turk, of course, laughed his ass off.

"Fifi! What the hell are you, kid, a stripper?"

"What the hell are you, curator of the Topkapi?"

"Huh?"

Everybody immediately shushed us because there was my mother, sniffling away. "Please. Phoebe is a dear, sweet child. She . . ." My mother was so choked up that my old man started yabbering again before the camera man could get back to him.

"This is our baby, Maribeth, who will not be able to

sleep tonight unless Phoebe is there to read her a bedtime story."

Old Zit-face yelled out, "Ha. Her old man is trying for a friggin' Emmy."

"Yeah. He don't know I'm reading his copy of *The Joy of Sex* to the little dummy."

We were shushed again, and this time the camera panned in on old Blob, who was laughing her head off and waving her rotten Pooh Bear like a God damned maniac.

The reason I call my kid sister Blob is because I saw a fifties horror movie on TV called *The Blob*. All through it, they played a song that went:

> It leaps,
> It creeps,
> It slides,
> It glides,
> Across the walls,
> The floor, the . . . etc.

The song describes my sister perfectly. If you're presently living with a two-year-old, believe me, you've got my sympathy. One thing about old Blob, if she saw a ninety-year-old paraplegic get flattened by a steam roller, she'd laugh like a hyena. Naturally, the director wised up and went back to old Meredith.

"Now we will speak with little Phoebe's best friend, Miss Marlys Hightower."

"That's MS. Marlys Hightower," Marlys piped up from the background.

"Right on, Marlys," I said, but I didn't hear the first part of what Marlys had to say because of that pea brain, Zit-face, who looked as though his head was going to explode.

"Holy, fuckin' shit. This God damned kid's best friend is a God damned nigger."

Well, not being one to argue with a cretin like Zit-face, I said, "Marlys is black. I'm white. You're purple. So what."

"Whadya mean, purple?" He was a perfect straight man.

"Purple! Like the disgusting color of your eight million zits." I instinctively ducked behind Lettie, and as Zit-face leaped out of his chair at me, old Turk yelled (saving my life), "Shut up, the both of ya. I wanna catch this." And we went back to Ms. Marlys.

"My dear beloved Phoebe," Marlys crooned, "is my best and truest friend. She is warm and dear, with a personality which combines the courage and strength of Susan B. Anthony, the bravery and determination of Harriet Tubman, the sincerity and charm of Eleanor Roosevelt, the brilliance and mystery of Virginia Woolf, the fortitude . . ." Naturally, she was cut off fast, right when her oratory was about to reach the heights that only her idol's speeches could: Doctor Martin Luther King, Jay Are.

They closed with a video-tape of all the kids in my neighborhood holding up a banner saying Bring Back Phoebe. Those old buddies of mine sure looked like a bunch of refugees from a Galapagos work camp except, of course, for old Duwayne Duwyer who was in the back row with a shit grin on his face and giving everybody the finger.

Anchor man Jim Jensen then read the special police information number if anybody knew of my whereabouts, and with a promise of Warner Wolf making a total ass of himself, Lettie snapped off the set.

"Hey!" Old Zit-face was right out of his chair again.

Too bad he was a sports fan, as if old Warner Wolf knows a God damn thing about anything except hockey, which is not a sport in our country.

But Lettie being in charge, old Zit-face might have been a four-year-old. "We've got to get rid of this kid. Things are gonna get real serious. I'm gonna call Hairy Gene and the boys, and we'll leave tonight. Pack up."

That Lettie was a regular drill sergeant, because Turk and Zit-face jumped up and started gathering their junk together with the Monsoons'. Lettie told me they were going to leave me off about a half a mile from Kentucky Fried, and she'd give me a dime to call my old man from the phone booth.

"Will you be afraid to wait in the dark, Phoebe?"

"Are you kidding?"

It was all settled, and at eleven-thirty that night, there I was walking down Route 7, heading south from the Colonel's. I was even kind of sorry to say goodby to old Lettie, but honestly, old Zit-face and Turk were not my kind of people.

By the way, at the phone booth I didn't call the old man. Would you? I mean, after all, which would you prefer to drive home in? A police cruiser or a crummy, old Porsche that had a three-to-five chance of breaking down?

They zoomed me right home for a large, weepy scene with my old man and lady. All the commotion woke up Blob, and she came wandering out of bed with her filthy Pooh. When she saw me, she started screaming like a banshee and waving old Pooh madly in the air. Naturally, she bammed me in the eye with it.

The cops were all excited and asked me a hundred questions a minute, but I'm not very good at descriptions (they didn't even know who James Coco was when I told them who Turk looked like). Anyway, they were pretty disgusted with me when they didn't get any last names, or the car's license number, but even though I may not be agent Double-o-Seven, I'm not an asshole, either. I told them I knew the number at Hairy Gene's and the boys. I had watched Lettie dial it.

Well, they all marched out the door, PDQ, just as two reporters came running in. The reporters were basically interested in whether old Zit-face or Turk had taken "liberties" with me, particularly now that I sported a black eye, but that made my old man all nervous so he threw them out immediately and carried me up to bed, piggyback, like when I was a kid. I, of course, bonked my forehead against the overhead door moulding. I knew I was too old for that sort of stuff, but I didn't want to upset the old man considering the circumstances.

So now the summer is over, and my old man finally gave in and took us on vacation. We went to Amish country. Naturally, we didn't see any Amish, but our motel did have a swimming pool with a sliding board, and those invisible Amish people sure cook good pancakes except for that pile of apple butter on top which I would scrape off. Pancakes with a big pile of apple butter look like something I personally dubbed "Shit on a Shingle." So what with the pool, it wasn't a total loss.

As for Lettie, Zit-face, and Turk, they're all down in the old hoosegow waiting trial, but do you think my old man will take me down to visit them?

Ha!

THE END

§ § §

Ben put the journal down at the end of the short story, and nibbled his thumb nail before he asked, "You wrote this at thirteen?"

"Yeah."

"Why don't you want to be a writer anymore?"

"I like people too much. I don't like to be alone."

"I'm alone when I paint, but when I finish something, I have a big blowout with about a thousand people."

"I'm glad that works for you, Ben. I have to force myself to stay on an even, consistent keel. I can't be alone or bored for more than a day maybe, or I do crazy things . . . like get kidnapped."

"And like get pregnant."

"No, I got pregnant because my IUD wasn't up to snuff. You don't have to read anymore. It was a dumb idea." I took my journal off his lap. He took it back.

"I haven't read in five years. I forgot how much I enjoy reading. Just one thing, though."

"Yeah?"

"Am I reading fiction or nonfiction?"

"Docudrama."

He laughed, tucked me under his arm, and turned back to my journal.

§   §   §

So did you believe all that crap? Believe it. Most of it. I really was kidnapped, but the story you just read was just a little short fiction based on my experience as a kidnap victim. I sent it to the *Seventeen* magazine short-story contest. Never heard anything, though. I didn't expect to. *Seventeen* girls do not read words like goddamn and fuck, if you get my drift. But if I'm going to be a great writer, I figure I need the practice. Getting back to *Seventeen*, I read somewhere that *Seventeen* was the last magazine in the U.S. to quit airbrushing out belly buttons. All those tall, skinny, beautiful models perfect in every way except for their holeless tummies.

And getting back to the kidnapping, let me tell you what actually happened, and in the process I will also tell you about a man named Tyrus who affected my life more than anyone else with the possible exception of Ted Williams when I realized I could never play major league ball. Ted Williams thrust me headlong into the feminist movement. It's a long story, but it's incredibly exciting and involved, and although there have been a tremendous amount of kidnappings in literature where no one really gets hurt, mine is the first story to be told by the actual victim herself. Not *him*self, *her*self.

Literary kidnappings never involve girls. It actually makes quite a difference as you are about to hear.

It was after the news. Remember when Zit-face complained about missing the sports? That's where my short story and my true experience split up. Let me tell it to you as if it was happening right now, so you'll get the actual feel of it, okay? Okay.

So, I asked old Lettie, "Lettie, will you take me with you?"

"Of course not," she answered.

"Listen, Lettie, I don't want to become a robber like you guys, not that it isn't chic and all. I mean, Robin Hood, Anthony Vesco—you're in the same boat with a lot of class people—but the thing is, I would like to write a really great article about the life of your average, everyday crook. You know, with interviews, pictures . . ."

"No pictures."

"Silly me. No pictures, naturally."

"I thought you wanted to be a dancer."

"Oh, I do, really, but you've got to have something to fall back on. Like, how you've got crime. Some day I'll be all rickety, and my boobies will be hanging down to my knees, and . . ."

"Nature has treated me rather well."

"I'll say. But I just can't imagine spending life after forty like old Madame Poritchova—we call her Madame Prosciutto—teaching bratty little girls how to plié when they would rather be taking gymnastics or tennis, and buying those giant-size tights with no size number that just say "Statuesque" instead. What do you say, Lettie? This could be my big break . . . my exclusive . . . my—"

"Sorry kid. I gotta think of your parents."

"No, really. They'd understand. I'll drop them a note explaining that this is a voluntary kidnapping . . ."

She was shaking her head when who do you think saved the day himself? Old Zit-face. He came running in to tell us that there was a Connecticut newsbreak, and old Jim Jensen was describing their getaway Ford. No doubt that nosy Mrs. Fermin across the street had been sitting with her binoculars in front of her bedroom window taking in my dance routine and saw the whole thing. Naturally, she waited three hours to call the cops so that the kidnappers would have time to pack me in cement and dump me into the old Housatonic. She'd always wanted to even the score with me since the time me, Marlys, and the Pilitz twins sent her that anonymous note telling her she had twenty-four hours to get out of town or we'd piss on her statue of the black guy with the lantern that stares at us all from her front lawn making us nauseous. But after all, she did get even with us since we were only eight years old at the time and never thought that by using Mrs. Pilitz' stationary which said at the top, "From the desk of Loretta Pilitz," we'd get caught. Of course, the Pilitz twins got it the worst, so I can't really complain.

Anyway, once Lettie realized that the cops were looking for their car, she went immediately into action. In fact, the three of them really started jumping, and I pitched right in helping to load up the Ford with the loot. You should have heard them. They were going to go out and lift another car. Imagine. Lift another car. Easy as, "Lift the rug with me, Blob, so we can get old Willy out." Willy is my gerbil. He'll be all right when I'm gone. My mother will remember his water, but Blob will kill him for sure, now that I think about it. Not that she'd out and out squash him to death or anything, but I just know she'll do the one thing I've told her we can never, never do with him—let him out the front door.

But who knows? It's summer. Maybe old Willy will make it. Just so long as he doesn't try to make friends with sick Alice, the Monsoons' asshole cat. And I know I won't have to worry about Sarah Bishop. She's my hermit crab named after a famous Connecticut hermit of long ago. Hermit crabs are scavengers. When Blob lets her out of her box, she'll be able to scurry around at night and find plenty of spilled Cheerios to nosh on.

Guess what? Lifting a car turned out to be easier than lifting a rug after all. Did I say car? We lifted a goddamned Chrysler van. The gigantic kind with the purple stripes over jet black, and the Grand Tetons in the rear window. We just drove up next to it in a big, long driveway, tried the door, and we were in business.

I said, "Hey. What if the people in the house see us?"

"Not to worry, kid, no one's home."

"How do you know?"

"That's my job."

"Oh. But what if the neighbors hear us?"

"What neighbors? This is Fairfield County."

"What if a cop comes by?" I mean, you should have seen us unloading the car and nonchalantly stuffing everything into the van, slamming doors like mad while Turk revved up the Ford engine to jump the van. Imagine trying to jump start a Chrysler off a Ford.

"I told ya, kid. Quit worrying. This is easier than takin' candy off an old lady."

"Baby."

"What?"

"Nothing. But listen, what if these people have a security guard, and he comes walking out of those woods with a shotgun?"

"You must think we're stupid, kid. I'm packin' a little somethin' here. Right here." He patted the side of his belt which was hidden under his big, fat stomach.

"That would be murder."

"Phoebe?"

"Yeah, Lettie?"

"Clam up."

"Sure."

There are some people you don't cross. Lettie is one. Frank Sinatra is another.

§ § §

I still can't get over the fact that stealing a van is a hundred times easier than sneaking a Twinkie past your mother. Even if she's in the basement doing the wash, your mother can hear you tiptoeing across the kitchen with a Twinkie.

So in the end, Lettie decided to tolerate me, said she

had no choice for the time being. But I told her I had it all planned. I'd drop a line to the folks and let them know I'm following a story that would make me famous. Lettie said it'd be okay because she'd have Turk mail it from the Bowery or some place. We're also going to cut my hair, and dye it, and get me some glasses like Lettie's (minus the rhinestones), and, as it turned out, I was about to have one hell of a summer vacation after all.

Chapter Two

I found out a lot of stuff during that ride in the van, like Zit-face's first name, for example. It's Galooch. Can you stand it? "Eh, Galooch. How ya doin', Galooch?" And these people aren't even Italian. I don't know what they are besides poor. That is, I had to assume they were poor what with wasting their time stealing the Monsoons' cheap crap.

Do you know how many back roads, how many dirt and rock paths there are that pass for roads once you cross over into Westchester? I mean, it's shocking. Three thousand bucks in taxes for a quarter of an acre and a fake colonial, and the bastards don't even pave your road. You want to get to work in a rainstorm? Forget it. Sit in the mud till the sun comes out. I mean, honest to God, the part of New York that old Turk drove through—and we're talking less than an hour from the city—looked like the Punjab.

Later I had a frightening thought. What if Lettie and these guys were stealing because they had a drug habit?

"Hey! You people aren't on drugs or anything, are you?"

"Drugs? Whatcha think? We're crazy? Drugs are for niggers and brats like you."

"Eh, Galooch," I said, "how come you're a racist?"

"I ain't no racist. I know a lotta niggers. It's just . . . shit . . . what's a nigger ever done for me except take my job?"

"What job?"

"Yeah, Galooch. What job you ever had?"

"Shit, Turk. You know what I mean. It's a manner of speakin'. Ya gotta have black cops, black firemen, black this, black that. I mean . . . shit. Us whites are all gonna be out on the street if we don't stop them."

"Listen, Phoebe," Lettie said, "you can't talk to Galooch about stuff like this. He's thick-headed. But don't worry. Galooch is all right. He sees a guy layin' in the street, he's right out there givin' the poor fella a hand. He don't see if the guy's black or white. He'll risk his life for anyone in trouble. He's just afraid of blacks . . . ya know? Ever since they started all that salutin' and bushy hairdo stuff."

Okay, Lettie. I get it. Even my friend Marlys would get it.

§   §   §

We headed directly toward Queens. To a little street in front of a little house squashed between two other little houses that looked exactly alike except for their colors; ours was pink. The one on the right was blue, and the one on the left was mint green. Also, ours didn't have an imitation grotto in the front like the other two, just a plastic deer with his nose in a birdbath. Between each house was an alley, maybe wide enough to get your bike through.

"Okay, everybody, we'll unload and dump the van."

We piled out, and Turk put a ton of stuff into my arms, and I followed Lettie up the steps. If Archie Bunker had answered the door, I wouldn't have blinked. The houses were just like the ones at the beginning of "All in the Family." The only difference, I would have to say, is that across the street there weren't more identical houses. Just a chain link fence, and about fifty feet below the fence the Belt Parkway. Eight lanes. What a racket. What fumes.

I said, "Lettie, how can you stand all this noise?"

Lettie said, "What noise?"

Once all the Monsoons' stuff was up on the stoop, Turk told Galooch to put the van in the Pan Am parking lot. Galooch left. We went into the house.

Inside the house was an old lady about fifty, or fifty-two. She hugged Lettie.

"I told ya, Mary, ya didn't have to wait up for us. C'mere, Phoebe, I'd like ya to meet my sister, Mary. Mary, this is Phoebe. She's gonna have to be with us for a while."

"Hello, Phoebe dear. Would you like some lovely hot cocoa?"

"Yes, please." These two were sisters? Mary had black and white frizzy hair, and a red print housedress with a purple polka-dot apron over it. She had on slippers that looked like they had been chewed up by a Ger-

man shepherd, and little yellow ankle socks. I was sure
that if Mary ever got dressed up, she probably wore a
girdle with those long rubber garters to hold up her
stockings—like my nana. Panty hose haven't been uni-
versally accepted. She shuffled off to the stove. It took her
about an hour to get across the kitchen. The kitchen table was made of metal. Never saw anything like it in my
life. It had worn-away pictures all over the top of it, and
it felt very cold under my elbows. No place mats. Then
Lettie took off her orange beehive and gave it a good
shake. Yes, they were definitely sisters. Lettie had black
and white hair, too, only it was all damp and plastered to
her scalp.

"What size do you wear, kid?"

"Wig? Gee, I don't know, I've never . . ."

"Your dresses. What a comedian, eh, Mary?" Mary
laughed.

"I'm just into a twelve—I'm small for my age—but I
don't wear dresses. I prefer . . ."

"Twelve? Okay. I'm gonna have a nice bath, grab a
little shut-eye, and then tomorrow I'll go into town and
buy you some duds. And don't forget, you have to write a
letter to your folks first thing in the morning. Mary, have
you heard from Harry?"

"Yeah. Harry, Gene, and the boys are going to Chicago tomorrow. They'll unload your stuff early, before
they take off. They've got a big deal goin' somewhere."

"That Harry. He's always got a big deal goin' somewhere. So, Phoebe, write the letter like you're in Chicago, okay. Turk and Galooch will mail it from there."

You know how in police shows "the boys from the
lab" are always about a hundred and two years old? I
guess with anything having to do with crime, the lower
echelon is referred to by the term "boy."

Meanwhile, I couldn't wait to get going on the letter. What a job of creativity it would take. Mary came back across the kitchen with a cup of cocoa for me and coffee for Lettie. The cocoa was stone cold. Took her longer to get back across the kitchen than it had on the trip out.

"So, Phoebe, what kind of stuff do you like to wear?"

"Actually, Lettie, I'm glad you asked. I haven't had a dress on since my first holy communion. All I need is a couple of pairs of jeans and a few tops."

"Okay." She pushed her chair back, stood up, and stretched. While stretching, she took a whiff of her armpit. "Phew, I stink. Put Phoebe up in my room, Mary. I'll move in with you."

"Geez, don't do that," I protested. "I'll sleep on the—"

"Forget it. Give me and Mary a chance to chitchat. Look in my dressing table for some paper, Phoebe. I'm gonna get in the tub. Phew!" Before she left, she pulled her dress up over her head and threw it into the sink with the cocoa pan. It had been ripped only under the arms, but I thought I heard a few extra threads pop as she yanked it off. She strolled out, holding her hairdo in one hand. Her underwear absolutely must have come from Frederick's of Hollywood.

"Now finish your lovely hot cocoa, Phoebe, while I do up Lettie's dress." It took Mary forever to get out of her chair, but she made it, and somehow, I don't know how, she managed to reach the sink. She turned on both faucets, and squirted Joy all over the dress, and bobbed it up and down twice. Then she held it up, stared at it for about three years, and made her way to the back door. The dress left a trail of soap bubbles across the linoleum. "I'll just put this on the line to dry." It was about two o'clock in the morning when she went out, and I swear to God, it felt like two in the afternoon by the time she got back. I was yawning my brains out.

"Follow me, Phoebe, and I'll show you Lettie's room." We went through a swinging door, and nearly bumped into the dining-room table as we passed the living room to get over to the stairs. Didn't I tell you it was just like Archie Bunker's? We went up.

"That's the bathroom" . . . shuffle, shuffle, shuffle, . . . "that's Galooch's room, and Turk's" . . . shuffle, shuffle, shuffle . . . "that's my room. . . ."

I peeked in the open door. There was a great big German shepherd lying on her chenille spread. "It's okay, Dodge, just a friend of Lettie's." She threw him one of her slippers. He caught it without moving an inch.

"This is the door to the attic. There's nothing up there but bats. So don't ever, ever go up there, will you, dear?"

"Sure."

"And here's Lettie's room."

Jesus Christ was it ever. Early bordello. Lettie had one of those chairs that curve up and down and back again. The kind those blonde movie stars in the thirties used to slouch across. Romans, too. The color scheme was red and silver. The tassels that hung from the bedspread and curtains were the silver part. The rest—the entire rest—was red. Not red chintz, either. Red satin. Of course, it wasn't real, authentic satin, but you know the shiny stuff they line coats with? That was the stuff. The bed was huge, and had a canopy that touched the ceiling; not the kind of canopy that fruity little girls have. The kind that Ebenezer Scrooge had in the movie that hung down all over the place. In fact, it would make you think of the beds in the emergency room where the nurse comes and wings these drapes all around you in about one eighth of a second. Only difference being that the emergency room drapes are all splattered with blood, and old Lettie's looked covered.

"Now you get some sleep, and tomorrow after you've had a lovely breakfast, you can write your letter. And when Lettie gets in, she'll find you a nice spot for your lovely new clothes." She left smiling, completely accepting me as if Lettie brought people home with her every day of the week. But who knows? Maybe she does.

I was tired, and I knew I'd go out like a light, but I first wanted to get that letter out of the way. I found Lettie's notepaper, and wrote to my Mom and old man with this large quill she had sticking out of a fake bottle of ink. Don't you love it? A ballpoint quill. So here's the letter:

Dear Mom, Dad, and Blob,

Copy this letter before you turn it over to the fuzz, because if you don't, we'll never see it again, and I'm going to need it to get information for my article, not to mention my memoirs. Move over Oriana Fallaci.

As you know, I was kidnapped, but it was completely accidental. I just happened to be in the wrong place at the wrong time. I know I shouldn't have even been on the Monsoons' front porch, but that's really a minor infraction. How could I have possibly known there was a burglary going on? Anyway, the burglars panicked and took me with them. Naturally, they wanted to return me to you right away, but I talked them into letting me join their band—not that I intend to participate in any of their future operations. I simply want to delve into the lives of honest-to-God thieves. I'm sure you realize that this is an opportunity I can't pass up.

I have just moved in with one of the robber's sisters. She is quite beautiful, has a lot of class, and doesn't know her brother is a burglar. She thinks he's a stockbroker with Merrill Lynch. I have a little turret room in her charming Victorian house, and it's perfect for me to write in: quiet, papered in the palest apple green, and overlooking Lake Michigan. Won't the kids die of jealousy? The lake looks just like Long Island Sound (grim, right?) except that the shore is lined with ugly skyscraper condos. And it doesn't have those posts sticking up all over that mark the lobster pots. But I'll save the descriptions for another time since you're probably more interested in my well-being.

Although the people I left with are thieves, they're surprisingly pleasant. I suppose it's not fair ripping off people like the Monsoons, but don't forget that the Monsoons are insured, and insurance companies rip off more people in a day than these robbers could in a lifetime.

Naturally, I can't tell you much about them except to assure you that they will do me no harm and that they are not armed. They're just simple folk who realized at one point in their lives that they just couldn't be happy in nine-to-five jobs, working late, not getting paid for the extra time, and never taking vacations. Like you, Dad.

Mom. I know you're terribly nervous about this sort of thing, but if that quack doctor of ours is giving you Valium, or Librium, or Crapium, flush it all down the toilet. I don't want to come home to an addict. I'm absolutely okay, and you have nothing to worry about. Remember the time I snuck into the rectory cellar and stayed there for three days doing my exposé on priests? I came home, didn't I? I was fine, right?

Now just tell old Blob that Phoebe will be home soon, and remind her that it's like the time I went to live in Father Hickey's cellar only this time I might be gone just a tiny bit longer. In my desk—top drawer—is a story I wrote. Take it out and read a few pages of it to her every night. It should take about a week. I'll try to mail her another when I get a chance to write one. The story is called "The Littlest Faggot." Don't read the other stories in the drawer.

Also, now is not the time to try to get her to stop dragging the pooh around. I know it's ragged, and I know it's got dried throw-up on it, but so what. In three years the kindergartners will laugh her out of town if she shows up in school with it. If Blob wants to sleep with something that smells like liver bile, that's her problem, not yours.

So listen, I'll write a lot, and please tell old Marlys to send me eight million letters in care of Robert Jones, American Express, 11 Rue Scribe, 75009 Paris. France.

Tell Grandma that I hope she birdies all her holes, and Dad, when you see Nana on Sun-

day, give her my love if she can figure out who
the hell you are.

Love, and eight million
kisses,
Phoebe

§   §   §

I mean, can you stand it? Lucky old Marlys. Aside
from the fact that she will adore sending letters to gay
Paree, just imagine poor Robert Jones (and there should
be at least one Robert Jones there, buying new traveler's
checks). He's sure to be picked up by the Sûreté, and
God, wouldn't Peter Sellers love it if he were only still
with us, bless his heart. Shit, when I think of how all the
angels and seraphim and cherubim must be up there
laughing their asses off at old Detective Clouseau, I could
just die of jealousy.

Chapter Three

"Phoebe, are you awake?"

"Sure," I lied.

"Why didn't you give me the journal right where Tyrus enters the picture?"

"Why didn't James Joyce start *Ulysses* right when Molly enters the picture? Tyrus is coming in a minute. Anyway, I need to break into this slowly."

"But you're not reading this, I am."

"I'm watching your face, aren't I?"

"Go make us some cocoa, okay? And Phoebe?"

"Yeah?"

"Who the hell are these people?"

"Tyrus' relatives. Doesn't it say that?"

"I think that this docudrama tilts perhaps more toward drama than docu. For example, you didn't write that last paragraph when you were thirteen."

"What paragraph? Let me see."

"The one with Peter Sellers. He didn't die until 1980 or '81."

"Oh. Well, I must have just taken a peek at that part a while later and tacked on the paragraph. That's nothing. Writers do that all the time."

"But . . ."

I was already in the kitchen rattling those pots and pans.

§　§　§

Dinner at Lettie's was remarkable, to say the least. It was at noon. I'd slept through breakfast. Actually, the dinner was a goodbye party for Turk and Galooch since they were going to Chicago with Harry. Lettie said she'd have gone, too, but she wanted to rest her dogs for a couple of days and show me a good time, besides. Naturally, I can't wait to find out what her idea of a "good time" will be about.

That Mary sure could cook. When I came downstairs at eleven, she asked me my favorite food. I told her pepperoni pizza with extra mozzarella. Well, would you believe she actually made me a pizza with her own two hands? It was a hundred times better than Luigi's, which is my all-time number-one pizza. Galooch had a steak that was four inches high and hung over the side of his plate all the way around. Its outside was burnt black, and the inside was so raw that it still had a few ice crystals peeking out. On the side he had a loaf of garlic bread about a yard long. Through the whole meal butter and blood dripped down his chin. I offered him a piece of pizza. He said, "Sure, kid," and tore off one whole side of my pie. Naturally, he stuffed the entire piece into his mouth at once.

Turk had pirogies, galumpkes, and a huge bowl of sauerkraut with cut-up kielbasa in it. Mary and Lettie each had a big dish of Chun King chicken chow mein over instant rice.

Now here's the strange part. Just before Mary sat down, she came out of the kitchen with a tray. On the tray were three glasses of what looked like root beer and three bowls of something I couldn't see. She took them upstairs.

"Who's that stuff for?" I asked. My God, you'd think the police had walked in. Everybody dropped their forks, Mary stopped right in her tracks, and they all stared at me.

"It's for Dodge," Lettie said.

Then they all smiled and said, "Whew!" All at the same time.

"He eats upstairs?"

"Phoebe, when we're not here, Dodge is all Mary has."

"Yeah, kid, so mind your beeswax."

"Sorry, Turk, I didn't mean to be nosy." Dare I ask how the dog drinks soda out of a glass? Three glasses, yet. Maybe the dog entertains a lot, right? "My Uncle Bubs has a dog, and he puts a milk bone in his own mouth, and then the dog jumps up and grabs it and eats it."

"That's disgustin'."

"Isn't it?"

"Your uncle's probably got all kinds of germs."

"Does he ever."

"Imagine giving a poor, damn dog germs."

I figured maybe Dodge was real old and had trouble with the stairs. And I'm sure you know how dog owners are. Just look at my Uncle Bubs, to say nothing of my Uncle Edmond, who thinks he is one.

For dessert we had hot apple pie with Cool Whip. I took just a sliver since it was about ninety-five degrees, and I associate apple pie with Thanksgiving and blizzards. After dinner we all sat outside in the backyard. The backyard was a vegetable garden except for the one small area around the back steps where we sat. On one side of the steps there were about a million garbage cans, and on the other side was a cozy circle of lawn chairs, the kind that are advertised in the New York *Times* at about two hundred bucks a pop, and that's not including the price of the cushions. They were slightly used, however, but anyone who has enough money to spend that much on a goddamned lawn chair deserves to have it stolen. My mom has Indian chairs. Not sheet Indians. Feather. These guys in a big dump truck pulled up on my street one day and said they were Indians from the Hoot tribe and they were selling hand-customed lawn furniture. The furniture was a bunch of split logs nailed together with pieces of rust that passed for nails. Everyone on the street was giggling and poking each other in the ribs until my mother said, "How much?"

"Ma," I whispered, "you'll get slivers up your arse." But I knew my mother would buy them. There's a little glimmer of rebel in her. Not much, but some.

One of the Indians threw a chair over the side of the truck and it landed on our front lawn. He said, "Twenty-five bucks." Then, he threw down a bigger chair and said, "Love seat, thirty-five bucks."

While my mother was writing a check, asshole Mr.

Monsoon steps up, winking at all the neighbors, and says, "How much is that in wampum, Chief?"

So the Indian says, "Fuck you, Mack."

Old Mr. Monsoon had a choking attack while me and the Pilitz twins laughed our asses off. Unfortunately, my father choked, too, when he came home from work. He stormed into the house yelling, "What the hell is that pile of junk out back?"

I said, "That's your car, Dad." I said that not to piss off my old man but to take the heat off my Mother.

So everybody had a cold Bud, and I had a Coke, and they talked about the trip to Chicago and when Lettie would be able to meet up with them. A lot of your basic chitchat. Meanwhile, old Dodge noses his way out the screen door, and Galooch pours him a bowl of beer. He glops it up with his fat pink tongue, and noses his way back into the house. To sleep, I'd have to say. It was actually quite a nice little group, and they made me feel right at home. But all of a sudden, there was this loud, clear voice coming from up in the house. It said, "We are severely damaged at Pearl Harbor, Mr. President."

Everybody just kept on chattering.

"Who said that?" I asked, looking over my shoulder at the upstairs window.

"Said what?"

"Who said?"

"I didn't hear nuthin'."

"Somebody is talking to the President in your house. Something about Pearl Harbor, and I don't think it was Dodge."

"I didn't hear nuthin'."

"Probably some kid out front," Lettie said as she gave Galooch a long, hard look. First, he said, "Huh?" Then he said, "Oh!" He got up and went into the house.

"But . . ."

"Probably some kid out front, Phoebe."

"Oh, sure. Some kid playing Stratego or something."

I heard a fan go on in the house before Galooch came back. Hey, I'm just a guest, right? If your hostess is harboring the number-one man on the FBI's "most wanted" list in her attic, what the hell? For me it's more grist for the mill. The thing is, why would some criminal be talking to the President about Pearl Harbor, considering that Lettie surely didn't have the President up there, too? If Blob were here, I'd be saying, "Blob, old kid, this is getting curiouser and curiouser."

§ § §

That night I lay on the cold satin sheets, pressed my remote control button to Home Box, and watched what was supposed to be a snuff film. But I could see they didn't really kill anybody. Whoever made the film though—he should be killed. But it was either that or the Yankees. Just before I put out the plastic Tiffany lamp, I looked at my new clothes spread out on Caligula's chair; three pairs of jeans (Jordache, Gloria Vanderbilt, and pink Sassons), and a bunch of T-shirts with pictures on the front made of glitter. Marlys would have raved. She's more into fashion than me. Just as I was about to drop off to sleep, I heard that voice again over the whir of the fan, the one who had told the President about the difficulties at Pearl Harbor. This time it said, "*Achtung! Schnell, schnell! Jawohl, mein General.*"

Good God, maybe they have someone from the Baader-Meinhof gang up there. Needless to say, I dreamed of Mayor Koch giving me a ticker tape parade after capturing, single-handed, the most dangerous terrorist leader in the world.

§   §   §

"Phoebe, what's home box?"

"It's HBO."

"What's an HBO? Something like OTB?"

"Ben, when's the last time you went home?"

"Oh, a couple of years ago."

"HBO is part of cable TV. It's one of the channels."

"Nobody had cable when I was home. I was home after you wrote this."

"Oh, Ben, stop being so picky. It doesn't matter."

"I'm beginning to wonder. You're sure it doesn't matter?"

"Not a bit."

"If you say so." He shrugged.

§   §   §

The next morning I awoke to the mysterious voice. Back to English, unfortunately. First, he said real loud, "Fire salvos, men!" And then, after some mumble, mumble, "Commence mortar fire."

It hit me all at once. Not the salvos or the mortars, of course. I just knew exactly what the hell was going on. You've heard of *Arsenic and Old Lace*, right? The play with the two old ladies who have some nut living in the house who thinks he's Teddy Roosevelt? Obviously, it's the same thing here. Only what we have is George C. Scott up in the attic. General Patton himself. I knew that I was in a real tough spot. I didn't want to embarrass anyone, but I didn't want a salvo to land on my bed, either. I decided to wait for the right moment and ask Lettie, confidentially, to come clean.

I suggested we go out to dinner that evening. Lettie suggested Italian food. I think Lettie really likes my company.

"First, we gotta do something about that hair."

Fine with me. My hair is thin, stringy and a color that can only be described as shit-brindle brown.

"What are we going to do about it, Lettie?"

"Well, if we're going to do the town tonight, we should at least look related."

"Right."

"And you'll have to remember to call me Ma."

"And we'll have to change my name to something really upbeat like Antonia . . . or Oriana . . . or . . ."

"Son."

"Sun? Oh, son." Lettie had a giant pair of shears in her hand. I wondered if this wasn't getting a tad too adventurous. "Not too short, okay?"

"I thought bangs all the way around. Like little John-John Kennedy."

"Great." How do you tell these people that John-John Kennedy grew up? Nobody Lettie's age wants those Camelot days to be over, do they? She put a bowl on my head.

I've always worn my hair parted in the middle and pulled back behind my ears with a rubber band. It's easy, and it's out of my way. Sometimes my mother blows it dry, and it really looks terrific for about three seconds. Then it all clumps together and hangs straight down like a bunch of night crawlers. When Lettie took the bowl off my head, she combed it a little and held a mirror in front of me. First, I squinted so that I wouldn't be too shocked. Wow! I was the exact image of Dorothy Hamill in the middle of a sit spin. Very punky.

"Lettie, how about we paint some purple stripes

across it? Also, I have pierced ears, and we could put a safety pin in one ear, and a paper clip in . . ."

"Are you kidding? Who would think a woman such as myself would have one of those disgusting juvenile delinquents for a daughter. I mean, son." She haughtily brushed the nothing off the back of her shoulder.

"You're the boss."

"That's the truth."

She washed my hair in the sink and then stripped it. Stripped means she put this foul-smelling liquid on my hair, covered it with aluminum foil, and then opened all the windows. After about twenty years she took the foil off and washed my hair again wearing rubber gloves. It felt like acid was pouring down the side of my face. Naturally, I started screaming for a towel to wipe my eyes, but I gritted my teeth and stopped because it really set him off. "Him" meaning General MacArthur up in the attic.

"Torpedoes at the ready, men. Fire one! Fire two!" Took only two torpedoes to shut me up.

"One more rinse, Phoebe." Some day Lettie was going to have to come to grips with the war zone up in her attic.

She blew dry my hair, very professionally, and got out the mirror again.

Have you ever seen a brown-eyed albino? My hair was white. Kind of a moon white.

"Nice, Lettie, but somehow we don't look any more related than we did before."

"We will with this. This is the stuff I use on my wigs." It was L'Oréal hair dye. I couldn't believe L'Oréal put out a hair dye that was a color slightly more orange than Lucille Ball's curls.

"Ya know, Lettie, I've seen a lot of grown-ups with

that particular shade of red, but to tell you the truth, I've never seen a kid with it."

"No? Hm-m-m. I think you're right. Let me run down to the drugstore and pick up something a little more . . . a little more . . ."

". . . auburn."

"Yeah, auburn. I'll be right back."

She left. I took the soggy, smelly towel off my shoulder and threw it into the sink. I walked around. I ate an apple and watched Mary out the kitchen window hanging clothes on a line strung over the tomato plants. Her mouth was full of clothes pins. Naturally, she was working in double slow motion; an instant replay of a person hanging wash. The house was very still. I took another apple out of the refrigerator and threw it up against the ceiling as hard as I could. Damned if it didn't work.

"Dive, dive! Prepare to drop depth charges."

Fortunately, he was all settled down by the time Lettie returned. An hour later I was a strawberry blond. A strawberry blonde with tortoiseshell glasses. What with my new three-piece suit, white shirt, and clip-on bow tie, I was a knockout. My mother—old Lettie, of course—wore gold lamé with a little fake tiger-fur jacket. Now you know the precise color of Lettie's wig—the same orange as a fake tiger.

"How do I look, kid?"

"Fantastic! And your arrows really pull the whole outfit together."

"What arrows?"

"The ones going through your head." She immediately broke into eight million gales of laughter and punched my shoulder.

"Oh, Phoebe, you're a real card. Those aren't arrows. They're those chink thingamabobs. You know . . . like the geisha girls wear."

"Oh yeah. And if you eat Chinese, you can just pull them out and use them for chopsticks."

"That's right. I hope they never modernize those Chinese, or they'll be walking around with forks in their hair." She was serious. "Well, anyway, we're not eating Chinese tonight, and there's our cab."

"We're taking a cab?"

"Of course. You can't go to a fancy restaurant on a subway. Besides, the driver is a friend of mine. We get a cut rate. Free." We headed for the door, Lettie stopping first by the mirror. She gave herself a once-over, and then reached into her bodice and, one by one, pulled up her breasts so that the crack went up almost all the way to her neck.

"Good night, Mary."

"Have fun, girls," Mary called from upstairs.

"See ya later." Just as I shut the door, I "accidentally" kicked it quite hard, and old Lettie just continued to hold her head high though I knew she heard him.

Lettie got in the front door of the taxi, and I hopped in the back. The cabbie, Lettie's friend, was named Moe. They smooched seven or eight times, and I might as well have been invisible. Moe ignored me completely. Lettie sure was lucky to have a man like that. No questions asked. Just by the way he never glanced back at me I could tell that he wouldn't want to know anything unless Lettie wanted to tell him. To me, that's what love is all about.

While Moe went around the block eight hundred times with his off-duty sign lit, we went to a posh Italian restaurant in the theater district. The difference between a cheap-o Italian restaurant and a posh one is that a posh one doesn't have the plastic grapes hanging all over the place. In fact, the one we went to had real fig trees growing between the tables. Lettie got up after we ordered our Shirley Temple and piña colada to pick a dozen or so figs. She stuffed them into her pocketbook and told me Mary would love them. The waiter came, and Lettie ordered spaghetti and meatballs (not on the menu, but the waiter just kept smiling, and writing, and saying *"Buono, buono"*). I tried the osso bucco. Not bad, although Lettie told me she'd be afraid to give the slop I was eating to old Dodge.

So we generally talked about the rampant deterioration of everything and everybody until I finally decided that it was a great time to broach the unspoken subject. I mean, we were so relaxed and all. I said, "Lettie, just who is it that lives up in your attic?" She started to say "Huh?" but then she shook her head and changed her mind.

"It's a sad thing, Phoebe. A real sad thing."

"Yes, it is," I lied. I didn't think it was sad. I thought it was hilarious. "But who is it?"

"It's Mary's son. Tyrus. A retarded child."

"Tyrus? Mary has a son named Tyrus?"

"He's named after Ty Cobb, a famous ballplayer. Mary's crazy about baseball. She loves the Yankees." All backward people love the Yankees.

"Where's Mary's husband?"

"Never had one. Like I said, it's sad. See, Phoebe, our parents—Mary's and mine, and the boys'—were killed in the '38 hurricane. Stepped out the front door and were blown away. In those days, you never knew if a hurricane was coming until it got there. We didn't have weathermen. Then Mary told the rest of us that she was pregnant. She was sixteen. So we decided we all had to

stick together, and the only way four teenagers could
make it—I mean, we're talking about the Depression, the
war—was to steal. We've been stealing ever since, and
even though we ain't rich . . . what the hell? It's a
livin'.' "

"Don't you feel guilty about stealing other people's
money?"

"Nah. We only steal from rich people."

"The Monsoons aren't rich."

"Insurance, Phoebe. Besides, we never take people's
money. Just their junk. And when they put their claims
in, they make a lot of money."

I decided to get back to Tyrus.

"How old is Tyrus? Let's see . . . 1938 . . ."

"He's thirty-nine."

Wow! "Mary has had someone living in the attic for
thirty-nine years?"

"Not exactly. She used to take him out when he was
little. To the movies, the beach. But he stopped going to
the movies when Harry Truman was elected. All the
people in the theater where he and Mary went started
hootin' and hollerin' during the news—in those days we
had the news before the movie. It scared him real bad.
Then he got afraid of helicopters, and he ain't been out
since he was nine or ten."

"Why is he afraid of helicopters?"

"Who knows? Only God understands people like
Tyrus. He's a retarded child."

"What does he do all day up there?"

"Reads."

"Reads? Retarded children don't read."

"No?"

"No."

"Tyrus reads and listens to polka music. He has every polka record ever made."

"Does he read Polish books?"

"Now why the hell would he want to do that? He reads books on World War II." Aha.

"Can I meet him?"

"Oh no. He'd get scared."

"Of me?"

"Of everybody."

"So what happens to him when you all die?"

"How's that dessert you ordered, Phoebe?"

"Yummy, but—"

"What's it called again?"

"Zabaglione."

She snapped her fingers for the waiter.

"Yes, madame?"

"What's in this pudding the kid's got?"

"Ah-h-h-h . . . we have the cream, we have the egg yolks, and we have the Marsala wine."

"Trying to kill off the customers, eh?" She laughed. "Got any Italian ice?"

"I'm so sorry, madame, we have not. Perhaps you would like the fresh spumoni."

"That's ice cream, right?"

"Yes, madame, a sort of—"

"Nah. Never mind. Bring me the bill. Moe will take us for some cones at Baskin-Robbins on the way home, and I'll save myself a few bucks."

§ § §

"Phoebe, can I ask you something?"

"Sure."

"I'm just getting to the part where you're going to

meet Tyrus. I just finished the Italian restaurant. Will you really meet him?"

"Of course."

"You won't jump into another short story or some kind of epic poem?"

"I don't write poetry, normally."

"Phew."

"You need a break, right?"

"No, I don't. I just couldn't take a disappointment."

He put the journal down because his earlobe was in my mouth. I'd been staring at it for so long—Ben really concentrates so adorably when he reads—that I just couldn't resist any longer. But I admit that, in a way, I also wanted to make love because I had this last-minute panic about someone else knowing about Tyrus.

Making love beats yawning. Making love beats everything. And the way I felt after we made love—aside from feeling like warm oatmeal—was that I looked forward to Ben learning of this Tyrus part of me. He sure as hell knew everything else there was.

Chapter Four

I tied a white pillowcase to the end of a broomstick and practiced waving it. Lettie was out, and Mary was lying outside in the sun on one of the chaises. Lettie had told Mary that I knew about Tyrus, so I told Mary to have a nice rest and that I'd get her if Tyrus called. ("If Tyrus mounted an attack" was what I would have liked to say.)

Carefully, I opened the hallway door opposite Lettie's bedroom and started to go quietly up the stairs. I held the white flag in front of me and waved it just a little—the way the settlers do when the cavalry has left them to the Indians. At the top of the attic steps I opened the door a crack, stuck the broomstick through, and he immediately started yelling.

"Sneak attack, sneak attack. Fire at will, men!"

"It's not an attack. It's a surrender. Can't you see . . ."

"The yellow dogs don't know the meaning of surrender, boys. Continue firing, and remember—the only good Jap is a dead Jap."

"No, wait. I'm an American."

"Give the password."

"Oh shit."

"Inaccurate. Commence fire."

I retreated. He was throwing books at the door, and I could hear Mary attempting to hightail it up the stairs. I came out and met her in the hall.

"I'm coming, Tyrus dear," she called. "Phoebe, what did you do?"

"Nothing." Stock answer of every kid you've ever met, right?

"You can't upset the boy, or he'll get . . . he'll get very . . . very upset." She rushed past me. It was a crawl more than a rush, but for Mary it was damn fast.

Later I apologized, bringing Mary a tall glass of iced coffee and vodka, her daytime favorite.

"You're a nice little girl, Phoebe, but Tyrus gets excited so easily."

"But doesn't he get lonesome?"

"I don't think so. After all, he's a retarded child."

"He never goes out? At all?"

"Oh, Phoebe, it's those darned helicopters. I remember when he loved going out. Galooch would take him down to the train tunnels and they'd play on the tracks all day. But it's those helicopters."

"Do you know why he's afraid of helicopters?"

"I don't like to ask him. He gets so upset."

"So except for you guys, he hasn't seen anyone for thirty-two years?"

"He saw one other person."

"Who was that?"

"Someone from the Army."

"He knows so much about fighting that the Army sent someone to see him?"

"Oh no, Phoebe. They came when he turned eighteen. After they tried to draft him."

"The Army tried to draft Tyrus? My God, who'd they send?"

"A nice young doctor in a handsome uniform."

"Holy shit. Tyrus must have thought it was the blitzkrieg."

"That's what I was afraid he'd think. Lettie told me to tell Tyrus that if he didn't talk to the man, the Army would send him to Fort Dix for four years. That's in Jersey. But I told her that I would take care of it. I don't like to threaten Tyrus. I told Tyrus that General Bradley was coming to see him to get some information on the Jerries. That's the Germans, Phoebe, what we used to call them during the war. So, the handsome young doctor came one morning, and I took him up to Tyrus. He was nervous. The doctor. I told him to salute when he went in. Tyrus just stared at him. The army man told Tyrus that he'd be asking him some questions, and Tyrus was a very good boy. He listened so carefully to the nice army doctor except when he'd issue orders to his men in the field. He issues orders into an empty chicken noodle soup can. He thinks the soup can is a transmitter. Campbell's. Anyway, the army man ignored it pretty much. First, he asked Tyrus the capital of Italy. Tyrus said, 'Code word: Romulus.' Then he asked what 'perimeter' meant, and Tyrus got up and walked around his chair. Then he asked me to please leave the room, so I did because I could tell that I could trust him not to upset Tyrus. Two minutes later he came out and told me that Tyrus was emotionally perturbed, or something like that. Army talk for 'mentally retarded,' I guess. And he told me it wasn't anyone's fault. That made me feel real good. Oh, and just before he left, he said, 'You know, ma'am, he knew I wasn't a general. He asked me for identification, so I told him General Bradley couldn't come because he was in Washington with the President. He thinks I'm Bradley's adjutant.' "

All this, of course, told yours truly one thing: Tyrus was a hell of a lot more accommodating than he let on. Like my sister Blob or any other two-year-old. When push comes to shove, they're quite willing to give an inch or two.

"Listen, Mary," I said, "couldn't you tell Tyrus I'm a WAC or a WAVE? Lettie could go out and dig me up a uniform . . ."

"Tyrus would know you aren't a WAC, Phoebe."

"Not if I—"

"You're a kid."

"Oh yeah."

"But I have an idea."

"You do?"

"Do you know any polka tunes?"

"No, but I learned the polka in gym. Our gym teacher is such an asshole." He really is. All the money is in soccer, and he teaches us to polka. But then if the Olympic Committee considers ice dancing a sport . . . who knows? Although, I can't imagine anyone wanting to win a gold medal in polkaing.

"Gym teachers were like that in my day, too. I remember our Miss Hall. She used to make us wear our bloomers over our clothes because she thought they were so indecent, and they came down past our knees."

"What about the polka business, Mary?"

"Oh. Well, I was thinking we might get away with saying you're Jean Marie Kabritsky."

"Who's she?"

"You don't know Jean Marie Kabritsky?"

"Gee, I don't think so. Is she with a group?"

"She's a girl who makes polka records. Tyrus has all her records. She's one of his favorites. His other favorites are Stosh and Yosh Wischnesky, the Connecticut Twins. You must know them, you're from Connecticut. But I don't think Tyrus would believe that you could be Stosh or Yosh. Did I ask you if you knew any polka tunes?"

"The one we danced to in gym was 'Beer Barrel Polka,' but all I remember is:

> "Roll out the barrel,
> We'll have a barrel of fun.
> Roll out the barrel,
> Dum da da dum da da dum."

Mary said, "We've got the blues on the run."

"Huh? Oh, that's the other line, isn't it?"

"Yes, but Tyrus really likes the local tunes that Jean Marie and Stosh and Yosh sing . . . like . . . have you ever heard 'The Valushki Polka'?"

"I don't think so. What's a valushki?"

"Some kind of Polack food. Anyway, it goes like this:

> "Oh! My poor dear mother.
> Oh! My poor dear mother!
> Ate rancid volushki,
> What I gonna do?"

Old Mary started polkaing around the room, and she

grabbed me by my hands, and I joined right in. It's really fun to polka when you do it with an expert. My Uncle Norbert has this fantastic whoop he lets out when he polkas—he polkas without a partner—so I tried it out with Mary as we circled the couch for the seventh time, but that spoiled everything. I shouted, "Hayoo, Hayoo!" and Tyrus shouted, "Head for cover, men, native uprising in the villages."

Poor Mary had to fly up to the old attic, but by the time she covered the distance, Tyrus had gotten all his men under cover and had destroyed the entire village of Jumatra. I heard this in his report that he transmitted through the chicken noddle can.

$ $ $

It was another warm night, and we ate al fresco, once more, under the clothesline. Mary asked Lettie what she thought of the idea of my being company for Tyrus. Lettie said, "Of course, Mary. I've been trying to tell you that for years. Give Tyrus a little change. Phoebe, I've been trying to tell Mary for years that she should have one of those visiting nurses drop in once a week or something. She won't do it. Thinks the house is a mess." It is.

"Hey, Mary," I said, "don't worry about messes. Nurses are the biggest slobs in the world. Have you ever been in a nurse's house? All day at the hospital they have to clean up blood and piss and shit, so what's a couple of newspapers on the floor or a pile of dust under the bed to them?"

"All the same, it would get Tyrus upset." Mary looked down. Lettie looked at me and shrugged.

"But, Mary, he didn't get upset at the army doctor. And if he thought I was Jean Marie Kabritsky, I could go up there every day, teach him to play crazy eights, have him show me his books, all kinds of stuff. Mary stared at me through her thick glasses. She seemed to be wavering.

"C'mon, Mare, take the kid up to see Tyrus." Mary leaned her chin into her hand, thoughtfully.

"Well . . . do you know 'Too Fat Polka,' Phoebe?"

Chapter Five

I had a crash course in polka music starting with "Too Fat Polka," by Arthur Godfrey. They had the record. A 78 without so much as a scratch. A polka sung to the accompaniment of a ukelele. Wouldn't Don Ho just throw up? Not that his music is any better, of course. The names of these polkas are unbelievable, and if you thought the lyrics to "The Valushki Polka" were bad, you should hear some of the others. Good thing I learn fast. The next day Lettie got me a tambourine. You can always tell if the girl singer in a band is talented or not. If she's got a tambourine, pack up your gear and get the hell out of the joint. Anyway, you should have seen me: ruffles, peasant blouse, three dirndls, and eight million colored ribbons hanging down the sides of my head to match the ones hanging off the tambourine.

So I followed Mary up the stairs. I gave my tambourine a little tinkle as she opened the door and said, "Tyrus, I have someone to see you. Someone very—"

"Get it out," he shrieked. It. Have you ever been referred to as an "it"?

"Tyrus, it's Jean Marie Kabritsky come to visit, and she's brought you her latest record." Who but a dodo would believe that one? Maybe he really was retarded.

"Open hatch."

Mary opened the hatch. He was sitting at a desk. His back was to us. The entire room was filled with shelves of books and magazines, and the desk was covered with them. Peeking casually over his shoulder, I could see that he was reading the first issue ever of *Aviation Week*. In the corner of the cover it said 1916. Also on his desk was the most recent *Aviation Week* issued yesterday. Magazines folding left and right and this guy was reading one nobody ever heard of that's lasted seventy years.

"Jean Marie . . ." Mary whispered. I didn't pay attention. I'd forgotten I had a new name. She gave me a poke in the ribs. The tambourine clinked.

"Jean Marie, come around to the front of the desk. Tyrus can't look east, and he wants to see you."

"Why can't he look east," I whispered back.

"He'd get upset if I asked him that." I followed her on tiptoe while I took a gander at the back of Tyrus. He had black hair the same length all over (a quarter of an inch), as if he'd had his head shaved last week. He had on a short-sleeved retarded-person's shirt, and his arms were soft, muscleless, and dead white. The room had that kind of carpeting that they have in new-car showrooms except that it was stained around Tyrus' desk. Besides his desk, there were two other pieces of furniture; a bed, neatly made, and a night table with a lamp and a record player on it. Under the table were a stack of records. Everywhere else it was wall-to-wall books—zillions of them—and most were the giant kind you only see in library reference rooms. Almost every one was dog-eared.

We circled Tyrus' chair, and he looked at me under long black eyelashes. I tried to smile, and I gave my tambourine a little shake. His face was also dead white. Skin which hasn't been in the sun in thirty years is just like a new baby's after it's lost its pinkness. His skin reminded me of Blob's when my mother brought her home. Except for his left wrist. It was reddish purple, swollen, and callosed. I didn't need time to wonder why, because he suddenly started biting it.

"Now don't be nervous, dear. Try not to bite your wrist. It's just Jean Marie Kabritsky, like I said."

"It's the enemy." His voice rose with each syllable.

"No, honey, it's little Jean Marie." Mary looked at me and mouthed the word "sing." I perked right up.

"I don't want her, you can have her
She's too fat for me, hey!
She's too fat, she's too fat,
She's too fat for me, *hey!*"

I never took my eyes off Tyrus while I sang and beat on the old tambourine. His eyes were just so huge and black against that skin. His face was absolutely beautiful from the standpoint of an aesthetic like myself, but sad. So, so sad. When I finished, Mary asked him if he'd like to pick another number before I had to go. He said yes, but first, he wanted to take my picture. Mary told him that would be fine. I posed, tambourine held high. Tyrus opened a drawer in his desk and took out a real old View-Master. He looked through it and aimed it at me.

"Say 'cheese' three times."

"Cheese, cheese, cheese."

"Click, click, click."

"Mary," I said out of the corner of my smile, "why the hell don't you get him a real camera?"

"Jean Marie, I try to tell you—he's retarded." He took two more pictures.

"I have to do my trips now," Tyrus said, and Mary asked him if he would like me to come back and sing for him again. He said yes.

"When, Tyrus?"

"D day."

"All right, dear. I'll bring you your supper in a little bit." Mary steered me out the door.

"When is D day?"

"Any day with a four in it."

"Isn't that tomorrow?"

"Yes."

"Oh, good. He must like me. What are these trips he's going on?"

"Well . . . just a little routine Tyrus goes through to erase things that he didn't want to happen. Like if you mention the state of New Hampshire, he goes through this trip three times around his room, and makes these little honking noises, and then he's okay."

"What's the matter with New Hampshire?"

"It's the forbidden state."

Naturally, I could have asked her why it's forbidden, but the way I see it, you've got to get the information directly from the horse's mouth. I decided to bide my time. Mary just gets so nervous and embarrassed when she talks about Tyrus, and she's such a nice old lady, so why should I bug her? What I'm trying to say is this: at that point—when I'd decided to quit bugging Mary—I came to the decision that it was up to me to rescue Tyrus, and now that I had an in, and didn't have to worry about being beaned with a copy of *Jane's All the World's Aircraft* (which, believe me, must weigh at least eight million pounds), I decided to take the bull by the horns and rescue him. From what, you ask? From his obvious destiny.

Actually, let me be the first to admit that Mary herself had tried to rescue Tyrus once when he was five years old. Lettie told me. Mary took him to P.S. 42 to register him for kindergarten, but they laughed at her. Laughed her right out of the principal's office. Too bad they didn't have the ACLU back then. I mean, after all, doesn't the Constitution guarantee every child an education? It doesn't say anything about your having to be sane. I'll have to put that on my list of things to work on. Maybe Tyrus is eligible for some retroactive benefits.

The other time Mary tried to rescue Tyrus was when he was nine and beginning to stay in more and more and he started to get all these cockamamy fears he has—like helicopters, New Hampshire, facing east, etc. Mary took him to her priest, and the guy told her that it was a cross God gave her to bear for having sinned, and she's been bearing the old cross ever since while old Father Flynn spends two weeks every year at his church's retreat house on the beach in the Caribbean next door to the Hilton with its casino, floor show, and twelve gourmet restaurants. Can you tell how much it pisses me off?

Henceforth, I am going to look on this whole situation as a double-bubble opportunity. I can write an exposé on small-time criminals, as well as a tremendous human interest story about Tyrus. People really need to find out about this sort of stuff, and while I plan all this, I'm going to figure out a way to rescue Tyrus.

§ § §

Early the next morning there I was again in my ruffles and ribbons. I figure once Tyrus gets used to me, I can bring in my notebook. Mary told me I could carry Tyrus' breakfast in to him. She kept changing her mind about this decision, however, until Lettie said, "For Christ's sake, Mary, give the kid a chance with the boy."

"But what if he gets upset?"

"No, Mary," I said, "he won't. I promise I'll leave—I mean retreat—as soon as he looks like he's going to get upset."

"Promise me, if he starts to bite his arm, you'll leave."

"It's a deal."

Then I stood there trying like hell to keep a straight face as Mary gave me the following instructions:

"Now, Phoebe, today is . . . um . . ."

"Wednesday."

"Wednesday. The password is 'Omaha Beach.' First, knock three times and say the password. Go in, put the tray on his desk, pick it back up three times . . ."

"What happens if I make a mistake and I do something four times?"

"Omigod, Lettie, this won't work." Mary slapped her hand to her cheek.

"Sure it will, Mary. Phoebe, four is forbidden. If you do something four times, he has to make extra trips. Extra trips means his schedule is thrown off. He keeps to a very tight schedule, and if it gets way off, he has to start the day again. That means Mary has to get him another breakfast, remake his bed . . ."

"I get it." No wonder people around here go flying

when the phone rings. God forbid it should ring four times.

Anyway, up I went humming "The Monkey's Uncle Polka." I knocked three times and whispered, "Omaha Beach." The hatch opened.

"Here's your breakfast, Ty; three glasses of root beer, a lovely bowl of chicken noodle soup" (only one bowl—Mary must have put her foot down at some point), "and three chocolate chip cookies. Don't you like eggs, Tyrus?"

"No."

"Here, let me get my tambourine off your tray." I took it off, and he waited. "Do you want me to take the tambourine off twice more?"

"Yes." Oh well.

He got right down to business. Slurped down his soup and soda with the exact same piglike noises my old man makes, who of course has no excuse. Then he got up and hid his cookies in various nooks and crannies in the room: under the carpet, in his shoe, and over the door moulding.

"Rationing your cookies, eh?"

"Yes." He had on striped pajamas and convalescent-home slippers like my nana wears. I asked him if he wanted a song.

"No. I'm going to read."

"Oh. Which book?"

"*Queen of the Battles.*"

"That sounds good. What's it about?"

"All the great battles of World War II."

"Great in what context?"

"What does that mean?"

"Well, I mean, great in the sense of territory taken,

or enemy killed, or perhaps, as far as the battle brought about a turning point in the war."

"All that, see. Look." He opened to a page with a chapter titled, "The Battle for Kwajalein." There was a revolting photograph of dead Japanese soldiers rolling in the waves of this gorgeous island. The caption under the picture said, "In the words of our GIs in New Guinea, 'The only good Jap is a dead Jap.'" Now where have I heard that before?

"Tyrus, that's gross. Can't you show me another book?"

"Okay. Uncle Turk just got me the latest *Jane's Fighting Ships.*" Jesus, this Jane guy must be a really boring person. Tyrus scattered the pile of books on the desk and came up with this monstrosity of a book with a shiny new flyleaf. The price was still on it. Fifty-nine pounds sterling. Let's see. Two point three . . . hmmm . . . a hundred and thirty-seven bucks! No wonder poor Turk is a criminal if he has to keep Tyrus in hundred-and-thirty-seven-dollar books. I mean, I really can't believe he stole it. Even the best thief couldn't possibly sneak a book that size past the cashier at Barnes and Noble.

"This section is on battleships. I love battleships even more than destroyers. This is my favorite: the USS *Lexington.*" He showed me this page covered with little black and white pictures of battleships. Every single ship looked exactly like the one next to it, and I couldn't tell you what made the *Lexington* so special.

"I was on a battleship once. One of the old wrecks on the Hudson."

"Liberty ships."

"Yeah. About a million of them all lined up painted that foggy gray with white numbers. They were giving a tour on one of them, but all my old man cared about was the hatch covers." Tyrus looked at me curiously, and I just kept babbling on. "My old man wanted to buy one of those hatch covers so he could make it into a coffee table. Solid oak. Oak is in, Tyrus. He was all crazy over the idea that since the doors had little brass holes built into them, he'd have built-in ash trays. The holes were where you opened the doors."

"Hatches."

"Yeah, hatches. The old man couldn't get one, though. He looked into it, but then the Navy came and junked the ships."

"You don't know what they did with them?"

"Yeah. You can get all the hatch covers you want at United House Wrecking in Stamford at about a five hundred percent markup."

"I meant the liberty ships, not the hatches."

"Oh. I don't have any idea, but if I had anything to do with it, I'd have them towed out to the middle of the Atlantic Ocean and set adrift. I mean, they really looked like ghost ships anyway, ya know? Then you could kind of track them, or even let people claim them. First guy to find one gets to keep it. Now if I found a liberty ship, I'd—"

"You're crazy." Tyrus smiled.

Tyrus' smile lasted maybe an eighth of a second, but he did smile, and when he did, he looked like a normal human being. And he was right. I am crazy. I like to be crazy, although I must admit I looked a hell of a lot crazier than I actually am what with that getup I was wearing. It's my belief that kids and mentally ill people have quite a lot in common.

"Tyrus?"

"What?"

"I'm not really Jean Marie Kabritsky."

"I know."

"Oh, good. I am so relieved that you didn't believe it. These people you live with—your mother, and your aunt, and those uncles—they think you have no sense at . . ."

"You're her twin sister. Joan Marie Kabritsky."

Well, shut my mouth. He didn't bat an eyelash. And his face was like a dog's who's been waiting all day for you to pet him. His eyes were so damn incredible—so gorgeous, but so piercing. Not scary piercing, frightened piercing.

"Yep. Joan Marie Kabritsky, that's me. Jean's twin sister. Call me Joan, Tyrus. I'm not as good as she is— never made it big on the Polish wedding circuit . . ."

"I'll call you Enola Gay."

"What's that from? That's familiar."

"That was the name of the B-52 that dropped the first atomic bomb."

"Great. Listen, Tyrus, I'm a pacifist. How about Libby? Short for Liberty. That way, if anyone hears you talking to me . . ."

"The original Enola Gay was named after the pilot's mother." He pulled a book down from the shelf. An immense book all tattered and torn. I bet he'd read it eight million times.

"What's that book called?"

"The American Encyclopedia of War Planes."

There's a book that never came out in paperback. He started reading it, and I left him to walk around the room to see all his other books. I began noticing that there was other stuff in the room, too. Between the books on the shelves were a few framed autographed pictures of my twin sister, and in one corner was a table all piled up with model ships and planes. All gray. The Pentagon must get a deal on gray paint.

I looked more carefully at the models. Each one was covered with a ton of hard dried glue lumps where the pieces had been joined together. These models were the real authentic kind that come with a hundred million pieces in the box. And the pieces all look exactly alike. I could just imagine Tyrus picking up those little bitty pieces and sticking them on one by one. They were all in the right spot, but they were crooked and cockeyed.

"Tyrus, you made all these models, didn't you?" No answer. "You did a fantastic job. What patience you have."

"I did a very bad job. I always drop a lot of pieces on the floor, and then I have to get down on the carpet and find them."

The goddamn carpet was gray. "Do you have to drop the pieces two more times once you find them?"

He nodded his sweet head and said softly, but with a stiff upper lip, "Affirmative." My own lip quivered.

"I get my next model on the twenty-fifth. I'm getting the USS *Lollipop*. Here's my glue." He opened another little drawer. I don't have to tell you what the disgusting tube of glue looked like. I planned to tell Lettie to make sure she gets Tyrus a new tube of glue with each new model. That's the least Tyrus deserves, damn it.

§   §   §

Now my in was legitimate. Forget the polka crap. Me and Tyrus made the USS *Lollipop*. He never once looked at the directions. Just opened one of his books and told me where to glue everything. The only problem was that the windows in his room were shut, and before I'd thought to let in some air, we were both high as kites, giggling from the fumes. That Tyrus sure knew how to giggle, and when the last piece was stuck on the USS *Lollipop*, he said, "Please leave," very politely. Progress? Maybe.

Chapter Six

Tyrus wasn't crazy. Certainly wasn't retarded. Wasn't emotionally disturbed or brain-damaged. They mainstream those sorts of kids into art and music classes at school. None of the Special Ed kids I grew up with were anything like Tyrus.

I think Tyrus started out as kind of a strange person like Albert Einstein. The kind that doesn't talk until he's five, and when he does, the words are so advanced you have to break out the old dictionary to understand him. But what kid wouldn't be strange raised by four teen-aged hoodlums one of whom was not dealing with a full deck. And sometimes, while talking with Lettie, I had to question even that possible shred of normalcy. I believe

Tyrus went from strange to weird to a lot weirder because his mother loved him too much. She loved him too much to send him out into the world where all the other kids would make fun of him. Now she loved him too much to let some social worker get him a job sweeping out a factory while the tool and diemakers hid his lunch.

I could live with Mary's overprotection. Besides, she didn't have anything else to do with her life, so why not spend it loving the only person who would ever love her back? But unlike Mary, I had extended vision. I could see all the horror that would befall poor Tyrus in, say, twenty years. As badly as I felt for him, I must admit to taking some pleasure in the fact that I suddenly had a mission. A legitimate mission where I could really do something worthwhile for another human being.

Having a mission meant more to me than having a horse or a private phone, and don't forget we're talking about a pubescent girl here, and everybody knows how they are about horses and private phones. But what could I, a pubescent (not to mention insolvent) girl do for starving babies in Chad, for Indians who wanted their land back, or for the Bates Mountain Elementary School that was going to close, like it or not? Absolutely nothing. But I could do something for Tyrus, and I intended to do it. I wasn't quite sure what, naturally, but I did know that first of all, I had to get him out of that house. And to get him out of that house for the first time since the election of Harry Truman. It took me two weeks, but I got him out, and then his entire life changed, along with Mary's, Lettie's, the brothers, and especially mine.

For two weeks I worked on Tyrus. We built boats and planes together, and I taught him poker. Mary and Lettie watched us play from the door, flabbergasted. They couldn't believe a retarded child could handle five-

card stud with such aplomb. Then I had Lettie buy us a
Monopoly set, and Tyrus really got into that. Naturally,
he renamed each of the properties. Forget Atlantic City.
The Boardwalk was the USS *Arizona*, and Park Place
became the USS *Enterprise*. And that old cheap-o, Mediterranean Avenue, he called the Fucker.

I said, "If Mediterranean is a fucker, what's Baltic?"

"A Messerschmitt."

Oh.

Finally, when Tyrus was really used to having me
around—would let me into his room without a password
and all that crap—I told him it was time for a heart-to-
heart talk. It was right after the Sunday night movie, *The
Miracle Worker,* which I talked him into watching with
me. Actually, I bribed him like I do with old Blob. I
promised him one uninterrupted game of Monopoly
right after the movie which, as everyone knows, could
easily last six or seven hours. Bribing Blob is much simpler—I just tell her she and Pooh can crawl into the sack
with me once the lights are all out. Then somewhere
between the time she falls asleep and the time she pees, I
schlepp her back to her own little bed.

Earlier I had asked Lettie if it would be possible for
Tyrus to have a little portable TV up in his room. She
said, "Sure." I said, "When?" She said, "How about right
now?" Old Lettie took me down to the basement, and
there were about eight million TV sets lined up on the
shelves, just like my nana's basement before she went to
the nursing home. Except Nana had rows of her famous
pickled cabbage cores, not TVs.

I quickly bypassed the Monsoons' shoddy GE, and
picked a nice little Sony (my grandpa, an expert, will
have nothing else).

Anne Bancroft and Patty Duke did the trick. Tyrus

watched *The Miracle Worker* with growing interest and comprehension. He leaned against me during the part where Anne had to be cruel and heartless toward Patty. There really were times when I wanted to put my arms around Tyrus and hug him like I do Blob when Pooh is in the washer, but it was all right because by now Tyrus knew I was crazy about him. No need to demonstrate my affection, because he would require two additional spontaneous hugs. You feel like a fool trying to act spontaneous when what you're doing isn't.

When the movie ended, I didn't put on the lights. We just sat there in the dark silently until I took a deep breath and said, "Ya know, Tyrus, you're another Helen Keller."

"I'm not blind," he said.

"Yes, but you do trips, and you won't look east, and you eat chicken noodle soup for breakfast." He looked at me. Blank. I hurried to keep talking because I didn't want to lose him. "That's just not the way things are done in life, Tyrus. It's not socially acceptable behavior, and you have to become socially acceptable because some day your mother is going to die, or as Anne Bancroft said to Mrs. Keller, 'What's going to happen to Helen when you're pushing up strawberries?' Tyrus, what's going to happen to you?"

He leaned against me. "Aunt Lettie will take care of me."

"Only on her good days. But she likes to take off and have a good time once in a while, and her idea of the fast lane is not racing up and down two flights of stairs every time you get upset. And don't forget, also, that she's going to die, too."

"Uncle Turk will—"

"Tyrus, even you wouldn't want to be taken care of

by Uncle Turk." Heaven knows if this family had a retarded person in it, Uncle Turk fit the bill.

He looked at me, and a little thread of the streetlight
outside came in along the edge of the shade and lit up
Tyrus' damp left eye. "Maybe I'll die first."

I swallowed the gagging lump in my throat and said
sternly, "Don't you dare lay a guilt trip on me, Tyrus.
It's not fair. I'm telling you this because . . . because I
love you, Tyrus." He leaned against me more heavily,
but I stayed stern. "Now I want you to think. What
would have happened to Helen Keller if that woman
didn't teach her to be a regular human being? What do
you think?" He didn't answer. "She'd have ended up in
some loony bin sitting in her own . . ."

"Will you take care of me, Joan Marie?"

Now that my eyes were accustomed to the dark, I
could see the terror in his. He touched my shoulder and
trailed his soft fingers down my bare arm. I knew he'd
have to do it three times, and I let him, but then I ran out
of the room trying not to cry—unsuccessfully. Yes, I
would take care of him, but not the way he was hoping.
If only he could know that what I was about to do would
give him the chance to be another Helen Keller when she
grew up.

Once I'd controlled myself, I went back up to his
room to make sure he didn't think I was mad at him or
anything. There was old Tyrus sitting in the middle of
the floor with the Monopoly board all set up. He smiled
at me and said, "You can go first."

This was the first time he let me go first.

§   §   §

I heard Ben's intake of breath and wondered what
he wanted.

"Phoebe?"

"Hmmm?"

"The part where Tyrus touches your bare arm . . . did you really run out of the room?"

"Sure."

"You didn't have . . . I mean, you didn't get into anything sexual?"

"Ben, for God's sake! I was thirteen."

"But you're precocious."

"I didn't become sexually precocious until this year. And Tyrus, believe me, was celibate."

"Just because you're emotionally disturbed doesn't mean you don't have a penis."

"Please, Ben. I loved Tyrus."

He sighed. "That's exactly the point. You have very naïve ideas about sex."

"What's that supposed to mean?"

"You ran out the door when Tyrus touched you, and you ran out the door during Marlys' stage act."

"I didn't run. It was disgusting. Admit it."

"Nudity isn't disgusting."

"Sometimes it is."

"Never."

"You're an artist. Your mind is twisted."

"Phoebe! If anything, art has untwisted my mind."

"Look at *Playboy* magazine."

"Beautiful naked women. What's wrong with that?"

"Ben, you just haven't been keeping up with the times. Nudity is more than it used to be. In *Playboy* they have pictures of women masturbating in front of mirrors. Some day you'll open the centerfold and say,

'What the hell is that?' And under the picture, it will say, 'Playboy Bunny Paige LeFay's cervix.' "

Ben cracked up. I didn't mean to make him laugh, but laughing is a great way to change the subject. Ben changed the subject from a discussion of nudity to a demonstration of nudity. Making love when you're pregnant forces a lot of inhibitions to end up by the wayside. If you have pregnant sex, and want to be comfortable at the same time, the best positions are really *incroyable.*

Once, Richard Burton, the movie star, not the explorer, said in an interview that sex is most erotic and pleasurable when the lovers maintain a sense of humor. He was right.

Later Ben lay back and resumed reading, staying naked.

§   §   §

God, when I think back. How did I survive it all? I told him, yes, I would take care of him, but not when his family had all died off. Now. Starting today. Well, when I said that, Tyrus straightened right up. Slowly, he opened his desk and took out his soup can. His back went ramrod straight, and he said, "Map out all the details for me, Sergeant, and report back at 1600 hours."

Dismissed, right? Right. But you can bet your booties I got the hell back to that attic at 1600 hours. I had to call my local army recruiter to get the info on what the hell time it was at 1600 hours, but I came back.

I mapped out every detail to him. I told him to be brave. I told him I was going to show him the world, and show the world him. In two days we were going for a little jaunt—a maneuver, so to speak. In fact, a secret maneuver. I just went on and on, and Tyrus ate it up. I won't say he freely and willingly put himself in my hands, but he understood what I was saying, and what it would mean, that he had no choice.

The excursion would be in two days on a Wednesday when Mary usually went out for groceries. We didn't have to worry about Lettie because she slept till noon with blinders and earplugs. I didn't know when we'd be back, so I wrote a note to Mary apologizing for upsetting her, but absolutely promising her that I wouldn't be upsetting Tyrus. I mentioned that we'd be in disguise so that she wouldn't have to worry about anyone recognizing me. I also apologized for breaking open her piggy bank. After all, we did need some money. Actually, I almost didn't apologize for that, figuring stealing would be the one thing they'd understand most easily. Tuesday night I didn't sleep a wink, and I heard Tyrus doing a lot of pacing, too. Mostly, I lay awake under all the dripping silver tassles thinking about the one hitch. There's always a hitch, right? Tyrus refused to compromise on facing east, and also, he said that if he spotted a helicopter, he'd have to duck into the nearest cover. He told me that if we were heading east, he would walk backward. I asked him what the hell all this shit was about east and helicopters. He told me that when he faced east he felt a cloud of sharp needles sticking into his face. Ouch. Fortunately, I, as you know, am ingenious. I told him I had a very simple solution although it meant another petty theft on my part.

§   §   §

So I'm a little boy again. Last night Lettie decided I could use a trim. Fortunately, the new haircut made my need for a disguise that much simpler. On the day of the great escape I was wearing jeans, a dress shirt—three buttons undone—and a suit jacket. If the suit jacket had been white, everyone would just have thought there goes another asshole kid trying to look like John Travolta. When Tyrus let me in, he was just about set to go. He looked like your basic mentally handicapped person: baggy chino pants, a short-sleeved shirt with flamingos all over it that must have belonged to Mary's swept-away father, and wing tips with dust in all the little holes. I wish some billionaire would donate enough money so that every mentally handicapped person in America could buy a pair of Converse sneakers.

"Have you got the helicopter and direction barrier, Adjutant?"

"Right here, sir." Wonder what happened to Enola? I held out Mary's economy-size jar of Pond's cold cream with the telltale label carefully soaked off. Does your grandmother use Pond's cold cream? Every grandmother I know has a great big jar of Pond's cold cream on top of her chest of drawers, right in the middle of the doily.

Then, of course, they've got those little teensy jars of Pond's scattered all over the entire house. My nana glops it on, and the stuff stays on her face all night, but it loses its white color as soon as you put it on—like Elmer's Glue-All—and then it looks like Vaseline. My mother once gave Nana Oil of Olay for her birthday. Nana tried it on once, and then put on a thick layer of Pond's right over it. She told me that Oil of Olay was a rip-off. She said if you are serious about keeping your face from getting wrinkled, you need a good thick coat of Pond's covering your entire face all night long. I personally prefer the wrinkles. Not only that, I sleep on my stomach. You absolutely have to sleep on your back if you want to wear

Pond's cold cream or you'll really guck up the old pillow, and your mother will kill you.

Tyrus looked into the jar.

"You want me to put it on you, Ty?"

"I am able to judge where I'm most susceptible to the needles, Adjutant."

He started putting it on. He didn't use a mirror, so he missed a lot and got quite a bit on his ears and hair as well as a huge glob on his nose.

"Now, Tyrus, we simply wipe off the excess, and you're completely protected."

"No. We leave it all on."

"Tyrus, it creates an invisible barrier. You don't need a lot on."

"I need a lot on."

"For Christ's sake, Tyrus, you sound like my goddamn nana."

"You are expendable."

"The hell I am, and by the way, you promised—no war talk today." I handed him a towel.

"I can't take it off."

"Tyrus, have you ever heard of a place called Willowbrook?"

"No."

"Well, believe me, there ain't no willows there, and there ain't no brook, either. It's where people like you go when their parents die. And they won't give you three glasses of root beer for breakfast if that's where you end up." I hoped Anne Bancroft found it easier to be tough with Patty than I did with Tyrus.

He wiped off the Pond's. He wiped it off without getting upset and without biting the hell out of his arm. Unlike Mary, I tend to believe in the effectiveness of threats when there's a hundred percent chance that they'll be carried out.

"Also, Tyrus, I have to put an Ace bandage around your wrist."

"Why?" Not "No." "Why?" A giant step in the right direction.

"Because most people do not chew on themselves when they get frustrated. They smoke cigarettes, or drink, or pop pills. All of the above are equally as bad as chewing on your wrist, but at least people don't stare at you, and the last thing we want is people staring at us. We have to remain incognito, remember?"

"What's an Ace bandage?"

"Don't worry, you'll love it. It's just a long, elastic thing that you put around a sprained ankle. They feel all warm and snuggly if they're not too tight. Let me go find one. I'll be right back."

I dashed down to the bathroom and opened the medicine cabinet. Eight million things immediately fell into the sink, and I quickly stashed them all back. No Ace bandage. I opened the linen closet. There was a neatly rolled-up Ace bandage next to a giant douche bag. I ran back upstairs with it just in time to see Tyrus taking a cookie out of the fan box in his window. I wrapped up his wrist. Then I unwrapped it, wrapped it, unwrapped it, wrapped it—one, two, three. I had to give in to him a little. After all, have you ever had needles flying into your face?

"Now follow me, Ty. Everything will be okay if you always follow me. We're going to have a goddamned good time." He saluted. Shit.

I taped the note to the TV screen since I knew Mary would be watching her soaps after shopping, but when I opened the front door, I saw that there was an unforeseen problem. It was very bright sunshine outside, and I realized I had definitely not thought of everything.

"Tyrus, I have to go find some sunglasses for you. You haven't been out in the sun in thirty-seven years. Now just wait one more minute."

"I'll have to do a lot of trips."

"Don't be silly. When we're inside places, you can take them off, and after three places it'll all come out in the wash."

Off I went to hunt. I really wasn't sure where to look, so I looked everywhere. I kept thinking: sunglasses, sunglasses, where does my Dad keep his sunglasses? In his car. No good. I went into Turk and Galooch's room. Get ready for this; they had bunk beds. I started opening all the drawers trying to find the junk drawer. Everyone has a junk drawer, right? So where do you throw an old pair of sunglasses? The junk drawer. Fortunately, old Turk and Galooch were on my wavelength, because I found a pair in a bottom dresser drawer mixed in with the batteries, pennies, and matchbooks with one match left. They were metal-frame aviator glasses, and I mean real aviators like a Pan Am pilot wears. Not only did they have a fancy *P* on one of the lenses (that's for Pierre Cardin in case you're not up there with the rest of us), but on the inside of the frames, they said 14k, (and *every*-body knows what that stands for). I wondered who they stole those from. They sure as hell weren't Mr. Monsoon's. His glasses have a designer Band-Aid holding the bridge together. *J & J* for Johnson and Johnson. Anyway, they were the most gorgeous sunglasses I have ever seen in my life.

So you should have seen old Tyrus when he tried them on. Terribly New York. With his black bristle hairdo and flamingo shirt he looked like Richie Rotten or

whatever that punk rocker's name is. And if anyone
looks mentally ill, it's those punk rockers. Old Tyrus
would blend right into the Manhattan scene. So stand
back, Big Apple, here we come: Joan Marie Kabritsky,
twin sister of that polka queen, Jean, and Tyrus Rotten.

We headed straight for the local branch of the Bowery Savings Bank, but Joe DiMaggio was nowhere to be
seen. I wonder how many people see old Joltin' Joe doing
those ads for the Bowery Savings Bank and then come
out of the bank singing "Where have you gone, Joe
DiMaggio? . . ."

"Take off your glasses, Tyrus, and let's go in." Tyrus
was petrified, but he still fired a salute at the old security
guard who was sleeping on his feet. The guard opened
one eye at Tyrus, but I distracted him with my most
dazzling Ginger Rogers smile.

"Hiya, pal," the guard said to me. Whoops. Keep
forgetting I'm a boy, right? I changed over to my best
John Travolta smirk.

I went directly to a teller, but she looked over my
head and said to Tyrus, "May I help you, sir?" Her little
nameplate said Miss Cupfer, but she looked more like
Miss Godzilla. Old Tyrus mumbled something about an
ambush while I cleared my throat real loud.

"Oh. Hello, dear. Are you ahead of this gentleman?"

"No. Actually, we're together. I'd like to cash in
these pennies." I heaved my paper sack up at her.

"Oh, my, my, my. It will take a good bit of time to
run them through our machine."

"That's okay, you won't have to bother. There are
2,752 pennies in this bag."

"I'm sure you're being completely honest, little boy,
but our policy . . ."

"Give me twenty-five bucks, and we'll call it even."

She laughed. "What's the matter? This is a bank, isn't it? You'll make almost ten percent." She laughed again, and then looked over at this drip sitting at a desk picking his nose.

"Oh, Mr. Waterhouse, this little fellow is just so adorable. Could you come over here for just a sec." She turned to Tyrus. "Is this your youngster, sir?"

Tyrus said, "Man your battle stations, boys, and prepare for a counterattack." Miss Cupfer made panicky motions, gesturing to Mr. Waterhouse to get his butt over to her window. Waterhouse sighed and stumbled out from behind his desk.

"What's the problem here, Miss Cupfer?"

"This darling little boy has broken his piggy bank and has offered to take twenty-five dollars cash for twenty-seven fifty in pennies."

"My goodness, young man, you'd lose quite a bit of principal that way. I'm sure if you left your money here, and came back in another hour—we'll give you a receipt, of course—we could—"

"My time is worth more than a lousy two fifty, Waterhouse. What do you say we make this deal? We have to visit my mother in the hospital, and visiting hours close real soon."

"Oh dear," said Miss Cupfer. Waterhouse took out his wallet.

"In that case, I think I'll take your word for it, young man, but I insist on giving you the exact amount." He leafed through his wad, held the money out to me and Tyrus, and said, "I hope your wife isn't seriously ill, sir." Tyrus stiffened.

"Superficial shrapnel wound to the left buttock, Colonel Waterhorse."

"Thanks, Mr. Waterhouse. C'mon Dad." I got the

hell out of there with Tyrus in hot pursuit. He didn't even bother to salute the guard.

"Tyrus," I hissed over my shoulder, "I told you and you promised—no war talk."

"Merely an injury report, Adjutant." We were out on the sidewalk.

"Civilians do not give injury reports. Nor do they receive shrapnel wounds. You could have shut up, and I would have told those assholes that Mom was having her tubes tied. Now try to remember: I do the talking."

We stepped down the stairs under the sidewalk, and I bought two subway tokens. I said to the token lady through the bars, "Which train do I take to get to the Statue of Liberty?"

"How the hell do I know? This is Queens, not the National Park Service." If you want to feel like a peanut, go to Queens.

"Then which train goes to Manhattan?"

"All of them."

"Which one will get us there quickest?"

"Whatcha think? The express."

"C'mon, Ty."

It was nice and cool in the subway. It was also filthy —I mean, the walls were covered with two inches of crud. A horrible roar came at us, and Tyrus blocked his ears. The train flew in. I looked to see if it said "Express." It didn't. It said, "Mayor Koch sucks crotch." Crotch was spelled correctly. The graffiti artists in New York are no dummies. The train stopped, the door opened, I looked in, and said,

"Is this the express?" Everyone inside stared at me for one eighth of a second, and the door shut in my face. *Vroooom.* Gone.

"Tyrus, we'll get the next one. And move fast. Those doors don't give you much time. Hold my hand."

"Negative."

"Don't start with that negative shit, Tyrus. Remember that cream we put on? It does double duty. It leaves a millimeter of space between us even when we hold hands."

Another train flew in. I grabbed Tyrus' hand. It was just the kind of hand you'd expect. Like a very big child's; smooth and creamy, with no calluses or bumps or scratches. I pulled him through the doors. At nine-thirty there are very few people riding the subway. Earlier that day the train carried four hundred thousand people to work. Straight across from where we sat was an advertisement for *A Chorus Line:*

"Dazzling," says Clive Barnes.

"Stupendously original," says Rex Reed.

"Breathtaking," says some other asshole.

"Rip-off," says I.

"What?" says Tyrus.

"Nothing."

"At least we're safe on this vehicle."

Did you ever dream someone riding the New York subway system would say something that ridiculous?

"Sure, Tyrus, you're thinking it's probably safe since it isn't two o'clock in the morning."

"No, I mean because we're under surveillance by the allied forces."

"We are?"

"Yes. I've noticed several reinforcements sent in by the RAF."

"Raf?"

"No. RAF."

"What does that stand for?"

"Royal Air Force. Where did you get your training, Adjutant. Montgomery's boys are easily identified by their berets."

"Oh. 'Royal' means 'British,' right?" I tried to sound impressive, and I thought I was, considering that I'd had no training at all except for *The Longest Day* on TV.

"I can see them from here." He glanced down at the end of the car. "Three of them."

I peeked around his shoulder. Three Guardian Angels were talking into their radios. Their radio antennas were about eighty feet long. I turned to Tyrus to explain, but I was a little taken aback by the fact that he had his Campbell's soup can to his ear.

"For Christ's sake, Tyrus, put that thing back in your pocket. And those aren't RAF guys. Those are Guardian Angels, a bunch of your basic, everyday kids who are trying to stop crime in the subways. Even Ed Koch has taken them out of his wacko classification."

"They're RAF."

"Tyrus, they're Americans. Can't you hear? They're speaking Spanish."

"With more men like Montgomery, the limeys could have gone it alone. Come in, Lieutenant Burrows-Finch, come in. Do you read me?" Tyrus pronounced it "Leftenant."

I gave up trying to convince him, and let him make all the contact he wanted with the Guardian Angels. We stopped about eight million times, and then we got lucky. We came into Manhattan from the bottom. I saw signs that said Battery Park racing across the wall, and I stood up and ran for the doors dragging Tyrus along behind me. We got out of the train and climbed up the steps to daylight.

Battery Park. Blue Harbor, white sails, the lady

holding up the old torch, Japanese tourists, the Verrazano bridge. . . . Jesus Christ! Did I say Japanese
tourists? I sure as hell did, and you guessed it: Tyrus was
gone. But I knew he couldn't have gotten far, since it was
thirty-seven years since he'd had any opportunity to run.
I made a slow 360-degree turn, and on my second scan I
spotted him lying on his stomach under a hedge taking
aim at three Oriental businessmen eating hot pretzels.
He was taking aim with a long stick with a few dead
leaves hanging off it. As I headed toward him, I could
hear: "Joe; get one for the *Arizona*. Ralphie, get the other
one for the *Nevada*. And I'll get the third one for what
they did to Hickham." I went leaping over the hedge and
damn near killed myself.

"Tyrus, the goddamned war is over."

"Watch out for a kamikaze attack. Keep low, Adjutant. All sailors have been put on alert."

"Tyrus, what about Hiroshima?"

"What about Bataan?"

"What about Nagasaki?"

"What about Corregidor?"

"They're gone. C'mon."

"Tough going, men, but we've scattered them. Remember the words of the GIs who took New Guinea:
'The only good Jap is—' "

"Now, you listen to me right now, Tyrus. When we
get on that boat, and get to the statue, there are going to
be Japanese all over the place. And Chinese. And Germans—"

"Germans! All right, men—"

"*Tyrus!*" Twenty people turned around. I tried to
calm down. "Yes, Germans. And Italians. And Indians.
(Sheet, not feather.) Every kind of people, and you can't
go around shooting—"

"International Red Cross area, men. Put away your weapons." I confiscated the weapon and threw it into the Hudson. "Has that area been designated as a weapon de-pot, Adjutant?"

I couldn't take it. "Shit, Tyrus, it's a goddamned stick, not a weapon, and it's floating away with all the other garbage. Now knock it off. You say one more mili-tary thing, and I'm taking off and leaving you here stranded. Got it?"

"Roger!"

"Piss-ant. You're a real piss-ant, Tyrus."

He followed me to the rip-off joint where you buy tickets to the statue after passing eight million shelves full of little clear plastic cases that you shake, and a big pile of snow that looks like dandruff falls all over a pa-thetic facsimile of the Statue of Liberty. Painted shit-brindle green, naturally.

§   §   §

Tyrus was like a little kid at the beach who has never been to the beach before. Or like a kid from Puerto Rico who can't resist tasting the snow the first time he sees it fall. Actually, my reactions were almost the same. I want to tell you, New York Harbor is utterly magnificent. There is nothing so fabulous as a harbor Mother Nature creates all by herself. And the palisades soaring upriver, and the skyscrapers almost close enough to touch, and all the mammoth ships at the pier, and the little tiny ships coming in from everywhere . . . It makes you realize that man and nature can actually complement each other's spectacle. All we need is a little more respect, because when this harbor is no longer polluted . . . bog-gles the mind, doesn't it? And what could the Golden Gate have that the Verrazano doesn't, aside from people jumping off. I mean, that bridge soars. And, of course, it's such a tremendously emotional experience to take a gander at the statue sticking up right in the middle of everything, holding the torch with her big, strong arm. The Statue of Liberty doesn't have a long, slim, lovely arm like Brooke Shields. It has muscles. It's what feminism is really all about, right? Boy, I couldn't wait to climb right up into her head.

Tyrus stood in the stern. (I learned port and stern while traveling with old Ty.) For the entire ride to the island he stared at the sea gulls. A bunch of sea gulls were following us because some kids were throwing Doritos out to them. Tyrus never took his eyes off them. Twin towers, huge jets getting ready to land, muscles . . . he didn't notice anything but those birds. Remember I told you how Tyrus has such long, gorgeous eyelashes? Well, as he gazed out at the sea gulls, I could also see what a beautiful curve his eyelashes had to them, and while I admired them, they seemed to glisten. Then he blinked, and a little tiny tear toppled out of one of his eyes. I really choked up, but I gave him a big smile and poked him in the arm.

"Hey, Ty, I think I'll go into the snack bar and get us some root beers. Three for you and one for me. Stay right here." I mean, I had to get away from him and make some cold, hard decisions. But I'll tell you this, when that tear rolled down his cheek, I knew just one thing: he wasn't going back to that attic. It took me one millionth of a second to decide that, although it took me quite a bit longer to decide how. A couple of hours, if you want to know.

§   §   §

"I can't read any more for now, Phoebe."

"That's okay."

"I'm beginning to feel a little afraid for Tyrus."

"I know."

"But I'll read it later."

"You don't have to."

"You've said that. I want to, but I think I'll have to prepare myself first."

I took the journal and laid it on one of Ben's shelves. "Whenever."

Artists take things so to heart.

Chapter Seven

Marlys arrived one afternoon in early December. It was sunny and eerily balmy—more of a March day when it's going out like a lamb. She handed me a folder with the name of the people who would adopt my baby typed on the cover. Just as I was opening the folder, and Marlys was digging into the Good Humors, a terrorist bomb exploded very near by. I knew it had to be close because my eardrums hurt badly and I was more aware of pain than a loud noise.

While we held our hands to our ears, the Pension Rapp shook, and Ben's garret took the biggest beating. The blurred little windows in the eaves shattered, and one of the balconies plummeted into the street. Marlys screamed, and I don't know what I did. We looked through the jagged window holes down where the balcony had been. Madame Besette was already outside, hysterical. A few blocks away we could see black smoke tunneling skyward and hear echos of distant shouting.

"That's Saul's," Ben said, oblivious to the destruction done to his art. All the canvases that had been suspended were lying scattered across the studio.

We bypassed the quaint elevator and ran down all the stairs, I as lithe as ever, surprisingly. The Greek boys were organizing an evacuation, and at the same time trying to calm the elderly couple trapped in the elevator cage, which was askew. Out on the sidewalk Madame Besette twisted locks of her red hair and babbled incoherently as she paced back and forth in front of the twisted, broken balcony. Great chunks of old brick clung to the inner side of it, but it hadn't landed on anyone, and thank God I never went out onto it when I had been so sorely tempted.

We ran down the Avenue Rapp passing the metal Art Nouveau building. The pear, and two artichokes besides, had rolled into the road, and there were dents in the sidewalk where they'd originally landed. We turned into the Avenue de la Bourdonnais, and took a left onto the Avenue de Tourville, where there was pandemonium. Debris was thickly strewn across the entire ground like the pigeon feed of the French bag ladies. Just as the Musée Rodin came into view, I noticed a shoe, kind of a trendy low boot that the students were wearing a lot. Marlys stepped in front of us, grabbed Ben's head and mine, and stuffed us into her armpits.

But her dancer's reflexes weren't quite quick enough. We all three had wondered and realized at the same time about the two white sticks protruding from the gory shoe-boot. Is it fibula and tibia, or fibia and tibula? That's what I kept asking myself as Marlys dragged us away. Marlys wrote me a year later to tell me that in her mind she kept thinking, Is that shoe mine? She said she was afraid to look down at her feet. Ben never said.

I didn't take my head out of Marlys' lapel, and I didn't open my eyes until Ben pulled me off her.

"Phoebe, we're at the Seine. You can look."

We strolled along the river, crossed the Pont Neuf, and finally sat down on a bench in the deserted Île de la Cité behind Notre Dame. Marlys and I listened to Ben rant and rave about how tourists come to Notre Dame and take a million pictures of the rose window when any nincompoop could see that the only part of Notre Dame really worth gaping at were the mammoth flying buttresses supporting the entire weight of the cathedral. He went on and on about sweeping beauty, architectural splendor, etc. Marlys and I just listened and stared into the water with the sirens drowning out all the Paris sounds except Ben's voice.

The goddamned flying buttresses reminded me of McDonald's arches, but I didn't say so, of course. And those horrible whining European sirens really got on my nerves, until finally, when Ben took a breath, I suggested we all go into Notre Dame where it was quiet. Marlys said she'd love to, but she really had to go home. I suddenly noticed that her skin had lost its translucency. It was gray like the Seine. She skittered back over the bridge and danced away.

So Ben and I sat in the church, where I found the flickering candles comforting. He talked about Jews, about how the French did their custodians proud by turning in a million Jews, and about one guy named Barbie whom Ben called the butcher of Lyon, who killed a lot of Jews himself, personally, and whom the French loved to help until Barbie began stringing up French Resistance fighters by their thumbs.

"Phoebe, you know that little school that we can see from the studio that made you say, 'Isn't it too bad that tourists are only here in the summer, and can't see the sweet little children in two straight lines, the smallest one is Madeline'?"

I didn't answer because Ben just went on talking.

"Well, Phoebe, when your grandparents, and mine, were doing without bananas and film for their Brownies because of the war, the headmaster of that school had all his Jewish students make a third line, and then he led them all along the Seine, across the Pont Alexandre III to the Gare de L'Est, where he put them on the train. He sent little messages home to their parents telling them that the kiddies were being relocated to a children's work camp where they would learn a trade to enrich their academic training. The work camp, Phoebe, was in Poland. Most of the children didn't live long enough to arrive there."

The candles continued to flicker in that silent, mysterious way that Catholic church candles do. And the statue of the Jewish God being tortured to death hung above the altar far down in front of us.

"Fucking frogs don't give a shit, still."

"But, Ben, a lot of Frenchmen must have been killed in that explosion," I said.

"Jews who live in France are Frenchmen, too, Phoebe. That's the point. Why can't people see that?"

"Sorry, Ben."

"Fucking chosen people. Chosen for what? For what?"

He was actually beginning to tremble. "Well, Ben, there wasn't much choice for God at the time. He had to make somebody the chosen people. He couldn't pick the Egyptians with all their jerky pharaohs; the Philistines weren't much. The Greeks and Romans would have laughed. I think the rest were all barbarians, so who could he pick but the Jews? After all . . ."

Ben bit my hand, which he'd been holding all along. He had wonderful ways of shutting me up. "Geez, Ben, I'm so nervous. I hope you'll bite my hand while I'm giving birth, because I'll really be nervous then."

"Let's go, Phoebe."

"Okay."

Truthfully, I hated to go. Notre Dame is very womblike. We walked up the Right Bank, where there is never any commotion whatever, until we got to the little walking bridge beyond the Avenue Rapp. Ben just walked right past the Pont de l'Alma, which leads into the Avenue Rapp, and I didn't mention it. On the bridge I noticed the folder under my arm. I had rolled it all up tight.

"Ben, it's not too cold. Why don't we go down to the quay and read the stuff in this folder from Marlys. It's about the people I'm going to give the baby to."

"Sure, Phoebe. I don't look forward to getting back to Madame Besette quite yet."

"And we'll have to stop somewhere and buy some heavy paper, or something, until we can get the windows fixed."

"I've got a closet full of empty canvases we can use. It'll probably be a long time before Madame will be able to line up a glazier. Parisian glaziers have struck oil."

I chose not to comment, just led bitter Ben down the steps under the bridge. We were facing the sun, and there wasn't a breeze off the river though it was December. It was quite nice. I opened the folder, and a thin piece of onionskin fell out. It had been protecting an eight by ten portrait of a couple who were the replica of the ever so handsome ex-President and his beautiful wife, Madame Giscard d'Estaing.

Her Coco Chanel suit was as old as she was, but in absolutely mint condition. She was blond—that country club, Lauren Bacall style as timeless as the suit. The husband was every human being's picture of a cosmopolitan diplomat: distinguished, impeccable, a little gray in the sideburns, and a subtle but deliberate sexiness to the eyes. They were both perfect, though slightly older than I expected.

The next photo was an aerial shot of the mansion Manderley that Rebecca dreamed she was back in—an enormous rectangular estate, practically a palace. It was surrounded by gardens, then woods, on one side the Atlantic, and on the other what looked like the edge of a cute little village. Taped to the bottom of the photograph was a brief description, brief being all that was necessary.

The desLauriers home in Normandy, one
half kilometer from the village of St. Aubin,
and twenty-five kilometers from Caen.

"I think she might be lonely there, Ben, don't
you?"

"Who?"

"My daughter. Or my son, too."

There I was, really beginning to humanize that
baby. I'd gone from fishie, to fetus, to baby, to son or
daughter. Ben didn't seem to consider it a milestone. He
rifled past the desLauriers' "home."

"Another picture, Phoebe."

I lifted the palace out of the way. Next was a Paris
boulevard—avenue, more exactly. *The* avenue. When
Jackie Onassis comes to Paris, this is the street where
she gets photographed. People in Ben's neighborhood
just let her have a stroll in peace. Anyway, this street
was the only one more prestigious than the one Marlys
lives on.

The desLauriers town house, no. 7, Avenue Foch.

"You won't have to worry about the loneliness part
after all, Phoebe."

"Right. The joint in Normandy is probably their
summer beach house. I just don't know if I want a rich
kid; I mean a little rich is all right, but my God."

Ben smiled for the first time since the bomb went
off. "Look at me."

"Yeah, yeah. I see you."

No more photos. "Listen to the report, Ben. First, a note from Marlys:

"Phoebe, I was going to have someone write out all the dope on these desLauriers people, but instead, Madame desLauriers has chosen to write a letter to you. It says everything, I think. All I can say, Phoebe, is that if I were an unborn baby and could choose any parents in the world, I'd have to pick these two, really. Love, Marlys."

I read Madame desLauriers' letter aloud.

"Dear young lady,
First, may I ask that you read this letter knowing that English is my second language. My husband, Eugene, and I are in the process of attempting to adopt a child. I am unable to bear a child because I have lost my fallopian tubes in two pregnancies. I am past the age permissible to apply to an "in vitro fertilization" clinic. It doesn't matter. My husband and I want a baby whether the child comes from another woman's body or my own. We are too old to allow our egos to influence our decisions. You, my dear, would give us the opportunity to know our baby from the moment of birth. You would be welcome to have the baby here at our home in Normandy with the best medical attention. I would feel privileged to shower you with as much emotional support as I could muster. In the case of an obstetrical

problem, we are just a short ride from an excellent hospital in Caen. I would accept any decision of yours. I would even be prepared for the possibility that you might change your mind upon giving birth, and keep the child. However, we would not allow to happen any claim of yours upon the baby once the child is more than two weeks old. We feel such a disruption might harm the child. Thank you for allowing this contact from me to you. Please call on me if you wouldn't mind speaking with me. I will be in Paris for the New Year. If you wish to reach me sooner, please phone me at St. Aubin.

> With fondest regard,
> Florence desLauriers."

All quiet on the western front, as Tyrus liked to put it.

Finally, I said, "Ben?"

"Yes."

"That settles a lot for me. Will you come to Lamaze classes with me so I can learn how to have this baby . . . I'm petrified."

"To go alone?"

"Yes, but mostly to give birth. And will you come to Normandy, too? I don't want to give birth surrounded by just strangers."

"Sure, Phoebe. From the looks of this folder, I doubt the desLauriers will mind at all."

"Thanks, Ben."

"You forgot about not thanking me again."

"My other thank yous were for taking me in. This one is for helping me give birth."

"I've always wanted to see Normandy, so I should be the one to say thank you."

"I love you, Ben."

"That's so much better than thank you. St. Aubin is probably one of those French coastal towns that are in all the travel brochures. We'll have a nice holiday there."

Ben pulled me around to face him instead of the Seine, and said, "Besides, I never want to be apart from you, Phoebe."

I focused on the cleft in Ben's bristly chin. "I don't think I want to deal with words like 'never,' Ben."

"It fell out. Sorry. Right now, I want you forever. Tomorrow, I admit, I could easily change my mind."

I swatted his arm, delighted at his first smiles since the bomb went off. "Let's go check on Marlys before we go . . . home."

He didn't realize that "home" is a word a lot like "never."

"Okay. That's a nice excuse for avoiding Madame Besette a little longer."

"She'll get a new Greek and forget the whole thing in a week."

"Too bad it's not that simple for the rest of us."

Chapter Eight

Paris was quiet as we walked to Marlys' house, or maybe the quiet was just relative. She was in, according to the guy who answered the door, but wouldn't see anyone. He had a camera hanging around his neck, or a light meter, and looked at us like we smelled of rotten fish.

"Just tell her it's Phoebe and Ben."

"*Merde,*" he mumbled, leaving us standing in the doorway.

"My God, Ben, she sure hangs around with a bunch of creeps."

"She has to, Phoebe. She's a star."

"Shit. I hope she gets away once in a while."

"She does. She has a lover."

"Don't be silly."

"I'm not being silly."

"Ben, if she had a lover, don't you think I'd know about it? Marlys has never really been in love. I've never really been in love until just a few months ago."

"That may be, but Marlys has a lover, Phoebe."

"Where? In China? I lived with her recently, remember? Believe me, there was no lover. She's got no time. She's never had time to be in love. In school she was always too busy with getting straight A's, and scoring record highs in achievement tests, and winning first prize in the Westinghouse Science Awards . . ."

Just then the photographer reappeared while Ben was giving me a curious look. The creep motioned us to follow him. I knew I looked a mess, but what can you do when you are six weeks from having a baby, and run out the door without combing your hair to see what happens when a bomb goes off and then actually see?

Marlys was in bed, her eyes all swollen. Barbara the secretary was sitting next to the bed with a cup of tea in her hand. Marlys, obviously, was refusing to drink the tea.

"You okay, Mar?" I sat on the end of the bed—not that circular beds have ends. Ben and the secretary gave each other knowing looks because that's the only way to describe it.

"Phoebe," Marlys asked, "why should I be rich enough to be protected, and not everyone else?"

"As President Carter said to Cassie Mackin—which lost him the election—'Sometimes life isn't fair.'"

Marlys wiped her hand across her forehead. "I remember that, Phoebe. God, how perfectly apropos. Do you remember that, Ben?"

"Missed that."

"Barbara?"

Barbara looked hurt. "I don't know a Cassie Mackin."

"She was a newscaster with a brain in her head. She asked Carter at a press conference how it could be all right for women with money to have abortions and poor women not. Now Cassie is dead, too."

" 'Too,' Marlys?" I said stupidly.

"Cassie and those poor people at Saul's. Nine people died, the radio said. Damn."

Barbara offered her the tea. "Please, Marlys. Drink some tea. Go to rehearsals. Don't stop. It never helps to stop."

I could tell Marlys got annoyed, because her nostrils flared as she spoke. "Listen, Barbara, mourning is normal. Just tell everyone I'm in mourning for some guy with no foot. I'll be at the show tonight. I want four hours to mourn. Phoebe, Ben, scram, okay?"

"Sure, Marlys."

"But come to Maxim's after the show. I'm having our own private little wake. It's Saturday, so wear your black ties. Phoebe, buy a dress, and for Christ's sake, go to a hairdresser. I want to be with my friends tonight. Oh, Barbara?"

"Yes?"

"Make an appointment with Roald for Phoebe's hair, and call Givenchy. I'm treating Phoebe to a dress."

"Excuse me, Marlys, that's very nice, and all—"

"Phoebe, believe me, you have nothing suitable to wear to Maxim's. Now be gracious."

"Oh, I'm extremely grateful and all, Marlys, but does Givenchy have a formal maternity line?"

Marlys looked at me and let out a tremendous hoot. Ben chuckled, and even Barbara smiled, though she wasn't the smiling type. I find most secretaries are short on a sense of humor they're so frazzled.

Marlys slapped her thigh. "My God, could you imagine the look on the Givenchy people if Phoebe walked in to buy a dress." She started to mimic the Givenchy people: "Perhaps, if we put een zee gusset here, here, here, and here." Her color was coming back. "Okay, Phoebe, go to that shop on the Rue de Gribeauval next to Chloé and get a maternity dress with sequins. Organize her, Barbara. See you at two o'clock at Maxim's. Goodbye."

We left, Ben for home to help out Madame Besette, and to rent a tuxedo, I presumed; me to some hairdresser driven by one of Marlys' lackeys. I got a cut, blow dry, facial, makeup, and Swedish hose. The latter was an obscene activity where they blast you with streams of water while you stand there stark naked with no book to hide your embarrassed face in. Stark naked is one thing; pregnant stark naked is another. But I had absolutely no choice. They just lead me through the old Parisian beauty treatment as if I were on a leash. The baby really loved the Swedish hose. She was doing triple underwater somersaults. The only thing I had serious difficulty accepting was the fake nails glued onto my bitten ones.

I walked into the designer maternity boutique with

my stunning new hairdo; stunning even to me because
of the golden rinse they put in it. My hair had sort of a
topaz look. I loved it. Also, I now had peaches and
cream skin with plenty of subtle makeup camouflaging
my features. From the neck up, I dazzled the little shop-
keeper, but the rest of me, I could tell, shocked her. I
took off the ratty pea coat I had picked up at Marché
aux Puces, and a T-shirt of Ben's which covered my
belly but was tight, and too big jeans secured with an
oversized safety pin. Thank God the woman was expecting me, or I'd never have gotten in that door. This
was a place that didn't use Lysol to deodorize the room;
all I could smell was Worth.

A little woman in a little dress with little pearls
around her neck said, "Sit down, please, madame, and I
will show you the suitable dresses for your dinner
party. But first I would ask your preference. Do you
like something to slim the pregnancy or flawn?"

"Flawn? *Je m'excuse.* I don't know 'flawn.' "

"Ah . . . flawn, no? Parade? Flawt?"

"Parade? Oh, flaunt! Yes, definitely flaunt."

The first dress I tried on flaunted my breasts much
more than my pregnancy. Pregnancy is an opportunity
for those of us flat in the chest to try on breasts. At first,
as Madame Besette had pointed out, mine had grown
higher, but lately they'd gotten bigger and bigger, but
my skin was too tight. Pale blue veins showed through.
Ben said only in a certain light, though. The dress was
scarlet with a high waist, of course, and fairly narrow,
so my stomach stuck right out. It was silk taffeta, that
elegantly wrinkled stuff. It was also strapless, and just

barely covered my magenta nipples. Pregnancy lends a great deal of personality to your nipples, I found.

"You see, madame," the little woman said, "your belly holds up the dress, allowing the low cut. You like?"

"I don't like," I told her. I really wanted to show some cleavage, but not the entire affair. Knowing me, I would reach over to pass the salt, and a complete breast would roll up and over, and onto the table. "Not strapless." Besides, magenta and scarlet clash, as any fool knows.

I ended up with a one-shoulder job that revealed all the side of my left breast only. I would have to remind myself not to lean to the left at all, but it was worth it because I loved that particular dress. It was silk, but loosely woven, like gauze. As if eight million black silkworms had crawled all over me for about three days, missing my right arm and shoulder. The skirt blew gently around my legs without benefit of a breeze. Very sensual. Also, it was shot with silver. Whenever you read about famous queens like Mary of Scots or Catherine of Aragon, they are always wearing dresses shot with silver. Silver hairs finer than the black silkworm threads.

"Wrap it up."

I happened to glance at the little slip of paper she wrote Marlys' name on. Eight thousand five hundred francs. No tax added on. Rich shops treat you to the tax.

I stopped at a dance studio on the way home, and picked up some silver ballet shoes. I was the only one who thought of shoes because I was the only one aware that all I had was my Adidases, and boots. I considered some glamorous high-heeled sandals, but since I'd be spending the evening listing slightly to the right, I might fall down with the heels.

Chapter Nine

Ben wasn't in his studio. He left a note saying he'd be out all night arranging repairs to the garret and that he'd meet me at Maxim's at two. I'd be picked up. I was tired anyway, so I went to bed in a chair with my head propped up by two tiny sofa pillows. I wanted to be sure and not mess up a single strand of my hair. My makeup seemed set, like a mask.

I ate the lipstick off. I must have had a food dream. Searching around the studio for something to substitute, I came across all these little packets of powder. I mixed a deep mauve powder with water, and painted it on. It was a good thing I stayed in the lines. My lips were stained mauve for the next week.

The Greek at the desk rang the alarm when I stepped out of the cage. Madame Besette came prancing out from behind her curtain. They exclaimed like mad about how *magnifique* I looked, and soon all the sleepy-eyed, bare-chested Greeks were out in force licking their chops as they made voluptuous gestures to one another. I leaned to the left to give them a tiny thrill.

As the limo pulled up, Madame begged me to wait *un moment,* and disappeared behind the curtain. For a second I thought she was going to return with a Polaroid the way mothers do before the prom. But no, she had some sort of brooch in her hand that she somehow stuck and pinned into the knot at the back of my head from which the twenty-five loops of shimmering golden braids swung down. It was an Art Deco sort of silver design. (I couldn't help but learn more and more about art living with Ben.) I just got a quick glimpse of it, and saw a winged, naked cherub holding a drape folded across his arms, probably waiting for God to step out of the shower.

Then my fussing audience made exaggerated shivering motions that I had no coat, and of course, I didn't. No one, not even me, had thought of that. Well, I had five minutes earlier when I automatically reached for my pea coat. I tried to explain in my developing Greek creole that I would just be outside for a few seconds between the doors and the limo, but they wouldn't stop buzzing. The problem, I think, was that Madame was certainly generous enough to lend me her hair decoration, but not her coat. Me and Polonius agreed with her. "Neither borrower nor lender be" is one of my primary tenets.

The chauffeur saved the day. A Bentley is a sporty Rolls-Royce. By "sporty," I mean slightly shorter than a Rolls. That's what came for me, and the chauffeur strolled through the front door of the Pension Rapp carrying an adult, dead polar bear. It was my coat, or more exactly, a white fur cape with a hood. I, in turn, flung it over my bare shoulder rather than put it on. I didn't ask, but I guessed the fur was from eight hundred bludgeoned baby seals, and God forbid I should run into Brigitte Bardot, though I am certainly on her side. I doubt she'd give me a chance to explain that I was a victim of circumstances and agreed solidly with her position.

They loved me at Maxim's. The dinner party included Marlys, her secretary, Ben, and twenty men. We didn't go to a private room, but filled one corner of the main salon and were reflected into infinity by the mirrored walls. In black I was sensational against the red velvet and the mirrors. Marlys, Barbara, and the men applauded my entrance; Ben was stricken with a paralysis, his glass of Pernod stopped just short of his lips. The polar bear was lifted off me and whisked away.

I loved Ben at Maxim's. He was clean-shaven, barbered, cologned, and took my arm leading me to my seat while whispering in my ear that the greatest turn-on for every human male was the exposed line which runs along a woman's armpit on down until it becomes the outer edge of her breast.

I whispered back, "Then it's a damned good thing I shaved." We laughed. I am in that school of feminism where we hope that equality means getting men to shave their armpits rather than women not.

As the twenty men at the table kept rising and kissing the back of my hand, Marlys said, "Phoebe, you look absolutely beautiful; I've just realized that there is a special kind of pregnant beautiful. I never knew that."

"It's all in the paint pot, Mar, but thanks. When do we eat?"

There are two things a pregnant woman does more than anyone else: sweat and eat. Fortunately, as we all know, sweat doesn't show on expensive dresses. Meanwhile, Marlys called out a French restaurant command. Hidden waiters went directly into action. I looked at the menu, and ordered *veau* something because I knew "*veau*" meant "veal." Marlys discussed her choice with her secretary. Barbara was looking rather glamorous herself. You just never know what you're going to get when those secretaries remove their specs and unravel their buns. Barbara was as white as Marlys was black; white-blond flowing hair, marble skin like the Venus de Milo, and white satin.

At Maxim's they bring out your food raw so you can give it the okay before they cook it. On a gleaming silver platter a proud waiter held under my nose two matching, bloody veal kidneys neatly nestled together. I stared at them, mesmerized by the revolting gory display. I thought they were bombed feet.

As any pregnant woman would expect, I didn't get to the ladies' room in time to vomit because I didn't know where the hell it was. I vomited in a dimly lit hallway on a rare Aubusson runner. There are no handy grates in the floor at Maxim's. The maître d' handed me an almond-scented damp white towel while two of his assistants casually rolled up the carpet and carted it out. Ben took me back to the table, and Marlys had such a good laugh it was almost worth it.

"Phoebe," she admonished, "you can upchuck at Miss Wright's but not at Maxim's! The thought of it!" Barbara didn't think it was the least bit funny. There is just no getting around it: throwing up will always be a private joke between Marlys and me.

We all temporarily forgot the day's horrors, and soon our entire party was laughing like mad, getting smashed on Dom Perignon, and eating the highest-priced food in all the world. I wondered how much they'd charge Marlys for the Cream of Wheat I was cautiously sipping off a demitasse spoon. When Marlys ordered it for me, I said to her, "If that waiter brings out the red box with the black chef on the front for me to approve, I'll spit." He didn't, and Marlys roared some more. The champagne went pretty well with my Cream of Wheat.

I tried to pick Marlys' lover out of the pack. It was easy to eliminate ninety percent of the men because they were all merely members of her court; a jester who was really a riot, but whose dog imitations were not on a par with my Uncle Edmond's. A couple of soothsayers who rather conspicuously tried to keep her mellow. A guy who I swear was a doctor from the way he'd look into just your pupils. Three others obviously adored Marlys, and she seemed to adore them, but they were all markedly similar, like Madame Besette's Greeks. Then it struck me. This was, after all, Paris. Now I knew why Ben hadn't gone into the subject more deeply. I leaned over and said to him, "My God, Ben, it just dawned on me who Marlys' lover is." I was about to point and say, "Him, him, and him," when I was overwhelmed by the sudden look of momentary and then alleviated distress upon Ben's face that turned his cheek muscles from taut to mush.

Ben said, "You're really so young, Phoebe, so naïve, and hopeful, and pat about everything. Anything that happens you neatly fit into your life like you're packing a suitcase. I was sure Marlys' lover wouldn't fit. I underestimated you. Apparently, she has."

A heavy black drape kept trying to open in my brain, but I refused to let it. "What, Ben? Who?"

He looked at me, knowing it was too late to take back what he'd assumed. "Shit."

"Ben, did you, just then, say 'her'?"

"Phoebe . . ."

"Good Christ, not Barbara."

"Well, who the hell did you think? One of these jerks?"

"Josephine Baker wasn't a fag," I stammered, escaping across everyone's laps, trying to keep from seeing Marlys. My one good friend, the one person whom I never hid anything from—wouldn't dream of hiding anything from. There wasn't a single thing about me that Marlys wasn't the first to hear about. I gave her everything. If she was a homosexual, what did that make me?

Horrible things kept charging at me from my uncontrollable brain: all those times we were together—naked together, sleeping together in the same bed. My God, we took showers together all the time. I refused to believe that Marlys could have gotten some sort of sexual satisfaction from what we did.

I ran. The Maxim people were prepared this time. Two waiters materialized out of dark corners and led me to the powder room. When I got there, I sat down in the nearest seat and wept. Of course Marlys didn't use our relationship for sexual satisfaction. But why couldn't she have told me? Why did she hide this from me? I guess it was a lot tougher on Marlys to handle being gay than it was to come to terms with being black.

I could have helped Marlys, really. I looked up and into the mirror. No, I couldn't have. The fearful look in my eyes told me that. I'd have failed her on that one, and she knew I would.

I blew my nose.

The powder room at Maxim's is just like Lettie's bedroom. There was even a quill in case you needed to balance your checkbook. Not ballpoint, naturally. I heard someone come in and assumed it was Ben, forgetting Ben wouldn't go into a ladies' room even at Maxim's. It was her reflection in the watery mirror. Blondie.

She said, "Marlys just told me she never told you."

"How long has she known?"

"That you didn't know?"

"No, that she's queer."

"Why, all her life, I imagine. I don't think she'd appreciate your using that term, Phoebe."

"Tough." I sure didn't need a lecture right then. Her accent was interesting. "What are you, Barbara, anyway? I mean besides a lesbian?"

"I'm a secretary, or more accurately, the manager of an important person's life."

"Where do you come from?"

"South Africa."

"Oh, joy. Apartheid does not apply when it comes to fucking, does it? Excuse me, I don't know if whatever it is you do is considered fucking."

"I call it love. Lesbianism doesn't apply at all in South Africa, and apartheid never applied to me."

I put my head back down on my arm. Love, my eye. Marlys was not in love with this woman.

"Will you be all right, Miss Desmond?"

"No, for Christ's sake, and please keep calling me Phoebe. When Marlys and I were little, we used to examine each other's crotches."

"I imagine all children do that. I examined the crotch of the little boy next door who I grew up with."

I lifted my head. "Weren't too impressed with what you saw, right?"

She laughed. She was one of those people who laughs sexily in her throat. "No, I must say I wasn't. He was interested, though."

"I was interested, too, but damn, I'm no lesbian."

"Marlys is. No one can say why, so don't bother to ask yourself."

"Poor Mrs. Hightower. Marlys is an only child. She'll never have grandchildren."

"Lesbians aren't neuters. Marlys plans to have several children. She plans to marry a man as well. A man who understands the situation. Artificial insemination is quite a simple procedure. Or she may adopt, like Josephine Baker."

"Josephine Baker adopted a dozen."

"Perhaps Marlys will control her maternal feelings."

"Really, Barbara, what man could understand that situation, anyway? Some crook who'd have to be paid plenty."

"Not necessarily. A man already wealthy. Ben Reuben has already volunteered, both his name and his sperm. But Marlys doesn't think children should have two artists for parents. What's the matter?"

"I'm getting out." The dirty bitch.

I collided with Ben in the corridor. They'd already put down a new, old Aubusson. I swept by him magnificently and said to some apparition, "My wrap, *tout de suite*. And *un taxi*." The polar bear arrived as Ben protested.

"Really, Phoebe, this isn't anyone's fault. Marlys—"

"Marlys is not the problem. You are. Why don't you become a veterinarian? Then you can rescue every helpless poor kitten that comes down the pike. Well, I don't want your ego-satisfying, phony-ass help. Marlys didn't want it, and I don't either."

I couldn't believe that I had been so naïve as to think that Ben was willing to do so much for me because he needed someone to make him hot cocoa in the middle of the night. He did it to ingratiate himself with Marlys. He had delusions of saving Marlys from her inconvenient homosexuality. I, obviously, was just another one of Marlys' inconveniences. Maybe he figured that if he did a sterling job on my case she'd let him take on her maternal difficulties.

Geniuses can be a lot more stupid than dumb people.

"Phoebe, let's just go home and talk about this. You're not giving me a chance to—"

"I'm not in the mood to give anyone chances, especially you. Please pass on my apologies to Marlys. I want to be somewhere alone. And somebody better break the news to her that her girlfriend is a shit-heel."

Chapter Ten

I stopped at the pension just long enough to give Madame Besette her hair jewel back and to jam all my stuff into the old duffel bag. The taxi waited, and took me to the Ritz, as directed, where I checked in with my journal tucked under my arm, the duffel bag at my feet, and the polar bear on because I was freezing. I signed in as Mrs. Jerry Lewis, hoping that if I didn't look like his new wife that the bell captain would think nobody looks the same once they become pregnant. I also hoped my husband wasn't in town getting another award from the French who love him so. I asked for a small suite, and they gave me a floor. Someday, I planned to pay Ben back.

I unpacked my three season wardrobe: pea coat, sneaks, three of Ben's painting shirts, two pairs of jeans, and leg warmers for when I needed to feel chic. Also three extra-large V-necked men's undershirts I'd bought to sleep in. Fruit of the Loom in French, but with the same bunch of grapes on the label. And my comb, toothbrush, and cosmetics (i.e., deodorant).

I wrote terrible gestative poetry in my journal all the next day, threw it away the following morning, and phoned Madame desLauriers. I invited her to tea in my suite. She insisted on my coming to her town house, but I prevailed. I wanted to see what she was like without the trappings. After all, she was to be my child's mother. I gave her the suite number, but forgot to tell her to ask for Mrs. Lewis if questioned.

I put on my leg warmers, unraveled my hairdressed braids, and had a very chic new do. My hair looked like corrugated cardboard, which is the rage.

She was led in by someone bowing, and wore another forty-year-old Chanel. She smiled, and said to me a little loudly so that the bowing man could plainly hear, "Bonjour, Madame Lewis. How nice to see you again. How is Jerry these days?"

Naturally, I fell in love with her immediately. Quite often you can judge a book by its cover. It seems that when she told the concierge that she would be visiting with the woman in suite 37, he said, "How lovely, Madame desLauriers. In her condition I am sure Madame Lewis would enjoy the company."

She told me everyone tried, discreetly, to get out of

her when old Jerry would arrive and she told them three days.

"Yes, Mademoiselle Desmond, Monsieur Lewis will adore the story, as will Madame Lewis."

"Please call me Phoebe. You know Jerry Lewis?"

"He has had certain business contacts with my husband and has been our guest at the sea."

"That's very nice."

"But I must tell you this—he will be here in three days."

I said, "I see." Time for me to pack it in once again.

We relaxed, drank *sirop de cassis*, and I disclosed my decision to give her my baby. That's all I said, and she waited expectantly before saying, "Please, Phoebe, I hope this will not sound insulting to you, but have you conditions?"

"What do you mean?"

"Well, we expected . . . that is . . . ?" She blushed, not out of embarrassment, but from her intense desire not to give me the wrong impression.

"Madame . . . Florence . . . there is no price tag on my child. The baby is yours because I think, and I hope, that you will love her."

"Excuse me," she said, putting her face into her hands. Naturally, everyone knows about yours truly when I am helpless over a helpless person's tears. No more *sirop de cassis* for me. Madame desLauriers forgot her uncontrollable joy, and once back from the gold-plated john helped me to lie down on the couch and washed my face with a thick Ritz towel. Always remember, if you want someone to quit crying, vomit.

She wanted to know if I would like her to ring for a

doctor, and I said no. Then she asked who my personal doctor was, and I told her, and she looked pleased.

"Phoebe, you must come to Normandy two weeks before the child is to come. I will have for you complete maternity care, and I know this doctor you have mentioned will approve of the transfer of your care to my own physician. He is a fine man in the forefront of obstetrical and female care."

"All right, Florence, I'll come. Spending the last two weeks by the sea will be good for me."

I thought of Ben. "Florence?"

"Yes, Phoebe?"

"I have a friend. Ben Reuben. He is going to attend Lamaze classes with me. I want him to come with me to Normandy."

"That would be easily arranged." Somehow her voice sounded skitterish.

"Are you sure?"

"Phoebe . . . this Ben. He is not the child's father?"

"No. Your husband, from the time I first saw his picture yesterday, is the child's father."

Her eyes refilled. "Thank you."

"But, Florence, for your piece of mind, the child's biological father never knew I became pregnant, and will never learn it from me. If the child, someday, wants to know her father's name, or rather the name of the man who impregnated me, it will be between her and me. But rest assured, he is very bright, boyishly handsome: brown hair, hazel eyes, six feet tall, athletic but slim, and a real son of a bitch."

Her gray eyes widened, then her smile wrinkled

the skin around her eyes. She took my hand. "I'm sure the child will have your personality, Phoebe. I couldn't hope for more than that."

"Thank you."

"Where is your friend Ben now?"

Now it was my turn to cry, and she put her arm around my shoulders and told me to tell her all about it if I liked, or just cry. God, she was the kind of mother everybody dreams of. All the mothers I know say, "Don't cry," or "Don't worry about it," or "Why get upset about nothing?" or "It could be a lot worse."

I chose to cry, and when I'd finished, she said, "I have my car. Would you like me to drive you back to Ben?"

"Oh yes. I would."

I started gathering all my stuff together and noticed her eyeing the polar bear. "This coat belongs to my friend, the dancer Marlys."

"Marlys?"

"Marlee."

"Marlee is a friend of yours? How wonderful. She is a clever, gifted artist."

Very clever. In fact, a clever, gifted artist who happens also to be a lesbian. Florence obviously didn't know who arranged the impending adoption, just as I never knew the real Marlys. But I think I am beginning to accept the real Marlys even though I'll never actually get completely used to the true her, I don't think.

Florence desLauriers, mother-to-be, drove a cream-colored Mercedes, and she knew it. Some day I hope to be as sure of myself as that woman.

In front of the Rapp Madame desLauriers touched

my arm and asked, impulsively, I'd guess, "Do you have any wishes as to how your child should be raised? What I mean to say is that my husband feels we should follow your wishes in such a matter as, possibly, religion."

I grabbed my bag and opened the door. "Tell your husband that decisions like that are meant to be made by the child's parents. When you buy a leg of lamb, you ask the butcher how to cook it, not the sheep who bore it, right?"

She didn't say anything. "I'd invite you in for a glass of wine, Florence, but I think this reunion with Ben might get a little heavy."

"I'm sorry—'heavy'?"

"Intense."

"I believe I understand. But Phoebe, do not suffer your desires. What I was attempting to say before was that Eugene and myself feel that your wishes, or perhaps dreams, for the child would be a great help to us in raising your baby."

"Listen, I'll think about it. But you've got to practice not saying things like 'your baby,' or just 'the baby.' Say 'my baby,' or 'our baby.'"

She gave me a sheepish smile. "Allow me to admit, Phoebe, that I have been practicing just that, though in French."

"Good. I will see you in St. Aubin at the end of January. I'll let you know the exact date."

"Fine. Thank you."

"Thank you for bringing me home."

At that moment she must have been glad that Ben was not the father. She'd have taken a shit-heel any day over Ben. He must have been looking out the window.

Suddenly, there he was, shaking me by the shoulders,
threatening to strangle me, and kissing me passionately
all at the same time. He hadn't shaved, and didn't give
himself time to put on his shoes. I gave him a meaning-
ful shove.

"Ben Reuben, I'd like you to meet Madame Florence desLauriers."

Ben ducked his head into the Mercedes. *"Enchanté,
madame.* Forgive me. I thought I'd lost her."

"Do not worry. Everything is fine. I look forward
to hosting you both. I will depend on you, Monsieur
Reuben, to help Phoebe look after herself."

"I won't let her out of my sight."

"I am grateful."

The car zipped off down the avenue, and Ben told
me that the doctor called to say our Lamaze classes
started tonight.

"Son of a gun, I'm just in time."

"Don't talk for one minute. I need you, Phoebe, but
only because I love you. At first, I admit, you were a
favor for Marlys, but now I love you."

"I love you, Ben." I did, but not as much as that
moment when I had first fallen in love with him. I guess
that's normal though, considering he'd wanted to marry
my best friend and father her child, which I knew now
but didn't know then.

When we got upstairs, we threw all my stuff on the
floor and made love all over the garret.

Then Ben said, "Can I finish the journal now? I
wanted to last night, but I couldn't find it."

I said, "I'll get the cocoa cups."

PART THREE

Chapter One

Liberty Island is a great place to sit and talk. Once we'd gone up inside the statue, we didn't make a charge for the boat as it was about to leave the way everybody else did. I happen to know there's a boat every hour and a half, but the tourists don't. We walked around the front of the statue, sat on a little ledge at the foot of the pedestal, and gazed out to sea. I spent all morning and through lunch devising a plan, and when I had it all worked out, I gave Tyrus all the details, sitting there on the hot ledge. Throughout my directions, he kept saying, "I want my mother."

It's very difficult to listen to a lost child cry over and over, "I want my mother." I did that when I was eleven into my pillow when my mother was in the hospital having Blob. I never got her back. I got back this frazzled, exhausted woman trying to spread herself thinner than Saran Wrap. Suddenly, there were too many of us and not enough of her.

I didn't give Tyrus these particular details because he wouldn't really identify, never having known a newborn. But I did tell him that we all want our mothers and that he'd continue to have his mother, only not at his beck and call. I assured him, though, that he'd absolutely have her right nearby. I thought of poor Mary. As Tyrus and I knew, it's swell to have a mother, but it must be awfully tough to be one.

Not unlike General Eisenhower exhorting his troops on D day minus one, I kept up this continual stream of verbal encouragement until Tyrus finally lapsed into his military chatter. That meant I had him, although for a while there I thought sure he'd bite right through the old Ace bandage. By now, I was adept at ignoring the biting. After all, I was used to ignoring Blob's temper tantrums. I mean, what's a little arm biting compared with a small girl in a pink pinafore holding her breath till she turns blue and passes out?

When we crossed back to the mainland, the last thing Tyrus said before leaving the boat was: "All right, men, this is your captain speaking. Man the lifeboats. Women and children first. And then it's every man for himself. Abandon ship!"

We went to a drugstore and bought a notebook, two pens, Magic Markers, tape and, a package of one hundred balloons. Then into a *bodega*, where I pointed out to the Puerto Rican grocer some bread, fruit, cheese, and cookies. He said,

"Peekneek?"

I said, "*Sí.*"

Tyrus said, "*Gracias, Generalissimo.*"

Last, we bought a bed sheet from a street vendor. He wanted five bucks for it, but he took three, and finally we got on a subway and went uptown to Columbia University, which I knew was in the vicinity of where I wanted to go. It was a perfect spot; the university, Riverside Church, the Hudson, International House, the West End Cafe—an area mobbed with people of every size, color, and shape. We walked up Broadway from the 110th Street subway station, cut through Barnard College, and found a lovely bench right facing our target. Our target was Grant's Tomb.

Tyrus and I were going to occupy Grant's Tomb, and by "occupy," I mean "take over." Like the embassy in Teheran, except we wouldn't take any hostages. Actually, I take that back. There was one hostage we'd have no choice but to take: Grant. But then he wouldn't mind since he was dead. I, Phoebe Dunkirk Desmond, was soon to bring the world's attention to all the mentally ill people in this country who are living in attics or overcrowded institutions, and hopefully, in the process, find someone who would promise to take care of Tyrus. And I had just such a person in mind. Someone who just might accept the challenge and who could use the publicity as much as we could.

I parked Tyrus on the bench, since it was such a perfect place for feeding pigeons. He proved to be as fascinated with pigeons as he had been with sea gulls. I handed him a chunk of bread, and he promised to stay put while I went on a scouting mission.

"Have you got a mine detector, Adjutant?"

"Sure do, Commander."

"Good luck then." He saluted. I looked around. No one was watching, so I returned the salute.

I circled the tomb. It didn't look like a tomb, it looked like a skinny Lincoln Memorial with a round top. But it had those great granite steps that make me want to tap dance my brains out like old Fred Astaire himself. I controlled myself and kept scouting. Across the portal over the entry way it said Let There Be Peace. Sorry, General, no peace today. Not if I can help it.

There weren't too many people around, mostly neighborhood mothers pushing strollers, some summer students from Columbia studying, and a few couples. However, I could feel myself being eyeballed by this wino who was sitting in the shade under Grant's horse. Don't you wonder if artists don't ever get tired of sculpting horses? I bet there isn't a town in America that doesn't have a statue of a horse somewhere along Main Street. Now I know it's probably unfair of me to refer to every dirty, scruffy old man with a squashed hat as a wino, but this guy did happen to have a brown paper bag in his hand which he'd take a drink from every two seconds.

"Hey, pal." He was calling me, I was sure. I looked over at him, and he crooked a finger at me.

"Yeah?"

"C'mere." God, but I always seemed to get involved with weirdos. I went over.

"How about a tour of the tomb? I got a special today —two bucks."

"Thanks. I don't need a guide."

"Ya can't just go in unless you're on a tour. Regular tours by some twerp who don't know his way around in there is five bucks. And believe me, you can't get into the good part unless you fork over the fiver."

"What qualifies you as a guide?"

"I helped remodel this place in '39." I was beginning to get the feeling that perhaps God does work in wondrous ways after all.

"Just because you carry hod, it don't make you an expert."

"True. But I also reside here."

"Reside here? How can you live in Grant's Tomb?"

"Easy. It's New York. You can live anywhere your two feet can get you. I got friends live in Macy's, the attic at the Dakota, tunnels, vents, you name it. Just a matter of findin' somethin' to your likin'."

"I'll give you fifty cents."

"Geez, a real spendthrift. What's your name, pal, Nelson? Give me a buck, and I'll give you the basic, no-frills tour."

"What are the frills?"

"One is where the can's at."

"I don't need you to find that. Okay, a buck. But you'd better make it worth my while. And I won't pay you till we get out." Wasn't I in luck, though? He stood up and stretched. How these winos can wear heavy tweed suit jackets on a sunny day in August I'll never know.

"What's your name, pal?"

"Nelson."

"Hey, I got a regular Milton Berle on my hands."

"What's yours?"

"Gramps. For security's sake." He tucked his long, stringy, filthy hair under his cap, maybe to look more like a real grandfather instead of a bum. The cap was orange and white, and said Bridgeport Hydraulic Company on it.

"Where'd you rip off that hat?"

"Details of my personal life ain't part of the tour. Now just sort of hang around the top step here with me, and we'll wait for the right moment to go in."

"How romantic. How can you tell when it's the right moment?"

"See that bus?"

"Yeah."

"That's our group pulling in. We'll mix with those characters, and that's how we get in. Uh-oh. On second thought, Nelson, we'll have to wait for the next bus." Together, we watched the Hasidic Jews pile out of the bus. Their hats were definitely not orange and white. Two more buses arrived at the same time.

The wino said, "Great. There'll be a real big crowd. We got it made, Nelson."

"I'll be right back."

"Hey. Where ya goin'?"

"I've got to check on something before I go in."

"Check on what?" He took a few steps back.

"My dog is tied to a tree. I want to be sure he can reach the water fountain."

"Hope it ain't a valuable dog, or it'll get ripped off."

"Nah. A mutt."

I rushed around the other side of the monument to Tyrus. He was through feeding pigeons. He was staring into a huge elm overhead.

"What's up, Ty?"

"I'm counting the leaves on this tree."

"Good."

Tyrus wasn't counting the leaves sadly or anything. He was all business, completely detached from his recent sorrow, and totally absorbed in his role as some general or other. I felt a little better. Tyrus was obviously able to adapt to a new situation just as long as his right wrist was wrapped up good and snug with an Ace bandage to keep him from injuring himself. "But I'm going to have to call in my engineers to booby-trap the thing. The enemy has commandeered the place."

"Which enemy?"

"Hitler's elite. The Alpine Corps. The damn Jerries are everywhere. Look. There's the leader right up there at the summit."

I looked up. Nothing like a few Nazi squirrels to occupy your time.

"Okay, Tyrus. I'm going into the tomb. I'll be back in a little while. Don't mount any attacks until I return. And don't leave the bench either. Somebody has to keep an eye on that Alpine group."

"Pillbox."

"Huh?"

"Pillbox, Adjutant. Pillbox. You called it a bench."

"Sorry. I will rendezvous within an hour."

"Roger."

"Wilco."

I ran off. The wino was squinting into the sun. Did you notice how winos are always squinting into the sun? He was about to be mobbed by about eight million senior citizens. A few of them even had their grandchildren. The wino spotted me.

"What luck, eh, Nelson? Let's go. They're just starting on in." He took me by the arm and whispered, "Just kind of hang in the middle of the group, and we'll stick in with these dummies until we get to the crypt. Once they're all looking down into the hole, we'll break away, and I'll show you the good stuff."

The tour guide, a wimp in a double-breasted blazer, was rallying us all together, and once he got some semblance of order, he began to shout instructions.

"Ladies and gentlemen, please pay attention! I want to give you a comprehensive idea of our schedule for the rest of the day.

"After our stop here we will board the buses and go downtown for a few blocks where we'll tour the Soldiers and Sailors Monument. Any questions?" An old lady holding a large paper cup filled with quarters raised her cane.

"Yes, ma'am?"

"Isn't this the bus going to Atlantic City?"

The guide cleared his throat. "No, ma'am. That was bus number 36. This is bus number 37. Now . . ."

"I thought all the buses were going to Atlantic City."

"I'm terribly sorry, ma'am, but we're running late, and I must get on with the tour. Please remember, if we all stay close together, you won't get lost. It's so easy to wander off somewhere when you have hearing losses and sight problems like most of you people." He sniffed. What a shit-heel.

"And so, ladies and gentlemen, the General Grant National Memorial was begun in 1892 and completed in 1897. That's right, folks, right through these pillars, please. The upper part was designed by the winner of an architectural competition, and the winning entry is a simplification of the tomb of King Mausolus at Halicarnassus where . . ."

Not one person was listening to him. Everyone followed each other through the doors chatting and sharing Life-Savers.

"God, it's gloomy in here," I told the wino.

"It's a tomb, dummy, not a disco."

"Don't get nasty now, Gramps."

"This beginning part is boring, Nelson, but be patient, and get ready. When I tap you on the shoulder, don't say anything. Just turn and come with me."

"Okay."

Everyone's voices were echoing against the marble, and terrazzo, and they were all complaining about the same thing—how they shouldn't have left their sweaters in the bus.

The guide droned on: ". . . and at one time, the tomb was one of New York's top tourist attractions. But with the lack of interest in the Civil War, in addition to the fact that the city couldn't afford to run the little British, red double-decker buses from Fifth Avenue, interest waned.

"As we approach the open arched vault, one floor below us, out of respect for the fact that this is a final resting place, I'd like to ask you all to keep your voices down."

"Ha!"

"What is it Gramps?"

"Tell you later."

The guide glared at us. I don't know why. Everyone else was yapping away, too. He cleared his throat. That was actually his way of saying "shut up!"

"As you can see, the sunken crypt is quite similar to Napoleon's tomb in the chapel of Les Invalides in Paris. But what many people don't realize is that our crypt holds twin sarcophagi—not only that of General Ulysses S. Grant, but also that of his wife, Julia Dent Grant."

"He exaggerates, Nelson," the wino whispered. "Napoleon's tomb is about a hundred times bigger."

A hand went up. An old guy with a fat, unlit cigar stump in his mouth said, "Would Mrs. Grant be any relation to Bucky Dent?" Everybody guffawed.

"Yeah, Louie. She's his sister." Guffaw, guffaw.

Gramps tapped me on the shoulder. We zigzagged carefully to the outside of the group to this iron door that a midget would have had trouble trying to squeeze through. Gramps took out a key and opened it with his back to it. He pushed the door open a little, and hissed at me to get in. I went over and through the door, and he was right behind me. Then he gently pushed it shut. Inside the door there wasn't a shred of light, but only for a second. Gramps clicked on a little flashlight.

"How'd you get a key to this door?"

"Shhh. Had it made in '39. Don't think there's another one around."

"Smart." I believed it. I could feel a heavy coat of dust under my feet.

"Shhhh. Everything echoes in this place. Nobody comes in here anymore, because I'm the only person left alive with a key. Now this here corridor leads up to a stairway that runs through the interior walls, up inside a pillar, and across the dome to the roof. And what a view! Wait'll you see, Nelson."

"Wait a minute. The roof? I don't want to fall off this thing. What a story. Girl falls to her death from the roof of Grant's Tomb."

"You're a boy."

"Oh yeah."

"I don't take no girls up here. Could get me in trouble, ya know what I mean? But rest assured, pal, the only way to get off the roof is to take a running leap. The top looks dangerous from below, but don't worry. It ain't. Ready to climb?"

"Roger."

"I hate the military."

"Sorry."

We walked for a little while, and then we started to

climb. I mean, if you think the metal steps in the Statue of Liberty are narrow and winding, you haven't seen anything. Good thing it was so dark, I would have hated to see what was down at the bottom of the stairwell. We passed several landings with catwalks as we felt our way along, and finally the stairs stopped. Above our heads was a door that was sort of a grate. It pushed open without a creak, and when I got my head through, the sight nearly bowled me over. You could see every inch of Manhattan, and on down to Staten Island and across to Jersey. In front of me was the Riverside Church's bell tower. Never mind the rooftops of Paris; the rooftops of Columbia University were just as romantic. Old Gramps made himself right at home, squatting down and taking a good, long swig.

"Terrific, ain't it?"

"Sure is." I tried to find Tyrus. I could see the elm tree all right, but he was somewhere underneath and I couldn't make anything out but leaves. "Do you take many people up here?"

"All the time. Kids like you—with honest faces—so's they don't tell on me. You wouldn't tell anyone about this now, would ya, Nelson?"

"Nope. Not me."

"Good. If anyone tells, I'll make it my business to find out who, and then I'll take care of him." Empty threat, I'd have to say.

"But why do you do it?"

"Gotta eat, don't I? This is my means of employment. My job."

"But you only get paid two dollars a trip."

"Five. You're a tightwad."

"Is that enough to live on?"

"I got real simple needs, kid. Independence and Johnny Walker Red."

"Oh. Would you like to make ten bucks for doing almost nothing?"

"What you call 'almost nuthin' '?"

"When we get down, wait about an hour, and leave that door down there unlocked for about ten minutes."

"No way."

"Why not?"

"I don't let no kid up here alone."

"But I won't be alone."

"Round up all your friends, right?"

"No. An adult. An adult who's lived in an attic all his life. I just let him out. I really would like to show him this fantastic sight. Then we'll leave. I promise."

"I believe you."

"You do?"

"Yeah, but how about I come along?"

"Geez, I'd love to have you, but he's awfully shy."

"Guess I'd be shy, livin' in an attic all my life. But ten bucks ain't enough."

"It's all I've got after I buy a flashlight."

"I'll give you mine. I can get another one wholesale. How much ya got on ya?"

"About twelve fifty."

"It's a deal."

"Thanks."

"So how'd you spring this guy from his attic?"

"Long story."

"Forget it then. I got more business to do. Ready to go back down?"

"Yeah. Are there many guards around this place when it's closed?"

"Two share the daytime shift, and one old coot

comes at night. The guy sleeps twelve hours straight. Convenient for me." He opened the trap door, and we went back under the roof. He was much slower going down than coming up.

"Why did you say 'Ha!' before?"

"Whisper, pal. Echoes."

"Why did you?" I whispered.

"When?"

"When we were looking into the crypt."

"Oh. Because they ain't really there."

"Who ain't really there . . . where?"

"Grant. And his wife. Bucky Dent's sister. Ha! That was rich."

"Are you saying Grant isn't buried here?"

"Shhhh."

"Sorry. But really, General Grant isn't buried in Grant's Tomb?"

"That's what I said, ain't it? About ten years ago. Middle of the night. Hearse pulls up. Some feds. Couple of cops. In they go, and the next thing ya see, they're bringin' out two coffins."

"No!"

"Ya think I'm lyin'? Why should I? I says to the old codger—the one who guards at night—'Where the hell they takin' the general?' He says, 'The descendents want him back. Want them buried in some churchyard in Ohio.' Couldn't stop them either. Rights. Probably figured the bodies were wearing some valuables. Wanted to get their hands on them. You know how relatives are."

"I sure do."

"Best part of my lifestyle is not havin' any."

"But, Gramps, I can't believe nobody knows this about General Grant."

"Well, the feds know. But they can't let on, or somebody will come along and decide to turn the tomb into condominiums."

"Bummer."

"You got it. Here's my door. Stop where you are." He switched off his light, bent down, and opened the door a crack. "Not yet." We waited. Finally, we could hear a bunch of babbling and moving around. "C'mon." We crept out and casually melted into a group of foreigners. Germans, I think. The shame of it was that the rest of the tour was such a drag, what with the guide speaking in German. Also, I was very anxious about Tyrus. Fortunately for me, the Germans were in a hurry to get the hell out of there. As if they knew or cared who General Grant was. I parted company with the wino, handing over all the rest of the money, and he agreed to unlock the door when the first group went in after four o'clock. He looked a little skeptical when I insisted he lock it again ten minutes later.

"That won't give your buddy much time to see the sights."

"I just want to take him up for a quick peek. He doesn't care much about views. Just for the thrill of it."

"I imagine there ain't many thrills up in an attic."

"Very few."

"Have fun."

"Thanks. I'll recommend you to all my friends."

"Don't do me any favors. I prefer to hustle my own customers. Gotta judge their faces myself, if you know what I mean."

"Sure. 'Bye, Gramps."

"So long, pal."

§   §   §

Tyrus was sound asleep on the bench. Poor guy. An excursion like this would take a lot out of anyone, but especially someone who hadn't had an excursion in thirty-two years. And I know I've made this point so many times before, but he really had the face of a baby. Not the five o'clock shadow, of course. Three o'clock shadow, actually. I waited for him to wake up. I love parks. Especially the ones in New York with all the different kinds of people. Suave-o's walking their Afghans, people in love with their arms around each other, addicts dozing, and little kids kicking the shit out of each other. I lay in the grass and was sort of dozing when I heard,

"Adjutant! Wake up, Adjutant."

"Jesus, Tyrus, I fell asleep. What time is it?" Tyrus began tracking the direction of the sun. "Never mind, I'll go find out. Don't move." I went and asked the suave-o with the Afghan.

"Twenty to four," she said, looking at her Piaget.

"Thanks, toots." I bent to pet the dog.

"Don't touch him! He's just come from the cleaners." Dogs are okay; it's their asshole owners who kill me. I went back to Tyrus.

"We've got a little time left. Now here's what we do. It's real easy, but listen carefully." Tyrus adjusted his headset, which was actually two yogurt tops. "We wait about twenty minutes, right? Then we go to the place where Grant is buried—used to be buried—well, never mind, we go through this little door. Then I switch on my light, and we climb up about a zillion steps till we get to the roof. Then we wait up there till the joint closes. I'll tell you the rest when we're up there. Got it?"

"What's the password?"

" 'Wino.' But listen. You reminded me of the most

important part. We cannot talk at all once we're through that door. Not until we're on the roof."

"Well, of course not, Adjutant. This certainly isn't the first time I've crossed enemy lines. And I'm going to have to remind you not to address your commanding officer in such a disrespectful tone or I'll have to find myself another driver."

"Yes, General."

"Commander, you nincompoop. I don't know where they're getting these noncoms nowadays. . . ." Tyrus went on yabbering about the decline at the Pentagon. He was being such a brick about all this.

As it turned out, I didn't have to worry about a watch. I could see old Gramps going in to unlock the door for me. He was trying to remain inconspicuous behind a group from the Belvedere School. Can you believe it? More good luck. The Belvedere School is for the mentally handicapped.

"Ready, Commander?"

"Roger, Adjutant."

"All systems go." He gave me a revolted look and then shook his head. I guess my reply wasn't in the old manuals. But he followed me, and as we crossed the grass, I scooped up a blanket and kept staring straight ahead. Naturally, I left the Sanyo so that whoever I ripped off can consider himself lucky that all I took was his dirty old blanket. Imagine leaving an expensive radio on a blanket in the middle of a New York park.

It's easy to get in and out of Grant's Tomb without paying. Those guides are like robots. They've done it all so many times that they just blab away while they stare vacantly into space. We got to the crypt.

"Okay, Tyrus. This is it. Be very nonchalant. Very,

very nonchalant." Do as I say, not as I do. I was quite nervous.

"Stop worrying, Adjutant. Once you've breeched enemy territory, the rest is all uphill."

"You'd better believe it."

The door was unlocked, and I didn't see old Gramps around anywhere. I got in, and Tyrus scooted right behind. I shut the little door without making a sound, and switched on the light.

"Is that an official blackout light, Lieutenant." Lieutenant? Was that a promotion or a mistake? Or are all adjutants automatically lieutenants? Who knows, but you can see why there are so many snafus everytime the Army tries to do something. They've got so much diddly stuff to keep straight.

"Yes, Commander. Got it out of my blackout kit. Now watch your step."

"I'm familiar with these new subs, Lieutenant. Now I know it's hard for you three-month wonders from Annapolis to remember, but I am an admiral, and you must address me as such."

"Sorry, Admiral." Isn't that Tyrus something? He didn't have the slightest bit of trouble hopping from one branch of the service to another.

We climbed, and although Tyrus did a lot of huffing and puffing, I still had to go very slowly. Also, keep in mind that the only exercise he gets is turning the pages of a book. I must say, though, he never complained. Once we got out onto the roof, he immediately broke into the widest victory grin, reminiscent of old Ike himself.

"Get the flag ready, boys, we've taken the hill and lost no personnel." He stood there with his hands on his hips, feet apart.

"Not to disturb you, sir, but we've got further instructions from headquarters."

"What is it?"

"Well, sir, when night falls, we are to advance below to the round ledge with the open pillars. We spend the night there in the protected area, and then one hour after dawn we must prepare to communicate with the enemy."

"And negotiate."

"Exactly."

"Sir."

"Exactly, sir. And how about some rations now, sir? Got to keep our strength up for the night ahead."

"Splendid idea. *Make camp, men!*"

I winced: "May I remind you, Commander, that we are in earshot of the enemy." God, every Boy Scout within eight million miles must have started setting up camp. And one other thing I want to tell you. When it got dark, and we had to go below to the open rotunda, Tyrus was very careful to remind his men to have some respect for the Italian antiquities in the area, meaning, of course, the pillars of Grant's Tomb.

Anyway, I spread out the blanket confiscated from the hostile local peasants, and passed out some cookies and fruit. God. A picnic on top of the dome at Grant's Tomb. If you ever come to New York, and you visit Grant's Tomb, look for a wino with an orange and white Bridgeport Hydraulic Company hat, have your kid flash him a fiver, and you'll get a day in the Big Apple that a king would envy.

Chapter Two

Not only was the night a spectacular one, also I discovered that Tyrus had another interest. Astronomy. Not astrology; that's the science of being a jerk and looking in the paper at your sign to see whether or not you're going to fall off a cliff. I'm a Pisces. A fish. So what, right? Tyrus was a regular encyclopedia of the New York nighttime sky. You want to know where Orion's belt is? Ask me. Old Tyrus could see those constellations as if the bears and the crabs were drawn from star to star in white ink. Me? I had trouble. I kept saying, "Yeah, yeah, I see it," when he showed me an arrow or a paw or whatever. But the only thing I was absolutely sure of (aside from the Big Dipper, which any asshole can pick out) was

Orion's belt. I mean, those three itsy-bitsy stars were so bright, and in such an evenly spaced line. And get this. Did you know stars have names? (Aside from the North, which all those Big Dipper assholes know, too.) Orion's belt consisted of Mintaka, and Alnilam, and Alnitak. I love it. Sounds like the names of three Eskimo brothers. Actually, Tyrus was disappointed. He said another month and we might have witnessed a meteor shower. Shit, I said, another month and we might have had a hurricane. Got to take the good with the bad.

Now I know I do go on about the sights of New York but my God, the lights are mind-boggling. The George Washington Bridge lights are gold this year because of its birthday. Gaudy to some, I'm sure, especially all those jerks who think it's cool to decorate everything in sight in "earth tones." I swear those golden lights seemed close enough to grab into your hands and let drip down between your fingers. Unfortunately, after an hour of gaping our brains out, we had to pack it in.

"Break camp, Ty. We've got to get below and start on those balloons."

"Break camp, men!"

"Tyrus, if I have to tell you one more time, I'll have a complete fit. Be quiet."

"May I remind you of my experience in battle, Adjutant. The sounds of the night bounce off the river, and become a natural diversion."

"Let's not take any chances, okay?"

"Roger." That Tyrus never really puts up too much of a fight.

We went down to the observation deck, the highest of three built around the tomb (not counting the roof, of course), and we blew up half the balloons to get somewhat of a head start. There wasn't the tiniest breeze, so we didn't have to worry about them drifting away. I got completely exhausted. Tyrus only did about five of them, because every time he blew one up, he had to let the air out and reblow it twice more. I held my temper, but I really wanted to brain him when his balloon kept making those little farting noises when he'd let the air out. I was sure that the guard would hear it, too, but from the way old Gramps described that character, he probably spent the entire night farting himself and would figure he was hearing an echo. And also, I had to do all his knots.

I'll bet you are dying to know what the hell we were blowing up balloons for, but don't feel bad if you can't figure it out, because the only people I can imagine who would have known immediately are Lord Peter Wimsey, Hercule Poirot, and Nero Wolfe, and they aren't real.

It was exhausting, so I spread out the blanket, and we went to sleep. Oh yeah. Just before he conked out, Tyrus said: "God bless my mother, God bless my Aunt Lettie, my Uncle Turk, my Uncle Galooch. God bless my adjutant, and God bless Dodge. [I beat out the dog.] And God bless all my boys in uniform."

He repeated all this three times. I said, "Amen," he said, "Amen, amen, amen," and then I said my own private prayer asking God to please make Tyrus cut the shit so I could get in my eight hours.

§   §   §

In the morning the first thing I decided was that our takeover shouldn't last too long, so we ate all the rest of our food for breakfast. It was going to be a hot one. You couldn't make out the sun coming up at all, just a white glare appearing through the haze, rising over the tops of the buildings. Actually, I think people should occupy buildings in tremendous heat; nerves are frazzled, tempers short—much more exciting, don't you think?

The CBS traffic-report helicopter lifted off from somewhere to the south, and soon the cars would start pouring in, including my Dad, unless the old Porsche conked out somewhere on the Merritt Parkway, which was the rule rather than the exception to his commuting schedule. I thought of my mother as I dripped peach juice down my shirt. She'd understand all this, I knew, and besides, I'd probably be seeing her by tonight. I couldn't wait to tell her about that Italian restaurant. Even though I loved it, I'll tell her it was awful. She always feels good when she finds out that something she missed wasn't all it's cracked up to be. I hope some day I'll be able to tell her the same thing about college.

I worked on the banner. I tore the sheet in two and took out the Magic Markers. Tyrus watched while he ate the last of the cookies. I love making block letters come out even, but I hate filling them in. When I finished, I unrolled the whole thing over the edge of the balustrade, hooking the edge on all those convenient little arrowlike things that you always read about people skewering themselves on. I'm sure my banner could be made out from below because there were only three words: Free the M.H. Imagine me sticking to just three words. I rolled up a poster board to use as a megaphone, and waited. They say waiting is the hardest part, but I found it quite revealing. An extraordinary amount of people went by—the early guys like the joggers and the dog walkers—and none of them noticed the banner, which was just as well because I needed a really big crowd to be truly effective. It's awfully easy, isn't it, to separate native New Yorkers like joggers and dog walkers from tourists. Tourists are always looking up at the skyscrapers, and natives are always looking down. So guess which group steps in the most dog shit?

At six fifty-six, according to a nearby clock on some tower, the daytime guard arrived, and he noticed the banner. He was exactly the first person I wanted to notice it. He walked up the white gravel path with all the pretty geraniums on each side, whistling "Dixie," and suddenly, he stopped dead. He had just lifted his right foot onto the first granite step in the wide, long staircase. He stared. And he stopped whistling "Dixie." Then he began to run up the steps, his mouth wide open, but with nothing coming out.

Bam! I jumped as hard as I could onto a yellow balloon. Bam! Bam! Two more. Holy shit. He ran back down those stairs like a goddamn maniac and on out to the elm tree, where the Alpine Corps continued to go about their business. He ducked behind the tree and shouted, "Help, help, help, help, help, help."

He forgot he was in glorious Gotham. A few joggers kind of glanced his way, but people didn't even seem to hear him, just kept munching their bagels. There was a vendor setting up his General Grant statue stand not twenty yards away, but he never broke his motion of standing each tacky statue in a neat line. Then the guard peeked around the tree trunk. Bam! I tried an orange one. And you should have heard old Tyrus.

"Idiot! You idiot! You're pulling the pin too soon. That kraut could heave your pineapple back at us before it has a chance to go off. Now do it like this." He held up an imaginary grenade, pulled the imaginary pin, and said, "One, two, three, D, five, six, seven, eight, nine, ten." And—*stomp!* He killed off another balloon. The kraut finally gathered up his wits and yelled for reinforcements.

"Hey, Chollie! Are you in there? Did they get ya, Chollie? Chollie! Come out!" Chollie, the night guard, came out peeling the skin off a banana. He ambled down the steps kind of craning his neck, looking for his relief.

"Whatsamatter, Ed? Ed? Where the hell are ya, Ed?"

"Quick, Commander," I said, "when I drop my arm, fire three rounds."

"Excellent plan, Adjutant." Tyrus got ready to jump. I knew he'd go for three rounds in a big way.

"Chollie, there's a guy up there firin' a rifle. A sniper. Head for cover, Chollie, quick!" Old Ed was screaming his brains out from behind the tree. Chollie just kept peeling his banana while he gawked around trying to figure out where his buddy was.

"Where ya at, Ed? You musta had some night. That's just some trucks backfirin' on the Drive. Why don't you come out from—" I dropped my arm.

Bam! Bam! Bam!

"Free the M.H.!" I shouted through my megaphone.

Boy, you should have seen old Chollie go rampaging down the steps with a big piece of banana sticking out of his mouth. Even though it was really quite a hysterical scene, I knew I had to remain serious. No backing out now. But, my God, Chollie was one of those guys with a great, fat beer belly and no hiney whatsoever. He got behind the elm with old Ed. They didn't both fit, naturally.

Now people began looking up, and by the time Tyrus and I smashed about ten more balloons, there were pockets of people all over the place huddled behind trees and balustrades, and stone lions. Then we heard sirens. So did Ed and Chollie. They gestured like crazy at this police car, and when it came to a screeching stop, Ed yelled, "Don't get out, don't get out. There's terrorists in the tomb with high-powered rifles."

"And machine guns," added Chollie at the top of his lungs.

"Up on the observation deck." They pointed at my sign.

Tyrus said, "High-powered rifles. What fool recruited that imbecile. *Fire one!*" He bashed a balloon. The two cops, who were by this time out of their car and scratching their heads, scrambled behind the back wheel of the cruiser. Just like a couple of real Keystone Cops. Can't blame them, of course. A cop in New York is braver than old John Wayne himself.

"Tyrus, we've got to reserve our ammunition for a while."

"Lie low, men. Let them come to us, but remain prepared to return ack-ack fire." Tyrus burrowed under the blanket and lay quiet. The balloons bobbled over him.

They came to us. By the dozens. By the hundreds. And rubberneckers by the thousands. That's why New Yorkers live in New York. For the action, and there's always some action somewhere. Well, they were there in force. Then the vehicles began rolling in: cars, police vans, ambulances, ambulance chasers (although it didn't take long for the old tow truck operators to realize that there wouldn't be any business for them). Finally, he came; the one guy I'd been waiting for—the commander of the hostage crisis unit. How could he know we had no hostages? You could tell this particular guy was the head honcho. He was the only cop in shirt sleeves, and he had about a dozen guys surrounding him the way the Secret Service does to the President. His adjutant had a giant bullhorn.

"You up there! You! Can you hear me?"

He had to be kidding. He almost blew my ears off. Sounded just like my gym teacher, Mr. Kroll, except Kroll doesn't need a bullhorn.

"Okay, you kids," Kroll bellows at us, "divide up into two teams. The losers have to do fifty push-ups, and the winners get to watch." Kroll wants to grow up to be another Vince Lombardi. Too bad he's already sixty-two years old.

Tyrus leaped out of nowhere and grabbed my megaphone. "Identify yourself," he said.

"Tyrus, for Christ's sake, give me that, and get back under the . . . I mean get back into the foxhole. Think of the morale if we lose our leader."

"You're a good man, Adjutant," Tyrus said as he retreated to the blanket.

"This is Captain Anthony DeTulio, NYPD. Why don't you come down from there and tell us what you're upset about." Sounded like old Mary herself, right?

"We'll talk from where we are, buster." I tried to make my voice sound tough and deep. Didn't work. At least eight million voices drifted up to me, all saying, "Sounds like a kid."

"Who are you?"

"Free the M.H.!"

"That is a kid, Evelyn," a voice said.

"That's right!" I decided to play it as it lay. "There are twenty-five of us kids up here in this building and we're all armed. One of us has a bomb strapped to himself, and he's ready to waste us, you, me, himself, and General Grant."

The first of the fire trucks rolled up. Firemen always have to get into the act. That's because they all wish they were policemen.

"What do you want? Who's the M.H.?" DeTulio yelled.

"The mentally handicapped across the nation." That sent the crowd to buzzing.

"How many kids did you say you got up there?"

"Several score." Confusion is always a good tactic.

"How'd you get in there?"

"Irrelevant."

"Where the hell are the National Park Service Security Police?" DeTulio asked the guy next to him. I heard him because he didn't switch the bullhorn off.

"They're behind the elm tree over there," I shouted.

"Do your parents know where you kids are?"

"Sure. Sleeping over at each others' houses. But listen, DeTulio, you're missing the point. We've got a mission here, and we'll only consider speaking to one person, so you're going to have to get him here."

"Who's that?"

"Senator Kennedy."

"He doesn't live here."

"No shit. Try Washington, try Hyannis, try Palm Beach."

"Which mentally handicapped do you want freed?"

"We will only talk to the senator, and we do not intend to give up this tomb until you get us into contact with him. In person."

"Okay, I'll see what I can do." DeTulio went into a huddle with his team.

The first camera crews arrived. Reporters had been there for a while, but hadn't been allowed to get too close. All the major networks were represented within minutes, followed by the local stations, of which there are about eight million in the Big Apple. The cameramen who were trotting around all over the place began to give the crowd some courage. All the nosey parkers hiding behind the trees and stuff started to peek out, so I stomped on several balloons. Need I say more?

"Did you scatter them?" asked Tyrus, voice muffled.

"Yes, sir."

"Carry on then."

I looked around me. The last fusillade had been a bad move. Things got real quiet. I could see sharpshooters on top of all the buildings at Columbia. I was sure they were too far away, but I didn't take any chances. I knew they probably wouldn't shoot a kid, but Tyrus was no kid—from a hundred yards he wasn't. But I guess he realized that things were pretty much in my hands now, because after a while I could actually hear snoring coming from under the blanket. He's something, that Tyrus.

Suddenly, from every direction came eight million hot dog carts, which really took the heat off and returned the crowd to its previous carnival atmosphere. And the pretzel carts, and the coffee wagons, and the stuffed grape leaf vendors followed. It began to turn into quite a party, and you could smell coffee everywhere. Luckily, I hate coffee, but when the guy came by with the roasting chestnuts, I thought I'd die. It smelled like Christmas Day. Then trouble. Not for me. For DeTulio. A big yellow bus arrived through the bus entrance, which the cops had neglected to cordon off. The day's first load of senior citizens started piling out into the parking lot while about eight million cops started running toward them in a frantic effort to get them back into the bus. The seniors paid no attention, naturally. They obviously had just woken up from a snooze, and were too busy trying to get the hell down the dangerous little bus steps without breaking a hip, and since every other one turned back for his sweater, who could pay attention to the

cops? DeTulio decided to appeal to my sense of human-
ity.

"Listen, kid, we've got sixty-six people down here
from the St. Stanislav Nursing Home. Now why don't
you come down from there and let them have their tour.
They came all the way from Poughkeepsie."

I aimed my megaphone at the bus.

"All you seniors from St. Stanislav, now hear this:
I'm very sorry to inconvenience you, but Grant's Tomb
is being occupied today by the Committee to Free the
M.H. Since the tomb is, consequently, under siege by the
police, you will miss your tour today. But believe me,
you should count your blessings. And might I mention
that from this vantage point I can see, one block down
Broadway, opposite Chock Full O'Nuts, a large green
and white OTB sign."

Good Christ, a veritable stampede. They careened
out of the parking lot lickety-split, waving up at me
while they hotfooted it across the park toward Broadway. It was just like the Senior Olympics when you see
those guys with their pacemakers running a four-minute
mile. They leaped over hedges and water fountains all
trying to be first in line to fill in their betting slips.

One of them thought to turn around and yell up to
me, "Hey, fella, can I play a double for ya?"

"Another time, thanks." God, if six and three come
in today, I'll kill myself—but back to the business at
hand.

"DeTulio! Have you reached the senator yet?"

"No. He's out sailing on Cape Cod Bay. Will you
speak to someone else?"

"Yeah. One of his sisters." DeTulio shook his head.

One of the CBS crew got out his own bullhorn. "Are

you Phoebe Desmond, the kid who got kidnapped last month in Connecticut?"

"Yeah, but I didn't get kidnapped. I ran away. Old lady Fermin is a pathological liar. How'd you find out?"

"Twenty minutes ago 'Captain Kangaroo' was interrupted with news of the tomb's occupation. Your sister recognized your voice and got your mother. We are trying to locate your father." Good luck. Try the Merritt Parkway. And how about that Blob? Wow, what a kid. "Are you being held hostage by your kidnappers, Miss Desmond? Have they forced you to do this?" My God, he thought I was Patty Hearst.

"No. And listen to me once more. I definitely was not kidnapped. When I read about Mrs. Fermin's testimony, I just played along with it in my letters home. Actually, all I did was go up to Danbury, and I took the bus to New York. I've been staying at the Y, where I met all the other guys up here with me. (The rest of my group was still snoring loudly under the blanket.) We want to bring the world's attention to the plight of the mentally handicapped who are being held hostage right here in their own country, and often in their own homes."

"What are the names of the rest of the children?"

"From here on in, I'll only talk to a Kennedy."

DeTulio elbowed the reporter out of his way.

"Phoebe . . ." Typical cop, always talks to you using your first name. I remember the time my old man got stopped for sideswiping a train. The cop said, "Well, now, Francis, how would you like to see if you can walk along that white line nice and steady." No one calls my father anything but Frank in the whole world.

"But, Phoebe, you can't really expect one of the Kennedys to come here if you're armed." Oh, brother.

What a jerk I can be sometimes. Imagine thinking old Teddy could come here under these conditions. But I was in pretty deep now.

"Sorry, DeTulio, I wasn't thinking. I'll have to decide who else I could speak to."

"How about your mother?"

"Forget it. There's nothing she can do about the mentally handicapped."

"Well, she's on her way."

"Figures." She knows she has to get to me before my old man does.

"How about a clergyman?"

"I'm not committing suicide, DeTulio . . . I mean unless, of course, my booby-trapped friend here decides to pull the old rip cord. Now I really mean it this time; I will not speak to anyone anymore. Please tell the Kennedy family that I would be willing to speak to their representative. I, and my group, will disarm if the Kennedys send someone to us."

DeTulio kept talking to me though. Probably was just following the instructions in his crisis manual. While he was droning on and on, I heard a long, slow creak. Naturally, I nearly jumped out of my skin. I broke the nearest balloon and whirled around in time to see my old wino friend sneaking out of the stairway door.

"Gramps! Are you crazy? You could get caught as an accessory."

He laughed. "Don't worry about me, pal. So, you're a girl, eh? Thought it was kind of strange that you weren't sure, before. Well, never mind, it ain't your fault. Just thought I'd bring you something you might find of interest." He handed me a little transistor radio. "Everybody in the world's talkin' about you. Listen." He turned it on.

The newscaster was saying, "Anywhere from fifty to a hundred small children, all wired with highly volatile explosive devices, have completely immobilized New York's Upper West Side in their crusade to bring the world's attention to the mentally handicapped. Grant's Tomb is the sight of . . ." I shut if off.

"You better get out of here, Gramps." He was snickering like a maniac. "How much for the radio?"

"Free, Nelson. Or whatever your name is. I'm going to be doing a lot more business, thanks to this caper, and the prices will skyrocket. That is, if you don't go ahead and blow the place. You won't, will ya?"

"Don't be ridiculous. Now cooperate a little and take a hike. Thanks for the radio."

"Don't worry, I'm cuttin' out. Is this the guy from the attic?" He looked down at Tyrus' shoes sticking out from under the blanket.

"Yeah, that's him."

"Don't like it too much up here, eh?"

" 'Bye, Gramps."

" 'Bye, pal." He left.

I listened to the radio for a while. They said my mother was being driven down from Connecticut while they continued trying to locate my father. Senator Kennedy himself came on, sympathizing with my cause and hoping that none of the children in Grant's Tomb would resort to violence. He agreed to talk to us if we came down. Tempting, right? Especially tempting because I had to admit to feeling a touch bored. Confused, too. If I threw in the towel now, what would happen to Tyrus? I was mulling it over and gazing at the crowd, which was also getting a little restless, when this eight-mile-long black limousine pulled up in front of the steps. I mean, right over the grass and on through the geraniums. De-

Tulio went over and bent his head into the window. The police formed a cordon around the limo, and the door opened. A tall, gorgeous gray-haired man stepped out. Not Senator Kennedy, of course, but someone important. His suit didn't have the slightest wrinkle in it like all the plainclothes cops, who were all sweating like mad and whose suits looked as though they were made of crepe paper. You know the cleaner's that does Detective Columbo's raincoats? Well, all plainclothes cops in New York must send their suits to the same place.

"Phoebe! We've got Senator Kennedy's brother-in-law here. He'll talk to you if—"

"Which one? He's got about eight million."

"Sargent Shriver."

"*Sargent Shriver!* Hey, all right!" I pointed my megaphone at the crowd. "Ladies and gentlemen. The man standing in your midst . . . in front of your midst, is the man who could have been Vice President of the United States. Instead, all you assholes voted for Spiro Agnew. And you almost destroyed our country in the process. Shame on all of you.

"Hi, Mr. Shriver. My mom voted for you guys. Not my dad, though. He's one of those *nouveau* Republicans."

"What can I do for you, Phoebe?" He didn't use the bullhorn.

"Come up on the elevator, because I . . . we really need to talk to someone who could understand our problems. Alone."

"Why don't you . . . all of you come down?"

"Can't. But I absolutely promise you—my word of honor—that if you come up, you'll be perfectly safe. My buddy has removed his batteries, so that the bomb is inactive, and I've put down my weapons. See?" I held up my hands.

"Okay, Phoebe, I trust you."

"Hold on just a minute here." DeTulio. "All you people in there will have to stand up against the balustrade with your hands up until Mr. Shriver, Detective Plock, and Officer Comerford get to you."

"DeTulio, I want just me and Shriver. The rest of my organization are manning their posts throughout the building. If I got them all up here, any one of you guys could get through."

"So how do those other guys know we've got a ceasefire here during negotiation?" He stumped me on that one, but just for a second. Tyrus came through.

"Tell them we've got transmitters." He held out his chicken noodle can.

"We've got walkie-talkies."

Meanwhile, during all this chitter-chatter, good old Sargent Shriver just walked across the park and up the steps, and once this was pointed out to DeTulio and he realized that Shriver was about to enter the building, a frightening thing happened. DeTulio started barking all kinds of orders, and every single cop went down on one knee and aimed their guns right up at me. God, it was just like Chips, especially the ones wearing those snazzy helmets.

I heard the elevator motor start, and then the little red light went on over the doors. The doors split apart, and Sargent Shriver nonchalantly said "Hi" before he made his way toward me through the bobbing balloons. I mean, you'd think he did this sort of thing eight million times a day.

"Geez, Mr. Shriver, don't step on one of those things, or all hell will break loose." Tyrus sat up.

"Has this man given the new password?"

"Sure he did, Commander. He's one of ours. In fact, I'm quite proud to introduce you to Sargent Shriver."

"Sergeant? Well, Sergeant, you're going to see a little promotion for yourself. It takes a dedicated man to infiltrate enemy lines solo. Plan on a medal as well, soldier."

"If you'll excuse me," Sargent Shriver said, "I think I'd better give a wave to the police officers so they'll know I . . . uh . . . made it across enemy lines."

"You won't give us away?"

"Just the two of you? No one else is up here?"

"Yeah."

"I won't."

"Thanks." I offered him my rolled-up poster board. He took it.

"Detective DeTulio. This is Shriver. Everything is under control."

"Now listen to me, whoever is up there. Harm Mr. Shriver, and we'll blow you out of there." Shriver winced.

"Give me ten minutes, DeTulio, and for heaven's sake, put down that bullhorn before you break my eardrums." Sargent Shriver casually leaned against one of the pillars and folded his arms across his chest. "Now give me the story, Phoebe."

I gave him the story. "See, it's simple, actually. Tyrus here lives in an attic while his mother takes care of him. She's old. I mean, she loves him and everything, but she thinks he's retarded; and when she dies, they'll probably put him in some horrible place, and you can bet that he won't be able to take his books and his polka records with him."

"So what is it you want?"

"I want two things. One, to call attention to people like Tyrus—which I think I've done—and the other, which is the reason I desperately needed a Kennedy, Mr. Shriver, is that I want Tyrus to go to that place that the Kennedy sister is in. The retarded sister."

"Ah. Our Rosemary. I'm afraid there is a very long waiting list to get into that particular establishment where our Rosemary lives. And, of course, it costs thirty-seven thousand dollars per year."

"I want the Kennedys to give Tyrus a scholarship. And it's my guess that there are certain names that never appear on waiting lists. But see, it wouldn't be a forever kind of thing. Tyrus is actually real smart. He could be out of there in no time. He just needs some sympathetic, astute doctor to figure out what the hell is wrong with him. No one knows what's wrong with him."

Out of the corner of my eye, I could see Tyrus watching me. He was putting up such a cool front. He was just as scared as I was behind his military fantasy. I told myself to stay strong—like that great-grandmother of mine—for good old Tyrus' sake. Still, I almost started to cry, but Sargent Shriver, what with his eight million sons, daughters, nieces, and nephews, knew I was going to cry.

"Now don't cry, Phoebe," he said as he put his arm around my shoulder. "You've begun a big job, and now you've got to finish it. As for your friend Tyrus, I'll see what I can do."

"I want you to promise me he can go where Rosemary Kennedy is."

"That's not reasonable." Not much like other adults, is he? Anyone else would have said "Okay, kid, it's a promise."

"Not a promise then, but a promise that you'll try. Hard."

"I will. I'll call my wife and see if she can speak with Sister Agnes. We'll all try. Is that enough?"

"Yeah."

"Okay. Now you must listen very carefully to me. You, too, Colonel."

"General."

"General. Please do not speak to the police or newsmen on the way to the precinct station. I'm going to try to talk them into allowing me to take you there in my car, but we might have to go with them. Especially if the FBI gets into this. We are in a national monument."

"That's okay. You don't have to. You've done enough. We'll face the police alone. Besides, you may be a famous person and all, but I don't think they'd let us go with you."

"They might. After all, I'm a lawyer."

"You're a lawyer? I didn't know you did anything. Aren't you rich?"

"Sometimes rich people work. I'm in corporate law, but I'll make an exception for you and the general."

"Wow. I just can't get over this. You mean you have an actual job?"

"Nine to five. We only play touch football on the weekends."

He had the cutest little twinkle in his eye. Lettie would have loved him. He was definitely a cross between Robert Redford and Paul Newman.

"I really appreciate this."

"My pleasure."

We followed him into the elevator, and as soon as we came out of the building into the sun, Tyrus raised his hand and made the victory sign although I'm sure everyone thought he was saying "Peace." The sharpshooters held their position.

Shriver called out, "DeTulio! Have your men put away their guns. These two are it. No one else is up there."

"You sure?"

"Positive." The cops stood up, and a lot of knees creaked in unison.

"Where's the arsenal?"

There wasn't a need to answer. A shining yellow balloon which a puff of breeze had blown up and over the balustrade floated down ever so slowly, and there was a tremendous silence until it landed at DeTulio's feet, where it popped with a nice, clear crack. A roar went up from the crowd, reminiscent of the cheers of baseball fans everywhere when Reggie "Zillion Dollar Contract" Jackson misses an easy pop fly. The cops put their weapons away rather disgustedly, but then they got to snickering. Like I said, it definitely beat picking up drunks out of the gutter. DeTulio came over to us, followed by about eight million cameras and microphones. He read us our rights. Sargent Shriver told him that we were his clients and offered him a ride back to the station with us. DeTulio looked at Tyrus and then back to Shriver. Out of the corner of his mouth he said, "Is this character dangerous?"

"Who?"

"The big fellow who keeps saluting my men."

"Nah," I interjected. "He's just mentally handicapped."

"However," Sargent Shriver added, "he does think he's General Patton."

"Why aren't you in uniform, young fellow?" Tyrus asked DeTulio.

"Yeah, Joe. Where's your uniform?" A couple of cops around DeTulio started ribbing him.

"Aw, shut up. You guys are all jealous. Get back on your beat."

"General," I said to Tyrus, "we can't talk till we've been debriefed."

"Jesus, Shriver," DeTulio said, "you didn't tell me that the kid thinks she's Omar Bradley."

Tyrus gave him what Barbara Cartland would call a withering look and then turned to me. "All right, Adjutant. I understand. Mum's the word, men."

DeTulio raised an eyebrow. Sargent Shriver shrugged. Me and Tyrus climbed into the limo. Not just any limo. A Fleetwood.

Chapter Three

I'm home. I'm also a household word. Every kid I know, and then some, has been over to take my picture. My friend Marlys is no longer allowed to sleep over at my house, but her parents will come around once they realize what a humanitarian act I performed. Merv Griffin called to see if I would like to do his show. My mom said no dice. My old man had a fit at my mom. He figured with a little exposure *Ladies' Home Journal* would pay me five figures for my story. For my education, he told her. Weakly. We all knew he wanted a real Porsche that worked. My mom said I should pay for my own college education working as a waitress, so I'd appreciate it. She also said to me, "Phoebe, will you please give me a year's break before you pull your next one?" Sure, I told her.

Old Blob acted like I'd never gone. I missed her. She learned two new terms: Remote Control Road Raker (which is a new toy she wants by Fisher-Price that costs about eight million dollars) and "motherfucker." I warned my mother not to let that Janey Carlson baby-sit for her, but she didn't believe me. "But Janey looks like such a nice girl, Phoebe." Mom's eating her words now. There is no such thing as a sixteen-year-old who's nice.

I found Sarah Bishop in back of my bureau. She was all dried up. Dead as a doornail. I buried her under our pine tree, but that goddamned Alice Monsoon dug her up and ate her remains. Old Willy made it, though. Every time you look out the front window, there's our Willy out on the lawn sitting up on his little hind legs sniffing the wind. By the time you get out there, of course, he's long gone. My old man keeps saying, "Those moles are sure out in force, this year. I'd better call Lawn Doctor." That Willy sure can make some great tunnels. I must say, however, that since gerbils are desert animals, come fall, when there's a little nip in the air, I fully expect to see old Willy scratching at the door dying to get back into his cozy Habitrail.

Since talking about what goes on at home is generally quite boring, let me tell you about Tyrus.

§ § §

Do you know that a person could actually live for a week or longer in Sargent Shriver's limousine. It has a TV, a refrigerator, and a bar. Me and Tyrus had three ginger ales apiece while Shriver and DeTulio cracked a couple of beers. It was hot in there till you felt the air conditioner. DeTulio said,

"There's going to be a stiff bail for the colonel here until it's officially determined that he's incompetent."

"General."

"Sorry, Mac. General."

"I've got my checkbook," Shriver said.

We left the limo out in front of this scuzzy building, and the flashbulbs were popping off a mile a minute. De-Tulio and Shriver kept saying, "No comment. No comment."

Tyrus kept saying, "It's over, boys. The big one is over."

I heard Phil Barnow say, who is my favorite local reporter, "I believe that the gentleman accompanying the first little boy to arrive from the tomb is Andy Warhol. Also, there's a very distinguished gentleman with the group who looks an awful lot like Stephen Smith, husband of Jean Kennedy, although I don't know what he'd be doing here." Obviously, old Phil hadn't gotten the full story on what had happened uptown. As if Andy Warhol would want to occupy Grant's Tomb. Andy Warhol must have come to mind when he spotted the Campbell's soup can sticking out of Tyrus' pocket, which was all Phil could see of him in the crowd.

Have you ever watched "Barney Miller" on the tube? The inside of DeTulio's headquarters looks just like it. Exactly. Except Wojo isn't there, of course. And—big surprise—guess who was sitting there? None other than old Lettie and her pal Moe, the hack. It seems she had arrived at Grant's Tomb just after we left, so the cabbie (who naturally knew all the short cuts) got her to the station ahead of us. She was sitting in the corner chatting with a couple of hookers who had spent the night there and were waiting for their rides home.

"Hey, Lettie!"

"There you are, Phoebe, you little rascal! You've got Mary crazy. C'mon, Tyrus, we're going home."

"Sorry, ma'am, nobody's going home just yet . . ."

"Who is this woman, Phoebe?" Shriver asked.

"Tyrus' aunt. This is Ms. Lettie Connolly. This is Sargent Shriver, Lettie."

"You're Sargent Shriver?" Lettie started patting at her hair, and she tucked her bra strap back under her sleeve. "My God, Moe, would you look at this. It's . . ."

"C'mon, Lettie. Don't embarrass Mr. Shriver," I said.

"I ain't embarrassin' him. Jesus, Sarge, I almost joined the Peace Corps myself. Really. I sent for all the brochures and everything, but the pay really stunk, ya know? Besides, I had a lot of responsibilities at home, so . . ."

"Right this way, please," DeTulio said, shoving us all into Captain Somebody's office.

It took only about an hour. Detective DeTulio explained to his captain that Tyrus was like one of those Japanese soldiers who turn up now and again on some Pacific atoll having been isolated for thirty-five years, and not knowing that the war was over and that the Japanese had surrendered. Only difference being, Tyrus didn't know *we'd* won.

Then my mother arrived. That was it. Tears, heartbreak, recriminations, urine. Old Blob pissed her pants. Shriver took complete care of the logistics. The captain seemed totally bored by the whole muddle, but don't forget we *are* talking about a New York City police captain who hears this kind of thing eight million times a day.

So in the end, Lettie took Tyrus home after Sargent Shriver forked over a check for five grand. He also gave me his word that he'd do what he said.

And my mother took me back to Connecticut. Once she'd gathered her wits about her and prepared to lecture me, she had a change of heart. My mother said instead,

"I can't believe how much you look like Maribeth with your hair that color. Maybe I'll have mine done, too. I never realized there was a hair color product able to match that wonderful shade."

"L'Oréal, copper-auburn. I think you should do it, Ma."

We looked over Blob's car seat at each other and had a good laugh.

I understand that just after we were all cleared out of the precinct, my old man arrived. Too late. Cost him twenty-five bucks. One doesn't park one's Porsche in a precinct captain's parking space.

§   §   §

Old Sargent Shriver came through, he really did. I got a call from Lettie about a month later. Tyrus got to go to a place which isn't the one the Kennedy lady is in, but another place in Westchester County called the Billingsworth Foundation. Sounds more like a chemical lab, doesn't it? They let Mary stay with Tyrus for one week, and then she's allowed to see him on weekends until he learns not to depend on her so much. Mary and Lettie had a tiny guest cottage on the grounds, and they were even allowed to bring old Dodge along. Lettie said Tyrus was learning to write and tie his shoes—all the things his small muscles had been protected from doing. She also said I wasn't to get in touch with him at all until the foundation contacts me, which of course was a very big disappointment. I immediately called the doctor in charge to ask him why, and he told me that as soon as my name is mentioned to Tyrus, he goes right into all that military jazz. The doctor sort of hinted that it might take years to convince Tyrus that he isn't General Patton. Depressing, right?

So I didn't get in touch with Tyrus. Almost. See, I didn't write or anything like that, but one day me and Marlys went with her mother to this new shopping center in White Plains called The Galleria. This particular shopping center is a little bigger than Rhode Island, and even has a hotel if you want to live there. There was a branch of that real expensive store, Neiman-Marcus, and they had all this stuff no one could afford unless he was Sargent Shriver. The thing that caught my eye was that they had a couple of model ship kits. The little pieces were made of pure stainless steel. One of the ships was the USS *Lexington*. Can you believe it? If you can, can you believe two hundred and seventy-five bucks? I asked the man if he would save it while I raised the money.

He said, "For a week, mademoiselle." Funny, I thought Neiman-Marcus was a Texas store. Not Paris. What a bunch of phonies in this world.

Anyway, I went home, and I sold everything I owned that my mother wouldn't know about: the first copy of *Ms.* magazine with Wonder Woman on the cover, which my Grandma had given me as a joke on my second birthday; my Barbie doll, which I had refused to take out of the box when I was five because it was so repulsive (a boxed Barbie doll is worth a mint); and my ten silver— real silver—dollars that were in the bottom of my bank, though I don't know who put them there. Marlys even offered to sell her record of Dr. King's "I had a dream . . ." speech at the Washington Monument. Is that a loyal friend or what? But I had enough because of the asshole doll.

Anonymously, I sent the *Lexington* to Tyrus. I hoped some nice nurse would help him to make it. I cried a little bit when I left the post office. I couldn't help it.

So September came, and school started, and even though I'd often wonder about Tyrus, I was awfully busy what with classes, and clarinet, and ballet, and religion, and the Committee to save Bates Mountain Elementary School. And you know how you get all wrapped up after that in Halloween, and Thanksgiving, and Christmas, one right after the other. But then it got to be January: late January when you just want to die of winter because you have yet to face February. It was freezing cold, and there wasn't any snow. My sled lay rotting in the garage. And there was such a lot of Canada goose shit in the pond behind the school that the water froze in soggy lumps. Consequently, my ice skates were rotting faster than my sled. As a matter of fact, next spring I swear to God that I'll put up a sign by the pond that says:

DO NOT FEED THE DUCKS
(By order of authorized personnel)

The reason I'll put ducks instead of geese is because the jerks that live around here think the geese are ducks. Also, I think "authorized personnel" will have more of an effect than "local police," what with all these nitwit, cop-taunting, teenaged vandals running loose.

But the worst of it—the very worst—which really got me so badly depressed that even Marlys couldn't cheer me up, was the fact that the last star in Orion's belt, old Alnitak, slipped down behind the top of Pine Mountain and was gone from my vantage point on the back deck. I strained to see it on my tiptoes from the railing, freezing cold in my pajamas. No snow was tough, but no Mintaka, Alnilam, and Alnitak was a gaping hole nothing would fill.

What I'm saying is this: I had reached the very bottom of the pits, and just when my mother began to notice and worry about me, a letter arrived with this postmark:

> The Billingsworth Foundation
> Wainwright Cottage
> P.O. Box 9
> Briarcliff, NY 10510

Here is what Tyrus said in a handwriting that looked like a right-handed person printing left-handed:

Dear Phoebe,

I like my school. My teacher is a girl. I like my school because my teacher is a girl and she sits with me when I see the doctor. The doctor is taking the needles out of my face. He said to me it would take a long time but have patience. There are so many of them. When they are out maybe you could come and visit me. My doctor said that's when you may come visit me. Would you come and visit me when the needles are out?

From Tyrus

P.S. I told my teacher I was saving the Lexington till you come. You are a good gluer.

§   §   §

Imagine sitting around like a jackass getting all leaked off at goddamned Canada goose shit.

Oh, Tyrus, a herd of wild elephants couldn't keep me away.

PART FOUR

Chapter One

When Ben finished the journal, I was sleeping, but I felt him cuddle up against me and nuzzle his face into my back. He nudged me around a little so that I'd think I woke up by myself.

"Did you finish, Ben?"

"Yeah. Are you awake?"

"Somewhat."

"Phoebe, I have a confession to make."

"I never listen to confessions."

He sighed. "Marlys told me about Tyrus. I remember when I was in college reading something about a kid and her retarded cousin occupying Grant's Tomb. Wasn't he your cousin?"

"Second cousin."

"Then who were all those other people?"

"Oh, I exaggerated my aunts and uncles. I always give people extra, more interesting characteristics. But, Ben, all the Tyrus stuff is true. All true. I used to visit him all the time, and when I saw that my Aunt Mary wasn't going to live forever, I took matters into my own hands. When I was a kid, I would do anything. I never considered the consequences."

Ben rolled me over so that we were face-to-face. "Writers are liars out of necessity. I got the impression before I read the journal that you'd never gone back to it since you wrote it. I think you led me to believe that."

"Well . . ."

"The Iranian hostage thing was after 1977."

"But, Ben, I only read bits and pieces of it, and I can never resist the urge to jazz things up a tad. I think I'd enjoy being a rewriter if there only was such a thing. I'd rewrite *Ulysses*, rewrite *The Snows of Kilimanjaro*, rewrite . . ."

"Don't get nervous."

"Sorry."

"Forget it. If rearranging your life through this journal is what makes you happy, then it makes me happy. The point is what did Tyrus have to do with not having this abortion?"

I turned onto my back and watched the ceiling for signs of breakdown. "A year ago, after Aunt Mary died, I got a telephone call from Tyrus. He had obviously suffered a relapse. He was all excited telling me he was going on a secret mission to destroy a key Jap outpost at Kwajalein. He told me he would soon be taking off in a small Wildcat—that's a fighter plane—from the deck of the USS *Lexington*. Tyrus said to me, 'This is a solo mission, Adjutant. Over and out.'

"I laughed and laughed. It had been so long since he talked that war stuff that I thought he was putting me on for old times' sake. Then I got to thinking; they were preparing him to make the big move to a community house in Larchmont with three others. I decided to call him back, thinking maybe he was really getting anxious about it. I waited till the next morning.

"I called him at his cottage, but the Billingsworth operator put me through to his doctor. That was unusual, because Tyrus had reached the point years before where he'd answer the phone just like any normal person.

"His doctor's name was Dillon, really a nice guy—like an old country doctor, only a shrink. The minute I heard Dillon's voice, I knew Tyrus had definitely relapsed. I said, 'Don't feel bad, Dillon. When you think you're General Patton for thirty-five years, it's tough to accept being just an everyday guy.'

"Dillon kept clearing his throat and clearing his throat, so I asked him what the hell was the matter with him. He sort of croaked, 'Tyrus only told you and me about his mission, Phoebe, no one else. Like you, I didn't think he'd really attempt it. Well, he attempted it, and he completed it. The USS *Lexington* was the roof of the administration building. When he was lying there in the parking lot, he told me a kamikaze attack was an honor, and he kept calling me "Emperor." Phoebe, all I kept saying, over and over, was "You're not a Jap, Tyrus, you're an American." '

"Then Dillon broke down, like I'm doing now."

The words were all sputtering out, and I was shaking uncontrollably.

Ben asked in his softest voice, "He died?"

"Ten minutes after he hit fucking Kwajalein."

I hope someone rocked Dr. Dillon in her arms, the way Ben rocked me. He said, "Shhh, shhh." But I kept talking.

"The one who carried on most of all was my sister. It was at the wake. My dad told her that when she finished saying a prayer, she had to go up to my Uncle Paul, who was Tyrus' father, and say 'I'm sorry.' So she told me she didn't say it because, after all, it wasn't her fault that Tyrus had died. But when she stepped in front of Uncle Paul, she was, of course, speechless considering her age, and he took her hand and said, 'Are you sorry?'

"I found her in the bathroom, hysterical. After I heard the story, I explained that Uncle Paul thought she was me."

Ben kissed my hot forehead. "Oh, Phoebe, how can you think you were to blame? It wasn't your fault at all."

"Theoretically. But if I'd not gotten involved, someone would have shipped Tyrus to the state hospital after Aunt Mary died, and he'd still be alive."

"Not necessarily. State hospitals have roofs."

"But they tie people down."

"So is Tyrus better off dead or tied down?"

"Dead."

"And if Tyrus didn't die, you'd have had an abortion."

"Yeah. I'll never kill anything else."

Ben braided my hair. "Phoebe, there's a tribe in Africa who—"

"The Fulani?"

"What?"

"Never mind."

"These Africans believe that when someone dies, his spirit is conceived again in the body of a new baby. You didn't kill Tyrus. He's that baby inside you. Shall I bring you some hot cocoa?"

"No. Don't leave me."

"Okay."

After a long while of clinging to Ben, I was sure he'd fallen asleep, and I had to go to the bathroom. As soon as I moved, he said, "I'm sorry about Tyrus, Phoebe."

"He's all right, Ben. He's going to be born at the end of January."

Chapter Two

It was my first year not to have Christmas. Ben doesn't celebrate it. Some Jews, believe it or not, do not consider Christmas a nonsectarian holiday. All I did was send presents to my family, which, of course, Ben actually paid for, not that that means he sold out. I, in turn, got some presents from them in care of Marlys' new secretary. Marlys was in Japan for Christmas. She sent me a note that she'd fired Barbara. She didn't mention whether she had a new mistress, too, so I imagine it was an awfully lonely Christmas for her, and I felt a bit guilty, but not too.

My parents sent me a mug with a bulldog on it

with promises of bigger presents when I got home. My sister sent me a candle holder she made in art class out of a Wisk bottle. It was lovely to smell Wisk. Countries may be alike in a lot of ways, but they always smell different.

Oh yes, Marlys returned the polar bear with another note saying she hated it, it was free from some fashion magazine, and throw it away if I didn't want it. I gave it to Madame Besette on Christmas Eve, apologizing that it was a used gift. She didn't hear the apology. She fainted. The Greeks ministered to her, and she wore the coat to midnight mass.

The lights in Paris are pretty at Christmas.

In December and January I did nothing eventful except go to Lamaze classes with Ben to learn the easiest method for getting a human, newborn head through a hole one hundredth the size of the head. The hole, we found out, will stretch open just enough about ninety percent of the time, though unwillingly. We read about the stages of labor, and how to relax and breathe correctly.

When Ben wasn't painting, we took long, long walks, because my doctor believes five miles a day shortens labor. Fortunately, I love to walk. Ben and I covered every street except the Avenue de Tourville, where we were afraid we'd still see the foot. But we did go back to Saul's the long way around. Saul's looked exactly the same except that the pretty pink ceramic umbrella stand just inside the door was gone. That was where they'd hidden the bomb. The stand had caught my eye because its glaze was the palest pink I'd ever seen, like a ballerina's tights. I thought it was beautiful.

Of course, Saul wasn't there either, but Sandra said he'd be back on his feet in about six weeks. I hoped that meant he hadn't lost his feet in the explosion. Sandra is Saul's wife. She runs the bistro for now, and the Jewish rye still tastes as good as cake.

I learned plenty about art. The metal building with the pear and artichokes missing is Art Nouveau, as are many of the beautiful entrances to several Métro stations. On our walks we'd often see groups of art students standing in front of the building learning about Art Nouveau. Ben told me to take a course at Yale called Post-Impressionism because it was me. I signed up for just such a course when my dean sent me the forms.

I never saw Marlys again in Paris, but I wrote her a zillion-page letter basically apologizing and saying I'd always be her best friend. She wrote me back a one-page letter saying she knew it and she should have told me.

Then it was time to pack everything together, and Ben and I rented a Citroën and drove to Caen. I decided not to tell the desLauriers I was coming yet. We'd stay for a week at a hotel that Ben knew of that had little bungalows on cliffs hanging over the sea, and a three-star restaurant. That way I'd have the opportunity to breathe in the salt air and spy on the desLauriers for the fun of it.

Chapter Three

I had no idea that when I went to Normandy I would
find Tyrus. What was I thinking of, I'll never know. I
knew all the D day beaches were in France, but I'd managed to forget that it was *Normandy,* France. The
desLauriers' estate in St. Aubin looks over an especially
lovely stretch of beach known to Tyrus—when he was
alive—and thousands and thousands of World War II
veterans as Juno. I set out to spend two weeks telling
Ben all about D day. The only part of the war Ben
knows is the Holocaust. And Ben set out to teach me all
about Calvados. That's a drink native to Normandy

geared to knock your socks off. It is made, unbelievably, of apples. They don't stop at cider here in Normandy.

Ben's hotel was more than he described. It had once been a luxurious farm. The owners lived in the farmhouse, where the three-star restaurant was, and the bungalows were actually all the farm's outbuildings. We drew the former dovecote, a short, fat tower, half-timbered, and with a hot tub instead of pigeon doo. Our two weeks there were like every human being's dream of what a perfect honeymoon should be except for one striking difference: I unconsciously began to prepare myself for my near-future separation from Ben while he in turn grew more loving, more protective, kinder, and, at the same time, increasingly dependent on my love for him.

For the first week we just ate and made love, and took long walks all bundled up against the dark, rough channel. As we walked across the tidal flats, white with frost, I would say things like "We're walking on men's bones." Ben would change the subject. He wanted to be just plain content; like the calm before the storm. I let him have his way for that week and took advantage of all the lovely *nouvelle cuisine. Nouvelle cuisine* is quite tasty besides being pretty, but I ended up ordering two of everything.

The first appetizer I had was reminiscent of the food Madame Besette's Greeks served to me my first night at Ben's. I had a half a pear poached in wine lying on a white platter. I didn't think of the metal one lying on the Avenue Rapp. The platter could easily have held a thirty-pound turkey. Next to the pear on the very lip of the platter was a lovely sculptured yellow vegetable with parsley delicately arranged beneath it to form a stem and leaves. It looked exactly like a wild primrose that you find along the shores of Long Island Sound. I ate the pear in two bites, then stabbed the vegetable with my fork, and Ben grabbed my wrist.

"Phoebe, you don't eat the primrose."

When you dine on *nouvelle cuisine*, watch your step.

We bought binoculars, lay on the bluff over St. Aubin, and watched the desLauriers go in and out along with numerous guests. I thought one guy looked a little like Jerry Lewis, but Ben said no. Sometimes a helicopter would land on the lawn, and all these businessmen would pile out with their briefcases. Other people who came were villagers with food deliveries. Most of these were women with eggs and milk and things like that. They always had children in tow, and actually so did a few of the guests. That gave me a good feeling. So did the horses. The desLauriers had an entire stable full. I imagined Florence in her beautiful riding clothes galloping along the bluff. I know she would love a baby. Monsieur desLauriers greeted most of the people at the door himself.

"Ben," I whispered, "I wonder what Monsieur desLauriers does for a living." You tend to whisper when spying.

"Looks to me like he has a full-time job just keeping track of his money, although he probably has his accountants do that."

"Hmmm."

"Want to climb down the cliff and walk the beach to Courseulles, Phoebe?"

"That's that cute little port with the oyster boats?"

"Yeah. We'll stop at a cozy spot and have some Calvados. I'm getting cold."

You drink Calvados warm, preferably out of your used coffee cup just after dinner. Ben and I drank it all the time, coffee or no. We loved it.

There were steps down to the beach cut out of the chalk cliffs. We passed a little sign between St. Aubin and Courseulles that said Graye-sur-Mer. I stopped.

"That name sounds familiar, Ben."

"What name?"

"The name of this beach. Wait a minute." I looked at the dunes behind us. To the left was the natural gap; to the right, the remains of the pillbox. "Oh my God, Ben. Quick. C'mon."

I pulled him by the hand toward the dunes.

"Where are we going?"

"We're on Graye-sur-Mer. Tyrus told me about this place. Hurry."

"Oh, Phoebe, I'm sick of hearing about Guam and kamikazes."

"This is the western front, you dummy."

He followed me through the dunes and up a short road to the first crossroads. The little artery coming from the beach became a bridge at the crossroads. It was a nice, neat sort of bridge with a scenic view. The bridge didn't cover a creek like most seaside bridges, but rather a swampy marsh that ran all along behind the dunes.

"I know this place, Ben. This bridge. Can I tell you what Tyrus told me about it? It's fantastic."

"Okay." The tone was "No."

"See, Ben, every soldier who landed on D day had

one specific job. Each depended on the success of the soldiers before him with their jobs, and later waves of troops depended on the waves before them. If somebody goofed, the whole sequence was thrown off. If you were a soldier who could see that the sequence had been thrown off, and you were next, you didn't say 'Oh, heck!'—you prepared to die. Anyway, there were these three British guys driving a fascine . . ."

"What's that?"

"A fancy tank. The British were very ingenious. They had all these recycled tanks, each with a different job. The fascines came on up the beach right after the flails and bobbins. The flails were tanks with a big steel drum attached to the front of them. Hanging off the drum were a zillion thick chains. When the drum rolled, the chains would beat the beach, detonating all the mines. Once the beach was safe from mines, then came the bobbins. The bobbins were tanks that unrolled hundreds of feet of steel mats so that if the beach had soft spots, the next tanks wouldn't sink, and neither would all the trucks, soldiers, and equipment about to land.

"With the fascines came the roly-polys, the petards, the crocodiles—"

"Phoebe, does this story have a point, and is it coming soon?"

"Just let me tell you about the roly-polys before I get to the point. The roly-polys had no turrets, just a flattened-out top. They'd cuddle up to the sea walls like a ramp, and the next tanks would just roll right up and over them while the poor guys in the pitch dark inside hoped the hell a potato masher didn't fall on them."

"I refuse to hear what a potato masher is. So what's the rest of the story?"

"Give me a chance. Anyway, these three British guys drove this one fascine. That was a tank carrying a tremendous load of logs. They were to drop their load if they came to a crater—these giant holes the Germans dug to stop the invasion.

"These guys followed a flail and a bobbin through the dunes till they came to this very marsh. This marsh that we're standing above right now. From the reconnaissance photos they thought the marsh was just a little stream. But it was covered with sea grass and looked dry. Before they knew what was happening, the tank started slipping, and they drove right into the marsh, got halfway across, and sank up to the turret, logs and all.

"But it was great, because the petards which carried portable bridges had bridges only thirty feet long. This marsh is fifty feet across. So they laid out two bridges supported in the middle by the sunk tank.

"Now get this, Ben. The bridge became famous because of these three guys making a mistake. After the invasion, Churchill crossed this very bridge, and so did Eisenhower and de Gaulle—even King George. Wow! Tyrus went nuts over this story."

"But what happened to the three British guys? Did they drown?" Ben was shifting his weight back and forth from one foot to the other.

"Well, almost. The tank filled up with water immediately, but they managed to pull each other out. They knew no one would help them because orders were to get your job done and not help anyone in trouble even if it was your best friend."

"Phoebe, that's horrible."

"This is the war I'm talking about, Ben. Stop to help your buddy, and two hundred guys behind you can't cross the bridge to blow up the pillboxes, so the Germans in the pillboxes kill the two hundred guys."

"Jesus Christ, I hope they pass the ERA. Women would be better commanders than men in a second."

"It's inevitable."

"What is?"

"The ERA."

"What about the three guys?"

"Oh. Once they were out, they ran over to the dunes for protection, but a mortar fell on them. Two died, and one only lost his arm. For D day, one out of three wasn't bad."

"I'm getting out of here. I can't stand this." He turned, hands jammed into his pockets, and clomped off the bridge back toward the gap.

"But, Ben . . ."

He ignored me. I got down on my hands and knees, leaned way over the bridge, and looked down into the swamp. Tyrus told me it would still be there. It was. In fact, the tide was so low that the top two inches of the turret were above the water right under me.

Before I left to catch up to Ben, I saluted. Tyrus would have.

§　§　§

Ben did drive me to the cemetery to pay my respects. I, who knew what to expect, was just as shocked as Ben, who didn't. Really high above what was Omaha Beach is the American cemetery. You drive up there and hit the brakes in shock. Extending forever, right up to the edge of the cliff, are rows and rows and rows of symmetric white crosses broken up every once in a while by a Star of David.

"My God, Phoebe, so many."

"More than six thousand, I think, Ben, because on the first day alone six thousand were killed."

"I can't help it, but think how six million would look."

"No one can imagine that. Six thousand looks like six million."

"Is the British cemetery just as bad?"

"No. They didn't lose nearly so many men during this invasion."

"How is that?"

"Remember all those funny tanks I told you about the other day?"

"Yeah."

"The American generals thought they were ridiculous."

"What did we use then?"

"Kids. They're all laying here now on this cliff. The greatest technical society ever to appear on earth decided to do everything by hand."

Ben walked a few steps away from me. His eyes got wet. Artists are very affected by this sort of thing because they can picture things in their minds exactly. We left right away.

§   §   §

We called the desLauriers, and they invited us to dinner. They wanted us to move in the next day, but I wouldn't till labor was imminent. I agreed to see Florence's doctor in Caen often so that he could predict when I would go into labor. He was to become a houseguest along with Ben and me. He was good. We moved into the desLauriers' guest wing three days before the baby was born.

I asked Monsieur desLauriers what he did for a living. He told me there was a great deal of family money. In fact, he offered to pay for the rest of my education, but I told him I was home free as far as Yale was concerned. But his job, he said, pouring me another cup of Calvados, was Minister of Justice.

I smacked my knee and said, "Ben, you big ding. You've lived in France for six years. Didn't the name at least sound a little bit familiar?"

Ben said, "I don't follow French politics." Ben follows just one thing: the Boston Red Sox.

Monsieur desLauriers said, "My dear Phoebe, I hope you don't mind that I am a member of the present Socialist government."

Silly man.

Chapter Four

One night while I was sleeping, leaning heavily against Ben's sturdy back, a loud explosion from somewhere in the east opened my eyes. I sat up and grabbed a handful of Ben's T-shirt.

"What was that?" Before Ben reacted, my first thought was D day, my second the foot.

He rolled toward my side. "What? What, Phoebe?"

"That boom. Like a tire blew out." I didn't dare say "Like a bomb" until I was sure. I went to the window and drew aside the thin lace curtain. The courtyard was empty, a band of pale light just forming on the horizon.

Placental fluid dripped steadily onto the carpet between my feet. I was what had exploded.

I reached over to my table, grabbed a handful of Kleenex and stuffed it between my legs. I wiggled over to the bureau to get some underpants.

"Was there a bomb, Phoebe?" Ben asked, scared and half asleep.

"No, Ben. You had a dream. Go back to sleep. I'm just going to the bathroom."

He was immediately asleep again, breathing sweetly. I put another wad of Kleenex into my pants and got into bed. I had no labor pains, and I was tired. It was twenty after two. The band of light wasn't dawn. Maybe it was Caen, or the aurora borealis. Whatever was happening could wait; I fell back asleep as quickly as Ben. It waited till twenty after four, and I got a cramp that woke me up. It was quite a hard cramp, but it didn't hurt and couldn't compare to a menstrual cramp you get when you're thirteen that the doctor tells you is all in your head.

I sat up. I had never been so excited in my whole life. I was totally unafraid—in fact, so excited I wanted to make hot cocoa with Ben. Instead, I tried to calm down and watch the clock to see how long it would be before the next one. I fell asleep. I dozed on and off until five, when I felt soggy. I went to the bathroom, flushed away the Kleenex, and got a towel to sit on. I kept dripping away.

By six o'clock the cramps were coming regularly, every five minutes, and though they still didn't hurt, I had to do my slow Lamaze breathing so that they wouldn't. I knew it was time to buzz the doctor, but I'd learned in Lamaze that I might not be allowed to eat during labor in case there was trouble and I had to go to Caen for a cesarean. So I said to Ben, "Ben, would you go get me a drink?" I was dying of thirst, but starving especially.

"Can't you get it?" he mumbled.

"No, and when you come back, I'll tell you why. And could you go down to the front door and get me a pastry? I heard the baker come."

Off he went, sleepwalking, really.

We munched some raisin buns, and Ben had brought me tea to drink. I said casually, "I've had some twinges, so I've been doing slow breathing."

He choked on a bun. "Twinges? What twinges?"

"Actually, my water broke."

He was out the door like a shot. I ate fast before Ben could get back with the doctor. I decided not to breathe during the next contraction in order to eat more proficiently. It hurt like hell. It felt like an iron grip fastened around my waist crushing me and pulling me apart all at the same time. I gritted my teeth the way you see Indian women do when they bite down on a strip of rawhide in the movies. Not only did that not help, it made things worse.

I took a last gulp of tea as the door opened. It was Monsieur desLauriers staring at me from the foot of the bed, shouting at his secretary to cancel all his appointments for the day. They both looked as though they hadn't been sleeping at all except for their silk bathrobes. The secretary must sleep with the notebook.

Madame desLauriers and the two nurses were fussing all over the room, Madame trying ineffectively to help. Nurses—French nurses, too—never let anyone think that anyone besides themselves can do anything. They wheeled in a table full of utensils. The doctor was sipping coffee, not quite awake enough to go into serious action. He just watched me.

"Here it comes, Ben." The desLauriers and the nurses went into shock and stood like statues. The doctor and Ben knew I didn't mean the baby.

"Deep breath, Phoebe." He looked down at his watch, new for the occasion.

I breathed deeply and went into my panting.

"Forty-five seconds to go." I breathed harder.

"Thirty seconds to go," he said rather loudly. It was because I was at the worst part of the contraction, but I knew that meant it was half over. You can get through anything when you know it's half over.

"Fifteen seconds left, Phoebe; you've got it licked."

I slowed up.

"Zero. All over, Phoebe. Relax."

It was. I smiled and said, "Hi, everybody. Morning, Doc." He loved it when I called him Doc. I loved him. He was French. They invented Lamaze. He told the desLauriers to leave so that he could examine me. Ben sat in the corner. Basically, the doctor snapped on a rubber glove, put his hand smoothly up my vagina, and said, "Between four and six centimeters, mademoiselle. Excellent. You are half there. Just four hours to go."

Remember my theory on being half there? I was ecstatic. I expected him to say eight hours. "But what about my water breaking, Doc?"

"The placenta is merely leaking. It did not burst, or there would be a cascade. Cascade? Yes, like a waterfall.

It will not be a dry birth, it will be a wonderful birth because of your lovely dispossession."

"Disposition. Thank you." Ben thumbed his nose at me. Jealous.

"You're welcome. I will leave you with the gentleman while I breakfast. You know, of course, the contractions may or may not get stronger, but they will become more frequent. It is normal, but call me whenever you like."

"Doctor?"

"Yes?"

"I don't want the nurses checking on me. It will destroy my concentration."

"Fine."

"And don't let the desLauriers in again. When the baby is here, I will tell you when to bring it to them."

"Very good. I will so inform them."

He left, I breathed, Ben counted. We got bored, so Ben gave me a back rub with two tennis balls. We learned to do that in Lamaze in case I had back labor. Back labor is when the baby starts pushing against your spine instead of your cervix. I didn't have it because I wasn't having such a dumb baby, but the tennis balls felt good just the same. When the contractions began to last a little more than a minute, my ears rang, but I couldn't consider the noise to be pain. I went to the bathroom for something to do and found that walking felt great. I walked out onto the balcony and froze. After that I couldn't stop shivering, so Ben went to get the doctor. I was worried because of the shivering.

"Mademoiselle," he said, "you are trembling with your excellent effort. Relax, relax, relax. That is the key.

And it is too cold to go out on the balcony." He felt inside of me. "A couple of hours left. That's all."

"Does 'a couple' mean 'two' in French?"

He put his hand on my forehead. "No more than two. You have such beautiful skin. It will not wrinkle. When you are fifty, you will look thirty."

"Thank you."

He kissed my hand and left. Ben didn't get jealous. He knew the doctor was soothing me at a time when soothing was paramount.

I could hear the desLauriers buzzing with the doctor outside in the hall, and then their footsteps echoed away.

The next hour was uneventful. The contractions were almost exactly three minutes apart. No surprises. I relaxed, I was in control of my breathing, and I watched my stomach rise up, pause, and fall down. It was a physical feeling unlike any other: an enormous muscle flexing of its own will.

The last hour was catastrophic for me as a human being. Nothing abnormal happened, but the contractions became so powerful that I felt as though a huge giant, a Cyclops, were picking me up and hurling me across the room. Hurling me down a cliff to smash upon the rocks below. But just as I was about to be crushed and split open by the rocks, the contraction ended. I was sweating like a horse. At the end of one especially long one, I said, "I thought I'd land that time."

Ben went and got the doctor. I was too wrapped up in what I was doing to explain to Ben what I meant, so he thought I was delirious. The doctor walked gently across the room behind the thrashing Ben. He felt inside of me during a contraction, and it hurt badly, and I screamed at him for not waiting till it was over. He apologized and said it was necessary, but just that once. I called him a fucking liar. He told me cursing had great merit, was an excellent, healthy reaction, and that I would surely have a beautiful baby.

Baby. I'd completely forgotten that I was going through all this because I was having a baby. Then something strange happened. An invisible hand reached inside me and began to tug.

"Something's happening, Doc."

"Ah. You now feel the urge to push, no?"

"No. Pull. And it's pulling all by itself."

He took my left hand. Ben was biting my right one. "Mademoiselle, I have never given birth, so I am not able to describe the sensation. But this pull . . ."

"More of a tug."

"This tug you feel. When it comes, you must sit up and bear down. Perhaps you will feel like fighting it. Do not, and the sensation will be pleasant. Monsieur Reuben may hold you around the shoulders and push, too. If you push during the tug, it will feel very good. It will feel delicious, like a great alleviation, an enormous burden being lifted from you.

"It will also be your hardest work. Hold your breath, and push for the entire time you feel the tug. During this stage of labor, some women achieve an orgasm. It is at this point that American doctors anesthetize their patients. They are unable to deal with orgasms."

I said, during my next space between massive tugs, "Jesus Christ, I sure could use an orgasm."

Ben said, "So the hell could I."

"Shut up, Ben." We laughed. The doctor sat at the foot of the bed and lifted my nightgown over my knees. On cue, the nurses came in carrying a load of laundry. One, who was more of a maid than a nurse, slipped a plastic sheet under my rear, plus a thick cloth.

"My feet are freezing," I said.

Ben jumped up and ran to his Lamaze notes. He said, "Coldness in the extremities. Delivery is imminent. Phoebe! Imminent!" He was hysterical with joy. Then he went rummaging around in the bureau while the doctor explained that the pressure of the baby's head was cutting off the circulation to my feet. Ben came back and wrapped my right foot in his blue Izod V-neck and my other in the Irish fisherman's sweater his mother had knit.

The doctor said, "That is very nice." I didn't know if he meant the sweater or the gesture.

The next time the tug came, I pushed so hard I thought I'd burst a blood vessel in my temple.

"The baby's head is showing, mademoiselle. Would you like a mirror?"

"Yes."

The maid-nurse went out, then wheeled in a full-length mirror. Ben said, "Louis XV."

They set up the mirror, and I saw the little opening about an inch across, and scalp with spare auburn down showing through. Mostly, though, I saw a ring of large purplish blue lumps just below the baby.

"What are all those disgusting blue lumps underneath?"

"I'm afraid," the doctor said, "that that is your rectum. Hemorrhoids which will recede after the birth."

I almost gagged. "Get the mirror the hell out."

"You are sure? I assure you, it is really quite a normal occurrence."

"Ben, did they mention hemorrhoids in Lamaze class?"

"No."

"Get the mirror out."

The maid-nurse wheeled it out. I could hear pacing in the hallway. The desLauriers must have been wondering what the hell was going on.

"Mademoiselle, if when you push you grasp your knees and lean far forward, you can see the baby born, but not the rectum."

"Fine, Doc, fine." I guess most of his patients don't want to miss a trick.

The nurse put a hot, steaming wet pack against my vagina. For the first time I noticed the pot boiling on a hot plate near the bed.

"What's that for?"

"To stretch the vaginal opening so that it doesn't rip."

"Is that what boiling water is for. I thought it was to keep the father busy. They don't do that in America anymore, Doc."

"I know. In America they prefer to cut."

"I wonder why."

"So do I."

It took three mind-boggling pushes to get the baby's head out. My eyes were shut. They screamed at me that the baby's head was out, but I had given up. All the energy left just drained right out of me as soon as the baby's head popped through.

"Can't push anymore, folks," I whispered.

"Push, push," Ben shouted in my ear.

"Just once more, mademoiselle. One last time, I promise you."

I gave a pathetic little push, and there was a loud slurping noise. I opened my eyes. The doctor reached over my knees with the baby and laid him on my stomach, which had automatically turned into a soft, mushy, cozy nest. His umbilical cord was white with aquamarine lines strung through like my nana's old clothesline.

Ben began crying uncontrollably. The placenta slid out, and the doctor cut it off. He tied up the stump over the baby's tummy. It obviously hurt the baby, because he cried out and shook his little fist. Then he whimpered sadly.

I said, "Don't cry, baby."

"I can't help it." Oh, that Ben.

The baby looked me right in the eye. I sat up, lifted him out of my depressed stomach, and held him to my chest. He blew bubbles. He sneezed. He smiled at me. I couldn't take my eyes off him. I said, "Doctor, Ben. I want to be alone with him for three minutes."

"In three minutes, mademoiselle, I will send the nurse back to clean you."

"First, send Ben."

"Very good."

They left. Ben was totally hysterical, his shoulders shaking wildly. The two nurses half carried him out of the room.

I said to my son: "Little baby, I love you. You are a

perfect boy. You have coppery, shiny hair like my sister. Like your aunt in America. I cannot be your mother because that would be cruel to you. You deserve a mother who wants you more than anything else. I want you, but I want too much else. I will always love you no matter what, and when you and I are ready, we will meet again, and you can tell me what your whole life that I missed was like, and I will tell you about mine. I love you, I love you, I love you."

Tears were falling all over the baby's naked body, but he didn't mind. He liked it. Ben came in, and he wasn't crying anymore. He took the baby, and hugged him, and kissed his lovely auburn hair. Very softly, Ben said my name. I looked away toward the window, and I thought for just a second that it had begun to rain. The glass was shimmering, the view out of focus. I heard the baby say something when Ben left that must have been goodbye.

I closed my eyes and saw my heartbroken mother sitting at the kitchen table watching John Lennon's record going round and round, the needle stuck in that same black groove, and heard John Lennon telling me over and over that nothing is real, like he tried to tell my mother.

Chapter Five

Ben told the doctor that he himself would give the baby
to Madame desLauriers so that afterward he could tell
me how it went. I didn't want to know. Not right away.

Within six hours after the baby was born I felt absolutely fine. Physically. More than fine—like a sheep
that had just been sheared. I wanted to run or skip. It
had been so long since I felt light. Ben and I were supposed to leave the next morning, but at twenty-five after
ten, when the baby was exactly twelve hours old, we
walked out of the darkened wing of the house, got in the
Citroën, and drove back to Paris. I did not look back,

grateful that I hadn't heard any baby sounds seeping through the walls.

We were part of the commuter crush coming into Paris the next morning. When we reached the Avenue Rapp, my breasts hurt, but that was all. The hemorrhoids must have shrunk back into position. Ben and I went to bed in each other's arms and slept twenty-four hours. We woke up, and I called Pan Am. Ben listened to my call, and he turned a yellowish green and went to the bathroom just as I finished making my reservation for that evening. The flight was to leave at midnight. I didn't know if I could stand waiting that long to get out of Paris, but I knew Ben would help me.

Ben had no intention of helping me.

I stupidly assumed all along that Ben knew I would have to leave France as soon as possible after having the baby. I admit that even I hadn't thought it would be as drastically soon after having the baby but I had to go home. I had to get away from the little throbbing voice in the front of my brain repeating over and over and over, "Go back and get your son." In France I had been pregnant, and was, in fact, a mother. At Yale I wouldn't be either of those. Now I know I'd been pregnant in New Haven, too, but being a little pregnant does not compare to being very pregnant. In Ben's bedroom I found myself still turning sideways and wriggling past the bed though there was plenty of room. I was through squeezing by things that normal people could get by without effort.

I truly didn't think Ben would be the least bit surprised. He'd helped me choose my spring classes at Yale.

He knew. But he came out of the bathroom and said, "Phoebe, I want that baby back."

I remember opening my mouth to say something, or maybe just to take a deep breath. Nothing came out. Ben looked like someone deranged. He paced.

"Listen, Phoebe, I went through that entire pregnancy. I witnessed that child's birth. I held him in my arms right after he was born. I love his mother. I'm as much the baby's father as you are his mother. If you don't want him, fine. I want him."

I watched him pick up the phone, unable to react. He asked for the operator and told her to connect him through to Caen. Finally, my muscles moved. I knocked the receiver out of his hand, and its casing cracked when it hit the bleached oak floor.

"What the hell are you saying, Ben? Why are you torturing me? What is this punishment for?"

"He's our baby."

"He's the desLauriers' baby."

"I'm going to get him. I'm going to go back and get my baby." He was actually ranting, staring right through me.

In the movies you slap a hysterical person in the face. I clenched my fist and smashed his jaw. Even though he tilted, he didn't fall, but he grabbed his face and held it. I groaned and doubled over, pressing my cracked knuckles to my stomach. I wanted to die with the pain. Ben put his arms around me, and we both cried, but for just a second. Ben pushed me away so he could get some ice. We sat on the sofa, and he held my hand in his lap while he pressed the bag of ice to it.

"Phoebe, please listen to me. Please . . . listen to

. . . me. This is not your journal. This is real life. In another three months you can't rewrite a page or two and then there's no baby. He's your child. I don't know how you can leave him like this."

I shut my eyes. It was the only one of my senses I could turn off, and I wished I could do the same to all six. "I am doing what I know to be the best thing. I want him very much. I want him in my arms right now, here. But I can't have him. I can't. I would make demands on him that no child should have to meet."

"Phoebe, Phoebe . . . are you sure? Are you really sure of what's going on? Has everything been just lines and lines of script you're writing down in your imagination? I won't let you do that to yourself. You might never come out of it." My eyes opened. He said into them, "You can't erase your baby."

His voice had become frantic. I didn't blame him for what he was afraid of. "Ben, I know it's real. It won't go in my journal. Not this. I'll . . . I'll just write a short story . . . a war story . . . about Graye-sur-Mer. The real story is just between you and me."

Ben took the ice off and kissed my swollen fingers. "I must have gone mad," he said. "I don't want the baby. I mean, I do want the baby, I do, but I want him in order to keep you. It's you I want. I want you to stay with me. Forever. Remember how we spied on the desLauriers? Well, it'll be easier spying on the baby because they'll take him out in a carriage, and out to the sea when he's older, and all that. We can take a lot of drives up there whenever we want and see how he's doing."

"You do that, Ben. Then write me and let me know."

"Please don't leave me, Phoebe. Marry me, and we'll have another baby."

"Okay, Ben, let's. But later. In a few years, okay? You're rich. You can come home and visit me a lot."

"This is my home."

"This can never be my home. I'm never going to come back to France again, ever."

He began pacing again. Not his madman pacing, his thinking pacing, like when he paints. "Stay a few more days. What if you start bleeding?"

"Princess Diana went home in twelve hours."

"You'll be in an airplane. The cabin might lose pressure. Then you'll probably hemorrhage."

He figured if "bleeding" didn't get me, "hemorrhage" would. I told him, "Then the pilot will say, 'Is there a doctor on board?' Naturally, Ben, there'll be at least a dozen. And I need to tell my mother something right away."

"Don't you want to wait and see Marlys again before you go. I know she's awfully concerned about you."

"I'll write Marlys. We understand each other. We may be shocked at each other's sexual preferences and habits, but we still understand each other."

"Please, Phoebe."

"No."

"The plane leaves at midnight?"

"Yes."

"Tonight?"

"Jesus Christ, Ben."

"How long is the flight?"

"I don't know. Six or seven hours."

"Will you make a deal with me?"

He was beginning to regain the normal tone of his voice. "Okay."

"If I get you a ticket on the morning Concorde, will you stay here with me all night and let me hold you?"

"You're talking twenty-five hundred bucks just to hold me."

"It's worth it to me. And you'll get to New York before you leave."

I sank into his lap on the wonderful cushy sofa.

"You're a feather, Phoebe."

"I know. The real me. Ben, you've never known the real me."

"I love you, real or otherwise."

"Ben?"

"Yes?"

"I'm not going to write to you when I get home, I don't think."

"I'm going to write to you."

"Okay, but I don't know when I'll be able to open your letters."

He held me even closer to him. "Will you meet me in the States, say, in a year?"

"How about five years, Ben?"

"Four."

"Three."

"All right, three," Ben agreed. "But please, Phoebe, two?"

"Okay." After all, I wasn't signing a contract.

"You'll meet me then?"

"Yes, I will."

"How about we meet on the baby's birthday? It'll be easier to bring up that way."

That got me sad, but I didn't want to discuss it. "Fine. And where shall we meet, Ben?"

"Is New York okay? In case I want to get right back."

"Sure. I'll even meet you at Kennedy."

"I thought Grant's Tomb, maybe."

"Shit, Ben."

"At noon. It's time you returned to the scene of the crime. Maybe it'll help you to return to this one."

"Oh, all right."

"Did you ever wonder if the wino was still there?"

"What wino?"

"The one in the journal."

"Oh, him. I made him up."

"Then how the hell did you get in there?"

"Walked in. The guard was real. He sleeps instead of guards."

Chapter Six

Naturally, when I arrived in New York, Ben had a private limo waiting to take me home. Everyone who gets off the Concorde has a chauffeur meeting him. I fit right in, just like I do at Yale. I admit to using all the sanitary napkins in all the Concorde johns, but I was all right. I left Paris at 10 A.M., got to JFK at 9 A.M., and arrived on my Connecticut doorstep at eleven. It was frigidly cold, but no snow. No one was home, but the hiding place for the key hadn't changed. I took a shower, and slept until my sister got off the school bus. I felt wonderful. Physically.

Her lumbering woke me up, so I was able to handle

her lunge at me. I had one suitcase full of clothes with Paris labels for her. She went hysterical and called up three friends, and they all tried on the clothes and gave me a fashion show. I shouldn't have been so surprised that I felt so old.

My mother, Maribeth told me, was at school fulfilling herself and wouldn't be home until seven-thirty. My mother is now a full time student at UConn, Stamford branch. She said Dad brought pizza home every Monday night, and I should have told everyone I was coming home so that he could have gotten half pepperoni.

He arrived, briefcase and pizza. My present to him was a case of wine; sixteen different kinds. We had Pouilly-Fuissé '67 with sausage and anchovy pizza. I feasted my brains out it was so scrumptious. Keep your veal kidneys, Maxim's. Dad seemed glad to see me. We were a lot like strangers who meet and hit it off.

My mother, like all college freshmen, looked all excited. She hugged me and called me her baby, and as soon as we were alone, she said, "I've become very honest since I started school, Phoebe. So I want to tell you that though I love, adore, and treasure your sister, there is something very special between every woman and her firstborn."

Can you believe she said that? Right away, mercifully, she asked how Marlys was, and I said, "Fine, and she sends her love."

That night my mother and I went out on the deck at midnight because I'd noticed it was snowing. It was those big, fat flakes that come to nothing, but watching them float down through the light of the outdoor lamp was soothing.

I said, "Ma, can I talk to you about your abortion?"

She smiled. "Don't feel you have to, Phoebe. I denied it and denied it, until finally I was able to admit to myself that you were pregnant. I wish you'd have come to me, but when I had mine, I wish I could have gone off to Paris for six months, too."

Now *there* was a shocker. I guess she knew because there is something very special between a mother and her firstborn. I took out two lawn chairs from the shed. "Sit down, Ma."

"What is it?"

"How do you feel about the abortion?"

"Every year I hate myself more for having done it. But at the time there was no other choice. So much was wrong with me. Having a baby would have destroyed me, Phoebe."

"If it would have destroyed you, then how can you blame yourself?"

"I blame myself for being so helpless. A grown woman, totally dependent on everyone but myself."

"Am I responsible for Tyrus' death?"

"Of course not."

"We were both victims of circumstance, Ma, and we'll always blame ourselves. It's human nature. But you know, Ma, I read that there are these African tribes that believe that when someone dies his spirit is born again into a new person. Well, Tyrus is now a new person and so is your fetus. They're both alive."

"Phoebe, what are you talking about?"

"A baby was born in France, and Tyrus lives in

that baby, and so does my brother or sister that never was." I stared into the light, and the flakes seemed to enlarge.

"What baby?"

"A really beautiful baby, Ma. A boy. With Maribeth's exact hair, that special burnished kind of . . ."

I never experienced my mother staring at me in ʝuite that way, and I knew I was unable to hide that great big empty, gaping hole inside me which nothing will ever fill because there is something special between a mother and her firstborn.

My mother cleared her throat or choked, and said, "Phoebe, I would have given anything to be able to go to a doctor and say, 'Take this embryo out and implant it in some poor woman who desperately wants a baby.' But to do what you've done . . . you have done the most generous . . . you have given the most precious . . . oh, Phoebe."

My mother tends to speak in superlatives when overwhelmed. "Knock it off, Ma. Every alternative was horrible. I did what was easiest on me."

Then it hit my mother that we were talking about her real and true grandchild. I could see the realization of that pull her cheek muscles into an unattractive sag. Now it was her turn to stare at the flakes. Her eyes glazed over, and as soon as she blinked, she said to me in her softest voice, "Don't tell your father."

"I hadn't intended to."

She sniffed, walked over to the deck rail, and kind of hung over it. I looked at her back, and my life fit all together like a jigsaw puzzle with very few pieces missing. "Ma," I shouted.

"What?" she asked, not moving.

"You have just revealed to me what I want to do with my life."

She turned. "I'm afraid to think what."

"No, Ma, you'll love it. A doctor. I'm going into obstetrics. A fertility researcher. I am going to find out how to transfer an embryo, a fetus even, from the woman who doesn't want it to the woman who does. I'll tell them tomorrow at Yale. Really, when you think about it, it's just one step beyond what they're doing now."

Finally, my mother had something she could grasp on to. "Can you change courses so easily, Phoebe?"

"Mother, this is Yale we're talking about. You can do whatever you damn well please. They'll love me in medical school. Medical students don't really want to be doctors. They want to be rich and noble—half in that order, half the reverse. I'll be a lovely change. Only . . ." My eyebrows knitted together. I know they did because my mother is one of those people who makes the same face as the person talking to her.

"Only what, Phoebe?"

"Only . . . now I won't be able to squeeze in Post-Impressionism. Ben really counted on my taking that."

"Ben?"